# MAI TAI
## TWO
## TIMES

### A NOVEL BY
# LUKE E WOODHEAD

First published by Luke E Woodhead, 2022

Copyright © Luke E Woodhead, 2022

The right of Luke E Woodhead to be identified as the author of this work has been asserted.

ISBN: 978-0-6454805-1-1 (eBook)
ISBN: 978-0-6454805-0-4 (paperback)

A catalogue record for this book is available from the National Library of Australia.

Cover Art by Sean Longmore Design
Edited by Irma Gold
Proofread by Just Right Words
Typesetting, internal design and eBook conversion
by Eggplant Communications

The story and characters in this novel are fictitious. Certain long-standing institutions and places are mentioned, but the characters involved are wholly imaginary and similarities to persons living or dead is purely coincidental.

For Helen and Conroy.
They know what they did.

And for that old Polynesian man singing Waimanalo Blues
while he whipped a disrespectful tourist with a length of
sugar cane. *Mahalo* ... that shit was hysterical.

# Contents

# Author's Note

This novel came to life as a direct result of the 2020 pandemic. Australia was in lockdown and uncertain times lay ahead; things were rough. And 2021 happened, and things got worse. But doom and gloom are not healthy for the mind and body, so while we were isolated and in desperate need of some sunny optimism, I wrote this story. Your passport to pure escapism. Sunshine in the palm of your hand. A bit like a glass of gold rum; something to soothe the soul.

If you require some context, this all probably happened in 2018. Simpler times. This is a story of experience and growth, because at various points in a man's life he will become lost. Usually in his mid-thirties to forties, when all men wish they were still teenage boys. But boys are idiots, even when they're grown men, and sometimes they just need to get it out of their system until they find the path again ...

But none of this matters.

*Mai Tai Two Times* is easy. Easy breezy. No effort required. My intention was to create a novel you could disappear inside at a moment's notice; a story you'd want to revisit over and over. Something you would find in an airport, and like crack, you'd be into it at the gate, on the aircraft, wedged in the toilet cubicle, or preferably while laying out in the sunshine during your beach holiday — although, if you find yourself in circumstances where an exotic holiday is looking like a distant dream, this novel can take you there instead. I bet you can already smell it, can't you? The sea. Tropical air so humid you can cut it with a knife. Coconut oil mixed with sweat and spilt beer … smells like paradise. Now, do yourself a favour and grab a cocktail, relax and enjoy. This won't take long. And if you get lost, don't stress, keep moving forward. It'll all make sense at the end.

# The Beginning

I was in the air somewhere between Sydney and Honolulu, six or more mai tais deep, and riding the jet stream of a questionable decision. Should I carry on with this fast track to alcohol poisoning?

'Another mai tai, sir?' asked the stewardess.

'Please,' I said and tried to present a smile that wasn't sleazy or gave away how much the drink was getting to me. I twisted my moustache and wondered when I was going to be cut off from the bar. Probably never, unless I decided to get rowdy — and that wasn't me. If anyone was going to get naked and ridiculous, it would be my Italian brother-in-law Mr Conroy. He sat across the aisle from me, enjoying the good life to its fullest, and in-between bouts of obscene laughter caused by a dirty joke he'd told about a French prostitute, he requested the same drink from the flight attendant. She returned a few minutes later with the cocktails and an extra can of beer. I figured it was for another passenger until she placed both drinks on the tray in front of me and said: 'Enjoy.' The responsible part of me almost told her to take it away, that I hadn't ordered the beer and it must be for someone else ... the other part of me thought, why the hell not? I could use a beer to even me out and cut through all this sugar.

The flight attendant must've thought the same thing. This was business class and they didn't make mistakes. Business class, which on Hawaiian Airlines is equal to first class. Unlimited alcohol for those in the fortunate position to be seated here, and I was making the most of it. One of the perks of being allowed to tag along on your wife's business trip to Hawaii. Not a bad turnaround two weeks after losing my job. And last Tuesday, another event was set in motion that would change the whole dynamic of this experience.

It had been about ten in the morning and as an observer of the species, I was sitting in my usual place on the outskirts, the empty barber chair of Caligula Beauty — my brother-in-law's lavish temple to hair and hedonism — listening to my wife and her twin discuss what the future had in store ...

'An architecture and design conference? In Honolulu. What kind of shiny scam is that?' Mr Conroy asked.

'It's a research expedition,' Elena replied. 'Hopefully it'll give me a fresh perspective — rekindle the fire I've been lacking. You *know* I'm damn good at my work, and I love it, but lately I'm having a difficult time remembering why.'

'That's not uncommon. At some point most people have laid in bed with the covers pulled up, knowing there's a hideous job lurking, ready to suck the life out of you until there's nothing left but the twisted husk of the person you once were.' Mr Conroy stepped back and checked his work … snapped his fingers at his assistant, pointed to me and said: 'The ten-year-old Cab Sav. The Barossa.' He then went back to cutting Elena's hair. 'Are these ten days in Honolulu tax-deductable?'

'Yeah. But it's only a three-day conference,' Elena said, tapping the side of her nose. 'The rest of the time we'll be on holiday. God knows I need it. And Eddie needs it so he can get his head right after all the trouble.'

'Indeed. Out of work for the first time in almost a decade.'

'Not by choice,' I said.

'What did you do?' asked a striking giraffe named Monique. She approached my chair holding a large glass of red wine, which she handed to me as if it were the Holy Grail. But that was Caligula Beauty. Good wine all the time. Highbrow, plush … exclusive. I was just a visitor with a backstage pass. It was doubtful if anyone here remembered or even knew what life was like on the middle-to-bottom rung of society, so I gave Monique an education on how the lowbrow made a living.

'I was a writer for a hack travel magazine … and in eight years those cheap bastards never dropped a cent on an airfare. So we wrote about places we'd never been to and used armchair research and a vivid imagination to share secret insider info on everything from the best hotels to the finest local restaurants.' I knocked back a third of the wine and lost myself in its depth until I realised Monique was still listening. 'The important detail is, it was all lies. But it was easy to turn a blind eye because it was pay to write. Until last week, when the whole shitty publication went bust and closed shop.'

'And no warning, no severance pay, and too late in the year to secure another writing gig. Can you believe that, Monique? An unfavourable position to be thrust into in one's mid-thirties, forced by some ice-cold fucks to face that frightening prospect — *what next?*' Mr Conroy said.

'That's the hard truth,' I said and finished the wine, 'but you take the good from the bad, and I now see it as an important stepping stone on the path to pro novelist.'

'The profession of choice for all insane people,' Monique said as she topped up my glass and then clip clopped away on a pair of outrageous eight-inch gold heels.

'She's got you nailed, Eddie, and someone in your delicate mental state will need guidance on this trip. So of course I'll have to go with you.'

'Your interest in my wellbeing wouldn't have anything to do with Jackie?'

'I'm wounded you think I care so little, but a chirpy bird did mention Jackie was in Hawaii. And if the film director is going to be in Honolulu, well, this is meant to be.'

'Ah, excuse me, what about the salon?' Elena said. 'Your clients have to book months in advance to see you, how can you just pick up and leave?'

'Easy. The people will wait for Mr Conroy. And why else would you have sent me your itinerary if not to tag along? This kind of event will require a high-class stylist, and someone with a high-balance credit card, we can't be seen driving around town in any old rental … It'll be rough on my clients, but it's a sacrifice I'm willing to make. Monique, book me on the same flight, will you? Business class. And I'll need a room in their hotel. The particulars should be in the itinerary.'

Monique held a tablet in front of me with the aircraft seating plan already displayed. She was either superhuman or a mind-reader, and I didn't know whether to be happy or pissed off. 'It's a good thing you're excellent company, you opportunistic bastard,' I said, and pointed to our seats on the screen.

Monique put Mr Conroy next to us. A couple of minutes later she also had him booked into the same hotel, and showed me just to confirm.

'Jesus. You're good. Roy has finally found an assistant who knows what they're doing.'

'She's a lesbian,' Mr Conroy said. 'That's why she's so damn efficient. I couldn't have a straight woman working for me, we'd never get any work done.'

'No. You'd be in court all the time for sexual harassment,' Elena said. 'By the way, if you're tagging along I expect to look amazing the entire time.'

But that was last Tuesday. Now the pieces were in play. We had our very own stylist and were headed for paradise, the best way to get our heads straight and plot the next step in our careers. Whatever that may be.

'Cabin crew, please direct the unwashed masses back to their seats. That's right economy class, this is your captain speaking, we kindly ask that you stow your crap and strap in, we're about to make our final approach ... For those of you in business class, it's been fun but the party is almost over, so I'd like to take this opportunity and thank you for flying with us, and we hope you enjoy your stay in Hawaii. The local time in Honolulu is 10 am and we are expecting generally magnificent weather for the foreseeable future. Have a fantastic day. *Mahalo*.'

It had been a sweet ride. Elena grasped my wrist and dragged me across her lap to the window. Deep blue sea lay below, and there she was, the island of Oahu. It was good to be back. Just seeing the brown mountainsides of the south west coast, before I'd even set eyes on white sand and palm trees, this stirred something inside me, something I'd been lacking recently — a sunny disposition with a dash of optimism. *Aloha*.

\*

Walking the Honolulu terminal feels like you're stuck in a sixties time warp, it's magnificent, even if it does feel like you've travelled several kilometres before you reach customs.

But it's a slog I appreciated. Walking that long lonely hallway was a chance to sober up, stretch my legs and get the blood flowing again after ten hours confined in a cigar tube. Although, the lay flat chair had made all the difference on the long haul flight. I felt so much better than the last time I'd flown here. I felt fresh.

I pitied those poor souls stuffed into economy. Had any of them slept? Had they even escaped the plane yet? Probably not. But any pity I felt was short-lived, it was so much better being me here and now. The last time I flew to Hawaii I had been one of those unfortunate coffin dwellers. Strapped down in a cramped seat behind some inconsiderate bastard who had no decency and had reclined his chair immediately after take-off and left it that way the entire flight. I had an aisle seat. A small mercy that allowed quick and temporary escape from the smothering of the bloated beast in front of me. This grotesque overweight slob bulged out of its tank top and leaked an odour that indicated he had not showered for at least forty-eight hours and had eaten a hot curry before boarding the flight. The guy smelt like he was rotting in his own skin. He slept in the seat like a gunshot victim, slumped to one side with his thick arm hanging into the aisle, his neck tilted at such a relaxed angle I had cause to believe he might have broken it. Was he dead? No ... but it would have been preferable. Then they would have hauled his stinking carcass back to the galley and I could have relaxed without having to use the complimentary sick bag as an air filter.

Business class was not anything like that hideous experience. It was another world. We had been afforded every courtesy, and when the time came, it was easy to remove a change of clothes from our carry-on luggage and disappear into the toilet cubicle to preen and primp and refresh ourselves for arrival. All decked out in pure linen, we now strolled at leisure along that long terminal corridor. Feeling good and looking good.

The first indication that the lower class had emerged from the plane was obvious. Our well-dressed trio was being overtaken by people who looked grouchy, bleary-eyed and sweaty. A sure sign of a ten-hour stint in the trenches. A man that looked like a grizzled university professor jostled past and managed to give Mr Conroy a shove out of the way, a seemingly impossible feat given the width of the corridor. Why was he so close to us? My own snobbery surprised me — but, why was he so close to us? When my good-humoured brother-in-law said: 'Slow down, champ, there's no trophy at the finish!' He was rewarded with an irritated glance over the shoulder and no apology. Was this gamesmanship? A form of intimidation to stop us from passing customs before him? I had an inclination to leap forward and crash tackle this aggressor, to rub his face in the filthy carpet and ask if he'd left his manners on the plane.

More of these insane people rushed by, moving at such a rate I thought we had stumbled into the midst of some strange foot race. There was an urgency in the air you couldn't help but be swept up in. Suddenly we were moving faster and faster, trying to stay ahead of the panicked stampede behind us. Would we beat them to customs before they caught up and trampled us to death under their resentful economy-class feet?

At customs, the border official thumbed through my passport and settled on a page with a stamp from my previous visit. They love to do that at passport control — take it nice and slow — gives you a chance to overthink things, like maybe you're not going to be allowed into the country. Or perhaps you'll be that impatient person who becomes frustrated with the border official, like the obnoxious couple at the counter behind me, arguing about how it was outrageous that people of their social standing were being forced to scan their fingerprints in the digital security devices.

'It's a ridiculous over-reach — we're not criminals! My passport should be enough, I'm not going back to scan my fucking fingers!'

'Also, I've just had my nails done and that machine will ruin them …'

'New international travel rules, folks, everyone has to scan before they can enter. No exceptions.'

It was true, only eighteen months ago this terminal had been a glorious throwback to a time when air travel was simple — line up, show your passport, visa and customs declaration form, and off you go. Damn, I miss those days.

But the world was evolving fast, fingerprint scanners had already been around for years and it would only be a matter of time before the latest biometric face scan technology arrived in Honolulu.

However, there was no telling the self-righteous couple at my back.

'We flew premium class, goddamn it! Do you realise how important I am? How much I'm worth? Oi, that journalist knows who I am, we were on the same flight — tell him, mate!'

I wanted to tell him to eat a dick for trying to involve me in his circus. Instead I shrugged at him and kept my mouth shut while he raged to the point of no return.

'You know how much I spent having my back waxed? On our matching spray tans?'

We waited for him to admit they also had matching bleached arseholes — my guess was someone would find out soon enough.

'*Fuck you, yank,* and *fuck this*, we're going through without the scan. C'mon, babe.'

The border official dealing with these puffed-up toads turned around and raised an eyebrow at the guy manning my desk — my guy nodded back and mumbled '*Six six six*' into his walkie-talkie. It looked a harmless gesture, but I had just witnessed a code red. There was now electricity in the air. They'd waited all week for a case like this, a chance to wield the big red one and stamp *denied* in a passport — even better that it was a pair of uppity arseholes. A few seconds later, three security officers swooped in and dragged the couple away, kicking and screaming. I knew those idiots would try to fight — and now it would be handcuffs, lubricated fingers in tight spaces, and an uncomfortably bright room until they were thrown on the first flight back home. No Hawaii for you. I knew better than to get pissy with *the man*. Manners go a long way in all situations, and besides, there's no need to be rude when you have just flown business class and feel crisp.

'Did that couple really know you?' the border official asked.

'I've never seen those people in my life,' I lied. They were sitting on the other side of the business class cabin and seemed to live for drama. Mercifully, their antics had been contained to their own small cubicle because throughout the flight they argued, drank too much, were rude to the attendants, and to our great amusement started arguing again right before we landed in Oahu. Now they were off to a jail cell, their accommodation for the remainder of a memorable island adventure. Oh, what fun they would have …

The border official examined the old stamp in my passport, flicked back to the photo page and then glanced up at my face. I smiled. He didn't. But apparently my face was okay, because he flipped to a random page in the middle of the document and with a deadpan expression said: 'Eddie Heads. Travel writer.'

'Bloody hell, you've got a good memory. Eidetic?'

'Nope. Your photo was attached to a piece you wrote after your last visit. I still have the article, "Liquid Aloha — At the Edge of Escapism." It made me laugh, especially that bit where you and your wife pretended to be on your honeymoon so the hotel would upgrade your room.' He slid a blank piece of paper across the desk. 'Can I trouble you for an autograph?'

This was surreal. I felt like a fucking rock star and happily signed; *Deep pockets don't mean shit at counter six six six. Respect the locals — E Heads.*

'That's great. So what brings you back to our fair shores? Business or pleasure?'

'This time it's a good old-fashioned holiday.'

He smiled and stamped my passport. 'Welcome back to Hawaii.'

Customs took almost no time. There was nothing to declare and all three of us had decided to travel with carry-on luggage only. There would be no need to wait an additional twenty minutes for any suitcases. We happily strolled by the empty baggage carousel, much to the irritation of the nudgey university professor. He eyed us with undeserved hate and tapped his foot on the ground, willing the luggage chute to vomit out his bag so he could race us to the taxi rank. This was the kind of ruthless wanker that would push you in front of oncoming traffic so he could get the first taxi or a better seat on the bus. No wonder he looked like such a miserable bastard, that was his whole life — *me first* and everyone else go to hell.

Mr Conroy observed his irritation with triumph and wanted to make the rude prick sweat until his bag arrived. 'It's going be a long wait for those bags, *bello*. We heard some of them were left behind in Sydney. Hope they didn't forget yours. *Ciao!*'

It was a cunning lie, I was so proud of him.

We had prearranged a shuttle bus to take us to the hotel. The driver waited near the terminal exit, accompanied by a large, bald-headed Polynesian man holding a placard with our names on it. Both men were decked out in bright red Aloha shirts. The Polynesian man introduced himself as Big Jim and greeted us with a warm '*Aloha*' and held a lei for each of us that he placed around our necks. He took our bags after that. I insisted on taking my own and tipped him as if he'd carried it anyway. I liked to travel light with a small leather duffel bag. It felt lazy and pretentious to have this man carry it, something that Mr Conroy had no problem with, and he happily handed over his cream-coloured Bric's Milano suitcase. Then he and Elena began debating who had the more stylish wheel-about. Was it her miniature steamer trunk? Or his practical and modern Italian? My opinion was of little value because I was a peasant who preferred to labour with his own belongings.

While they traded barbs, I talked with Big Jim and discovered that he was one hundred per cent full-blooded

Hawaiian. A rare thing in modern Hawaii. This was a fact he divulged to me with a great sense of pride and a depth of feeling I knew I would never understand, and that was okay, because I respected it. Big Jim was a good omen. It meant that the islands were in a welcoming mood.

# Oahu: Day One

My world had taken on sepia-tone warmth thanks to brown-tint lenses. A person could go blind here without sunglasses; the sun shone in a way it only does in the tropics. There's a certain heat that feeds vibrancy to the scenery. The light just lands differently, especially on water, and everything we drove past looked wet, although I could see no evidence of rain in the sky. Something about that just made the place feel fresh.

The shuttle arrived outside the Outrigger Waikiki Beach on Kalakaua Avenue. Our hotel was bang in the middle of the action — above a ground-floor shopping arcade that walked through to a famous restaurant on Waikiki, a good-time vibe called Duke's. To get to the hotel we took an escalator to the first floor.

The lobby was already jam-packed with conference attendees who had separated into several distinct groups. I made a quick assessment of the pecking order and could sense everyone sizing us up — my wife in particular. Elena stuck out like a glass chip in a car windscreen. Your eyes were just drawn to her. Short wavy blonde hair, sun-kissed features, dressed in breezy white linen. A real Australian stunner ... fresh meat. The regulars could smell it. We'd entered the jungle, and only the wily would survive.

The hard-core architects and designers were the least threatening. Gathered around the big outrigger canoe at the side of the lobby, these elitists were serious people wearing serious clothes because this was going to be serious work — for them anyway. Their Hawaii would be spent inside the conference walls, and it was doubtful the hard-core would ever feel the sand between their toes. Unlike the middle-aged, middle-of-the-road crowd. Easy to spot in the wild because of a bright Aloha or Polo shirt over belt-held shorts. They tended to be building contractors and product reps, here for the booze, the beach and the broads. And a three-day escape from the wife and kids, no doubt. I had no worries about this lot. The real snakes here were Elena's equals from the United States mainland. Women in the interior design business could be cutthroat. They'd turn into wild-eyed maniacs ready to spill blood and curse your ancestors if they suspected you'd come to pillage their land of its treasures — be that work or men — it didn't matter if you operated on different continents. Diplomacy was the key to success. But Elena knew jungle law — avoid the crazies and state the ground rules early. 'We're just here on a fact-finding mission and a holiday.' Yeah, that would work.

Still, I figured there might be a few unpleasant run-ins with the female attendees if my wife didn't tread carefully. We didn't need to get mixed up with the extracurricular activities of the obvious regulars. At the end of each day every last one of these women would be glammed up and blitzed on cocktails with the Aloha and Polo Shirts at Duke's. More than a few would be caught doing the walk of shame. And afterward, they'd freshen up, attend the next seminar, and do the dance all over again. They might have thrown a bikini in the suitcase, but hitting the beach was always a lower priority than spending free time shopping, shit talking, and stabbing each other in the back. That's how it always went at these events ... but you turned a blind eye. Stayed neutral. Avoided the crazies.

I navigated us through this odd collection of humanity until we reached the front desk, where the clerk explained: 'Things are hectic because of the conference. The cleaning staff are working as fast as they can to prepare for arriving guests but unfortunately you can't access your room until 3 pm.'

That was fine. Each of us had plans to fill the time. We took whatever gear we needed and left our bags with the hotel bag check on the ground floor. After that we separated.

Elena had to go back upstairs and register her arrival for the conference, attend the opening seminar, make friends, and investigate the situation. A gruelling few hours.

Mr Conroy had booked a hire car and needed to pick it up. Then our stylist would create a fuss because of some foul injustice he'd suffered. His goal was to be upgraded or awarded credit — and he always scored.

My own plans were less official. I was meeting Jackie for lunch, so I slung a small sailor-style rucksack over my shoulder and hit the street.

*

I walked along sun-drenched Kalakaua Avenue and enjoyed the heat on my shoulders and back, and felt my energy slowly return. Today I had not a care in the world. Drums and singing filled the air, a hula group performed on a stretch of grass outside the shops. As I crossed the street and passed a drug store and the Bank of Hawaii, it occurred to me that this was the most relaxed I'd been in years, and by the look of things that wasn't about to change anytime soon. At the end of the block, I stopped in the middle of a small triangle-shaped park surrounded by palm trees. In front was an angled street named Beach Walk, and the restaurant where my brother Jackie had agreed to meet me, the Hard Rock Cafe — all dressed up to look like a giant Polynesian hut, the kind of detail the islanders hated but tourists ate up.

'Whoop-whoop!' The bird cry came from a man with a chisel-shaped beard and long dark wavy hair, wearing fly-eye style sunglasses. This gangly goon spotted me from across the road, and with his arms raised in the air, ran at me like a rampaging chimpanzee. Cars slammed to a stop on Beach Walk and honked their horns. Someone yelled, '*Fucking idiot!*' But none of this slowed Jackie Heads. He picked me up off the ground and embraced me like a bear shaking a tree. 'Hey, brother!'

'Jackieeee … What's happening, dude?'

'Did you see that shit cunt honking me as I crossed the street? Anyway, better melting in this humidity instead of freezing my nuts in Vancouver.'

'When did you get in?'

'Late last night. Good flight too, no hobos or screaming babies.'

'Cool, cool. Where're you staying?'

'The Modern on Ala Moana. Nice little place with a view of the marina. No families, just models sunning themselves by the pool and good vibrations. But it's a rough hike up to Waikiki when you're not used to the heat or cardio-based exercise.'

'You don't look out of shape.'

'I've been hitting the weights and eating like a lumberjack. I'm always hungry. I mean, I could murder a burger right now. I reckon it's going to be that kind of trip bro, it's this heat, it makes a man ravenous … The restaurant is dead quiet. Let's eat!'

\*

We were seated underneath a crashing wave of electric guitars on the upstairs balcony of the Hard Rock Cafe. My brother disappeared into the bathroom and I ordered two burgers and two cocktails — the appropriate holiday beverage. I had been in desperate need of a cool drink for the past hour. The cocktails arrived just as Jackie returned. I took a long sip from my hurricane and felt immediately buzzed. How much alcohol was in this thing? I knew it was enough to make everything feel right. Jackie grinned and pointed at the air. Music filled my ears. The song was *One More River* by James Reyne. I looked across the Honolulu skyline and felt the warm breeze blow through the palm trees that lined Kalakaua Avenue. The vibe was good.

I turned to Jackie and said: 'You need to have a sip of this thing. I have a feeling the bartender was overly generous with the shots of liquor. I have pins and needles ... my feet are numb.'

'Whoo! No joke. Our burgers better arrive soon or we're gonna be off our face. Which reminds me, we need to address the pink elephant in the room. I understand my dear friend Mr Conroy is here ... Now, I love that man, but this is exactly the kind of environment where things will get weird if he's allowed to run amok. Some of us have work to do and that man is a bad influence. You need to keep him on a short leash or we're gonna come unstuck and wind up in prison.'

'You can relax. Roy knows why we're here. And as a stylist of high class and snobbery, he'll be on his best behaviour — most of the time.'

'It's the rest of the time that worries me ... Anyway, thank *fuck* you finally quit that bullshit travel journal. You were wasting your talent there.'

'I didn't quit. They went bankrupt.'

'Get the fuck out ... Still, they didn't deserve you. So how is unemployment?'

'I'm existing in that grace period where I can live off savings while I decide what my next move is. That's the whole point of this excursion, to get the head right with a little escape from reality.'

'Ha! You and an escape from reality is a recipe for trouble.'

'Trouble is a just matter of perspective ... So are you scouting Oahu or Kauai?'

'A bit of both. I won't bother you guys during the conference, I'll steal you away after it's done. And once we get to Kauai, I'm taking everyone on a driving tour. Should be smooth sailing. We'll explore, snap location photos and have an all-round great time. Food, beer, good company.'

'Sounds like a plan I can sink my teeth into. What's the new film about?'

'It's a romantic drama.'

'Oh, so something *new and different* for you.'

'Now, now. This one will be a classy and sophisticated picture. A period piece, very intellectual. The daughter of a sugar plantation baron falls in love with a native Hawaiian boy — sex and drama ensues. I'm going for a look that screams lust and passion in the islands. I want people to get lost in the romance ... With a kind of golden brown tone, like someone drizzled maple syrup all over the camera lens. You'll be able to feel the warmth coming through the screen.'

'That does sound appealing.'

'Which part?'

'Sex and maple syrup, delicious.'

Our burgers arrived and I hooked in. Despite his appetite, Jackie had always been a slow eater, a habit he now put into practice with the methodical chewing of his burger. He took the opportunity between mouthfuls of cheese and beef to enquire about current affairs. 'So, you're a lost boy again. Any idea what you might do next?'

'Not sure, but I've got ten days to figure it out.'

'Well, you better figure it out. You're a straight white male in his mid-thirties who is out of work; nobody gives a shit about you. So as far as I can see, you have two choices. You can learn an honest trade like Dad was always saying ...'

'What's the second option?'

'Or you put those writing skills to good use. And I've been thinking, what if I throw you a bone? Do a write-up for my film, a behind-the-scenes exposé. I've been forced to use an actress who is notoriously difficult to work with, and the bitch hates my guts, so there's bound to be drama. The good news is when the screaming starts you'll be there to record every juicy, blood-soaked moment ... Then you have my permission to sell the piece to *Rolling Stone* or whoever.'

'I appreciate the thought, dude, but I might be done with journalism. Forcing that shit out is like being a ping pong girl in Thailand. People are entertained and I might get a few dollars thrown at me, but it's thankless and dirty work.'

'At least think about it. I mean, what are you gonna do for money?'

'I have a couple of side gigs that pay ... what I really want is to write a novel.'

'That's cool, you've got time now. Although, are we worried about Elena?'

'I was, but she loves her work too much to quit. I think she just needs a break. A bit of distance from the computer is like being reborn ... And Elena has always known what the writing life is about. She'll only throw my arse out if I give up, and that keeps me motivated. But starting from scratch is a struggle, there is always doubt. What if I waste my time? Can I spend another five years in poverty? It's the kind of thing that makes me wonder, am I insane for sticking this out?'

'We're artists, insanity is a requirement. It's all in or not at all.'

'All I need is one good story idea.'

'The idea will come, probably when you least expect it. And it'll be original. You've never been a sheep. Hell, you've never even been a black sheep. You're that scraggly black goat standing on a pile of rocks screaming 'Hail

Satan!' Remember that guy? He'll find a story, he's a rock'n'roller. He's never been palatable or fashionable … fuck broad appeal. Write like that guy and those pages will be unfiltered, fire breathing joy.'

'You're asking me to channel Black Sabbath on a tropical island. Not easy.'

'Bah. AC/DC recorded *Back in Black* in the Bahamas. You're just feeling doubt because things have been rough lately. Or it could be jetlag. Either way, you're in Hawaii! Have a drink and stop feeling sorry for yourself … See, this is exactly why you should get back on the horse with the exposé. Writing *is* worthwhile. It's a fantasy most people never have the courage to try, and it's better than dying slowly in an office surrounded by two-faced puppets.'

'Elena says that all the time.'

'Well, she's right. None of us will ever take orders from cocksuckers on a power trip. We're not built for the nine to five; its suffocating. We need freedom to breathe.'

'This is different. You're not often filled with reasonable, thought-out wisdom.'

'I have my moments.'

'Hmm. This might be the first.'

I slipped into my usual sunny-side-up persona and any downhearted thinking vanished as quickly as it crept up on me. Jackie had spoken a lot of truth; an exposé was a way forward that made sense … at least until I had an idea for a novel. Hell, it would be easy to start scribbling some words while I waited for Elena to finish her seminars. I celebrated by having another hurricane with an incredible amount of alcohol in it. The drink burned in a way that was pleasurable and I eyed it warily, nothing but creeping madness in a tall glass. Two of these drinks was enough, a third would have induced the kind of mind-bending psychosis that would make the rest of my day a nightmare to navigate. Getting arrested for public drunkenness within hours of arriving was not an attractive option, so I sipped it slow and we caught up on life and more. Then Jackie had to get back to his hotel for a conference call with the film producers. We organised to meet the next day for a proper hang, but before we parted ways he gave me a present and said: 'I got you a little bit of pulp fiction, the perfect beach read. That should keep you out of trouble until tomorrow. Seriously. And don't forget what I said about our friend Mr Conroy.'

I still had some time to kill while Elena attended her induction seminar and our room was prepared, so I sniffed out the largest ABC store I could find. ABC stores sold everything, and the incredible thing about Honolulu was you could find one or two of them on every block. The one I chose was underneath the Imperial Hawaii Resort at the end of Lewers Street where the hula dancers had been performing. This would be a great place to acquire some much-needed sun protection. A hat was an absolute must, and I found a brown straw trilby with a black band, which matched my sunglasses and suited me down to the ground.

It was a keeper. Fifteen minutes later, I was packed up like a mule and set out for the beach with my rucksack slung around my body. The bag now held a tube of sunscreen, a small glass bottle of Coke, two miniature bottles of Koloa spiced rum and a five-dollar container of fresh pineapple.

I wandered along the beach like a pirate — barefoot, half cut and guided by the lingering remains of that monster hurricane. People watched me as I walked ... What I meant to say was, I people-watched as I walked. The swimwear trend leaned toward brightly-coloured board shorts and bikinis so small they offered no practical value except to show off. These people had come from all over the world to play under a special kind of sunlight that made even the most unfortunate soul look and feel better than they had any right to. Self-confidence appeared high on all fronts. Overweight and unattractive men swaggered around like kings, and every woman held her head high like a professional bikini model. It didn't matter what size, shape, age or race these people were because nobody here cared. There was no judgement. Would there be an uproar if some horny freak got his dick out and went berserk chasing shiny exposed arse? Of course, but that was the thing, everyone was so well-behaved. We were breathing some rare air here.

But this was also a test of character; could a man still find himself when it was so easy to get lost in all this incidental nudity? Sure. I had plenty of other things on my mind besides sex, and to linger on one thought for long was to miss all the action on offer. The beach looked like the human equivalent of the Serengeti migrations, an endless parade of near-naked bodies engrossed in a variety of sun worship rituals. I was inspired to look for a spot to relax and take in the sights, except the day was a scorcher, my feet were on fire, and I was reluctant to jump in the water wearing street clothes. So I abandoned the sand and returned to the Outrigger.

The hotel had direct beach access off a massive paved terrace that was filled with deckchairs and surrounded by a tropical garden bed. All the deckchairs were occupied by over-tanned lounge lizards or red-raw rock lobsters who had neglected sunscreen. I had no better luck finding a chair poolside, so I went back to the sand, stuffing pineapple in my gob as I tried to take the edge off the cocktails.

The universe likes to screw with you when you're vulnerable, which is a problem when you're tipsy, trying to float above hot sand, and allow yourself a perv at a big round bottom wobbling past. That was the moment I came unstuck. With my eyes elsewhere, I tripped over a large beach bag beside a woman and her husband who were sunbathing under a palm tree. 'Fucking balls!' Screams and pineapple chunks filled the air. I tumbled to ground and had a surprisingly soft landing on something plump and slimy. It was a flesh trap. I could smell the heavy scent of suntan lotion as I untangled from a mess of greasy limbs and spilled fruit, most of which had ended up all over the woman. Her husband immediately began abusing me.

'Moron! Why don't you watch where you're going? Look what you've done!'

'What *I've* done! Your bag was in the middle of nowhere, and look at this, I've lost all my pineapple! Do you know how much that cost? Five bucks, which is ten Australian, which is *twelve thousand lira!* My Italian wife will murder me for sure ...'

'Twelve thousand, you're mad! Wait ... what the hell's a lira?'

'I think we need to settle up, I'm owed for this disaster. Cash will be fine.'

'Whoa, I don't have that kind of money.'

'What about me! I'm covered in pineapple and there's sticky juice everywhere! It's dribbled into every crack ...'

'The ocean is right there, but I'm sure your husband would rather take you back to the room and clean you up himself. Isn't that right, sir? A little bit of top-to-tail action, eh?' I winked at the flustered man digging around in his wallet.

It was miraculous to witness the moment he understood what I meant, and goddamn, he wasn't going to let this opportunity slip away. It was a chance to show his woman how passionate he could be on vacation. He shoved whatever money he could grasp into my waiting hand, scooped his bewildered wife off the sand and hurried her back to the hotel. I looked at the crumpled bill in my palm — fifty American dollars — that man deserved to get laid after his generosity, or had I just become a pimp?

A beach holiday among strangers makes people act crazy, and this is no truer than when you're buzzed on rum. What a stupid situation to land in. Mental beyond reason. I picked up a wedge of pineapple, shook the sand off and put it in my mouth. Gritty, juicy and wholly unsatisfying. I spat it out in disgust. Then I remembered the fifty dollars and smiled. Cosmic justice is measured on balance, but was I ahead or breaking even? I got settled against the palm tree, cracked open the bottle of Coke to wash out the grit, and began to read the paperback Jackie had given me.

*Outlaw! Haunted by a blood-soaked past. Harassed by a gang of killers. A desperado battles to go straight in this smouldering tale of tension and extreme violence in the wildest of wests!* ... Written by Manny Checkerman, *Hell is a Hot Bullet!* was one of those pulp cowboy westerns originally published in the fifties, where the artwork on the cover was infinitely more entertaining than the story hidden within ... They'd branded Rick Trickle a cheat and a thief. He knew the only way to get clear of old debt was a six-gun blazing hot lead! ... I had to admit Rick Trickle was a relatable guy, many times over the past eight years I'd felt like a cheat and a thief writing bogus travel stories, and here I was again, barely a few hours into this Hawaiian adventure and I'd scammed some poor bugger out of fifty bucks. Not intentionally. Hell, it was alcohol-fuelled nonsense and fake outrage — wasn't it? I never expected him to hand me cash. This was not the way to get right in the head, but it seemed to be the way the universe was leaning, and after hearing Elena's stories about what they were entitled to with a conference ticket — free food at the upstairs restaurant and all you could drink from the bar — I decided to push my luck.

I was going to pose as a conference attendee. The level of cunning required to pull off such a venture would be somewhere in the league of Daffy Duck, Jack Sparrow or an idiot journalist who had drunk one too many hurricanes. So I was almost ready. My outfit already looked the part, a typical travel writer ensemble; unbuttoned shirt over a beach bum singlet. I pulled the new trilby down so it sat further forward on my head, and even though I would be standing in the brightly lit lobby, I kept my sunglasses on. It's easier to follow through with a fantasy from behind a mask. Or in this case, tell a bald-faced lie behind a pair of shades.

Fuel was needed, and after slamming both miniature bottles of rum, I felt confident and loose, ready to tackle this thing head on. I strolled across the lobby and made a line for the check-in desk beside the conference hall. The place was deserted except for the odd hotel guest. I figured everyone else must be sitting in on the seminar, which meant there was nobody around to question my intentions. That put a swagger in my step — or maybe that was all the rum. How many drinks was that now? Did it matter? Just don't fall through the floor man … steady and composed was the name of the game.

I was smooth and inconspicuous, mere metres from my destination, when I heard someone call my name. *Shit*, of all the foul luck ... Except, by some miracle, I was the only one who had paid attention. Not a single member of staff lifted their head. My disguise must have been working. Was I invisible?

'Eddie, you rascal, where are you going walking like that?' Mr Conroy had come up the escalator behind me and waved as he strode through the lobby. The slick stylist had changed clothes and now wore an outfit that looked more appropriate for the Italian Riviera than Waikiki Beach. This was almost too perfect.

'*Roy*. You're just in time ...'

'Ooh la la, it didn't take you long to adjust to the climate. Shirt unbuttoned all the way, already looking like a sophisticated slacker — how the hell do you tan so fast? Never mind. *Nice hat*. Where did you get it?' He adjusted the sunglasses on his brow and looked as though he lamented not having a hat of his own.

'ABC. I'll show you later. Do you have your phone on you?'

'Of course. It's in my pocket. Do you need to make a call?'

'No, you just need a prop. Come with me.'

We approached the conference check-in table and I smiled at the cheerful woman seated behind it. A tag on her chest read: *Hello. My name is Wendy.*

'Good afternoon, gentlemen. Are you here for the conference?'

'Yes. Unfortunately our flight was delayed and we're arriving a bit late. I take it we've already missed the induction? We're here to cover the event. I'm a journalist for the *Teak and Rattan Review*.'

'And what are your names?'

'My name is Eduardo Desah. And this is my photographer Pierre Conrad,' I said, amazed at how comfortable I was with the lie and how easily the phony names had rolled off my tongue. I looked over my shoulder at the confused expression on Mr Conroy's face and gave him a confident nod that I knew what I was doing. He gave me a nod in return. He'd figured out the game and was all in, just like I knew he would be.

'Eduardo and Pierre ... those are exotic names. Where are you from?'

'We're from Australia.'

'Excuse yourself, Eduardo,' Mr Conroy said in his thickest Italian accent. 'I am one hundred per cent Italian first. I don't count myself as a relation to those slovenly convicts.'

'Of course, Pierre. You'll have to forgive him, Miss. Frightfully stuck up, that one. My feet are planted a little closer to the ground. See, my heritage is also a quarter British, one-quarter Moroccan and a quarter Cherokee. Thus my olive complexion.'

'Ooh, I see, I've never met anyone from Morocco. What's it like?'

'Stinking hot, and it's a dry heat. You have to moisturise constantly unless you want to look like the leather goods in the bazaar, but a leathery complexion helps to blend in — stops you being hustled. Otherwise I wouldn't go alone, not unless you can get your hands on a good knife ... beautiful people though. Stunning country.'

'How exciting. I'll have to visit one day ... ah, where's his camera?'

'Pierre doesn't like to be overburdened with bulky equipment. He much prefers a streamlined approach to photography and uses his phone instead.'

'I have-a-the-cam-era.' Mr Conroy was holding his phone up to his face and snapped a picture of me and the surprised woman behind the table.

'It's a brave new world,' I said.

'Well, I'm sorry Mr Desah, I can't seem to find you or your photographer *or* your magazine on the guest list.'

'Bloody typical. Those lazy bastards in admin must have forgotten to forward our details. I swear this publication has gone to the dogs ... We're staying next door at the Royal Hawaiian ... here in conjunction with Elena Architecture and Design. Perhaps you've heard of them? They are a distinguished design firm from Australia. I'm sure you'll find them on the list.'

'Elena Architecture and Design ... give me a minute.'

Wendy scoured her list of names on the clipboard, flipping several pages until she landed on our salvation, 'Hmmm ... ah yes. And a representative from Elena will be able to confirm your involvement? Maybe later today?'

'Absolutely. I happen to be close personal friends with the head designer. I'll make sure that she touches base with you this afternoon.'

'Fantastic. Well, Eduardo, Pierre — here are your press passes. They entitle you to a seat at every seminar being held in the Leahi conference room for the duration of the event. You also have access to the Hula Grill and Plantation Bar, where all drinks are included with the price of your conference ticket.'

'Does that include-a-the-*cock*-tail?'

I could have smacked him. Mr Conroy drawled the words in a way that caused me to screw up my face and made the conference attendant blush. Thankfully I found the strength to keep it straight.

Somehow Wendy kept her head as well and hardly missed a beat, 'Excluding cocktails I'm afraid, uh, Pierre. The conference is sponsored by the beer company. And here are food vouchers for three meals a day. Present these in the restaurant and they will punch your card to confirm your visit. Enjoy the conference!'

'Thank you.' I extended my hand and shook hers. 'You have an excellent day, Wendy.' Smooth as butter. Wendy was all smiles as we left the table. We walked straight past the conference room and made an arrow line for the Hula Grill, where we grabbed our complimentary beers from the bar, settled in, and Mr Conroy toasted the health of free enterprise business conferences and a successful con at the con.

\*

Elena exited the induction looking dazed. I jumped up from my seat and called out to her from behind the plastic plants inside the restaurant. She brightened when she saw us waving from the Hula Grill, and a minute later she joined us inside.

'Well, that was a snooze fest and a wank off. What are you boys doing up here?'

'We got hungry,' I said. 'They do a really great fish taco here.'

'And already into the drinks, I see.'

'Free too. Not a bad afternoon's work thanks to your husband.'

Elena looked at us with suspicion and smiled. 'How did you scam that? I didn't know they were letting people drink for free who aren't going to the conference.'

'They're not …'

Elena cut me off. 'Never mind — guess what I got!' She fished around in her handbag and pulled out a pass and voucher like the ones we'd recently acquired from Wendy. 'I managed to get you in as my assistant. So you get a pass and a food voucher and you get free drinks here all day during the event. Pretty cool, right?'

'That is pretty cool. Kind of like these.'

Mr Conroy and I held up our press passes and food vouchers.

'What!' Elena kept her voice low. 'How the hell did you get those?'

'I'm a journalist,' I said. 'Here to cover your involvement at the event and write a corresponding article for *Teak and Rattan Review*, a small magazine based out of Australia. Which reminds me, you're going to have to play along and confirm with Wendy at the desk that Eduardo Desah and his photographer Pierre Conrad are here legitimately. You're aware our magazine is here to follow you, and are under the impression it has paid for our attendance.'

'Did you say *Teak and Rattan Review*?'

'I did.'

'Oh god … Eduardo and Pierre? Well, you definitely look like oddball journalists. How long did it take you idiots to come up with that?'

'It was spur of the moment. I couldn't stop myself. It's like my tongue was dripping honey — the sweet lies just kept flowing and Wendy happily lapped it up. But I'm almost certain it was my exotic Moroccan background that put us over the top.'

'You can be certain,' Mr Conroy said. 'I saw the moment her brain went on holiday.'

'*Moroccan background?* I swear you were working at that crooked travel journal for far too long … Will this work? What if they check the billing records?'

'Don't worry, hun, *Teak and Rattan Review* is on the brink of receivership and will suddenly become bankrupt if need be. You won't be held accountable if they come chasing money.'

'Unbelievable. Have a bit too much time on your hands today, my sweet? I don't think anyone is too fussed anyway. What kind of person would want to sneak into an architecture and design conference?' She stuck her tongue out at me.

'I hope you didn't pay for that pass, sister dear.'

'Luckily, brother dear, I did not, otherwise I'd be hitting *you* up for reimbursement. Jackie can have this pass, Eddie. That way we can all eat for free.'

We finally checked in. I was relieved Monique had booked Mr Conroy his own room instead of upgrading us to a two-bedroom suite. Now Elena and I could have our privacy and we wouldn't have to put up with her brother's more obscene habits.

Once the formalities had been sorted, we made our way to the elevators, crafty contraptions that could only be accessed using a swipe pad with your surfboard-shaped room key. It was a system that functioned about as well as you would expect — poorly. I lost track the number of times we would try to access the lift and have to wait while some unfortunate guest struggled because their surfboard wouldn't register on the swipe pad. Strangely I was never held up by this problem, the key worked for me every time. It was another sign that this journey was right.

Our room was on the sixth floor. Mr Conroy was on seven. We parted ways and got inside the room and opened the place up, spreading the curtains and doors wide to let in the sunshine and sea air. We had paid for an oceanfront room with a balcony. It was perfect.

*

Waikiki had to be one of my favourite beaches in the world. White sand and as wide as it was long. Low surf and incredibly calm. You could easily swim out hundreds of metres and still see the bleached bottom through the turquoise water, and the only dangers were the big catamarans coming and going. They'd run aground behind the hotels every hour or so, but getting hit by one of these was impossible because they announced their arrival well in advance through the deep bellow of a conch shell — a musical siren that blasted across the water and never disturbed the ambiance, it only increased the charm of the beach.

The day was coming to an end when we went down to the ocean for a swim. I stood at the water's edge and dug my toes into the sand and rolled my feet sideways, enjoying the pleasant sensation that occurs when sand granules touch those soft spots under the toes and along the arch of your foot. I looked to the jutting volcanic crater on the headland. Diamond Head. There was nothing obviously interesting about it and yet it was oddly beautiful, which is why it appeared on all the postcards, posters and advertisements. I couldn't help but stare, especially now at sunset, where the last light of day changed the colour of the crater from brown to purple. In the morning it would be pink, much like the architectural gem at my back that had stood as long as there had been tourism in Hawaii. The magnificent Royal Hawaiian Hotel. Elena and I would be welcomed inside those pink walls one day. Not this trip, but one day, when her husband was no longer a penniless writer.

A wax orange melted into indigo acid. That was the sun easing nice and slow into the Pacific Ocean for a long dip. I waded out into the waves and dove through the breakers until I reached the deeper water where it was so calm you could just float. There were no people here. I lay back and relaxed and let the tide carry me like a piece of driftwood while I watched the sky. It was so warm, like bathwater. I closed my eyes and breathed deep. These waters had healing properties if you let yourself go and allowed the ocean to swirl and flow and wash over you. This was what it was all about, what we came here for, to find some peace of mind. Aloha would do me fine.

This didn't last. I became aware of another presence in the water. I heard a powerful exhale of $H_2O$, like blowing through a snorkel to empty it. Bloody snorkelers. They had the whole ocean and they decided to surface right beside me. What was the matter with people? *Don't get frazzled. Don't overreact. It had only happened once. Remember why you are here, Eddie.* I calmed and opened my eyes, expecting to see Elena spring out of the water because she had been playing a trick. My wife liked to sneak up and jump on me, or drag me under the water … except she wasn't here.

Out the corner of my eye I saw a dark shape in the water and it was quite large. A smooth hump — mottled green and yellow in colour — surfaced. A small white head, speckled with black around its big black eyes, lifted above the water and took a breath. It was a sea turtle. I began to tread water so I could see it better. This was too surreal. I had never seen a turtle in the wild, and this one was close enough for me to reach out and touch. But I kept my hands to myself and watched the turtle adjust its position in the water so that our eyes met.

'Hello,' I said.

'*Aloha*. I hope I haven't disturbed you,' the turtle replied.

'Not at all. This is your home, I'm just floating on it.'

'Nice sunset.'

'You know it really is. And I've seen all kinds of sunsets, but there's something about Hawaii. It just feels better here, like it's somehow magic.'

'They call it *mana* on these islands. Something you've been searching for.'

'That's right … so, how do I find it?'

'Stop looking. Breathe. Live your life. You never know, *it* might find you.'

'Sounds like a plan. Take care out there.'

'You too. Trust me, things will only get better.' And the turtle dove beneath the water and disappeared.

Weirdness. Could it have been thinking the same bizarre thought? Did we have that conversation intuitively?

Telepathically? Or had we actually spoken the words? Maybe we did. If only the turtle had stuck around a bit longer; the stories it could've told me. I smiled and began to swim back to the beach, excited to tell Elena what had happened.

Later, when I had dried off, we were relaxing on the sand and noticed a crowd moving along the beach toward us. Something of supreme interest had captured the attention of a mostly male audience. All heads around us turned to watch this event. Wolf whistles echoed off the hotels and blew out over the sand and people took photos and laughed and cheered, and then we were among it — right in the thick of the rabble. Two lithe young women were the cause, strutters, soaking wet from head to toe and baring their pale breasts for all to see. What kind of boredom had led to this scandalous display of flesh? Honestly, I had seen better … but nobody else seemed to care, everyone loves a free show. We observed the spectacle closely. These girls were seeking attention from a specific camera, and the ringleader of this circus soon presented himself. A man was moving backwards along the beach, directly in front of the two naked girls, and not immediately obvious because of the crowd around him.

'What kind of smooth-talking creep convinced them to do that?' Elena said.

'Probably the kind that would call it art,' I said.

'I bet. The big sleaze.'

'Clearly he is no professional photographer, he's not even using a proper camera.'

But everything else reeked of money. Gold neck chain. White Capri pants with the legs rolled up behind his knees. Like the girls, he was topless and completely slathered in coconut oil. The air was thick with it — along with another smell, a woody tobacco that drifted from a cigarillo hanging out the corner of his mouth. I began to feel uneasy about the scene, everything was too familiar — the oil, the smoke, the wavy hair exactly like my wife's except it was dark ... I knew this man — *we* knew this man.

'Jesus Christ. It's Roy.' Jackie had warned me not to take my eye off the ball.

Then another commotion occurred and the mob scattered as quickly as it arrived. A pair of police officers had made their way onto the sand to clear the disturbance and have some stern words with the young ladies. No doubt they would discuss the possible legal ramifications that came from girls getting their boobs out on the beach.

'Disturbing the peace. Public nudity. Possession of deadly weapons with intent to use ... This isn't Europe, ladies, we have moral standards on Waikiki. You are over eighteen, aren't you? Good. We're going to have to get your phone numbers ... Why? Standard procedure. And what's your star sign? Scorpio? You know what they say about a girl with a sting in her tail ...'

But the police would never get a chance to follow this line of questioning because the situation was already beyond their control. There were too many bodies in motion. Skins fleeing in every direction. The trouble-making photographer had vanished and the girls had run squealing to the nearest hotel. Unfortunately, the cops began to question anyone left in the immediate area, which included me and Elena.

'Did you guys see who was involved? We had reports of indecent exposure caused by a pair of young girls and a greasy pervert with a camera ...'

'We saw a couple of naked girls running to that hotel. They were being chased by a fat bald dude in red speedos with sinister intentions. If you hurry, you might still catch them,' I said.

'What about him? He looks like he has something to add.' The cops looked at Mr Conroy, who hadn't fled. During the confusion he simply dropped down on the towels beside us and tucked his phone inside his pants — just another tourist laying on the beach watching the sunset. 'Did you see anything, sir?'

'*Mi scusi?*'

'Sorry, officers, but he was with us the whole time and doesn't speak English. He's Italian and naked ladies are the national pastime, so you can understand why he looks happy.'

That was all the convincing they needed. Consequently the police left the scene and we breathed a sigh of relief. Nobody was going to be thrown behind bars and I wouldn't have to call Jackie to pay our bail. Cool cool.

'You filthy old perv!' Elena picked up one of her sandals and threw it at her brother. 'What lies did you tell those girls?

I'll make you famous? Oh, baby, you're a natural, how about one more shot, this time on your knees?'

'Shit, that's a good guess. It's like we're twins or something. All I said was I'm a famous photographer, and they thought that was exciting and wanted to model for me. The girls were more than happy to be directed. You can't blame me for things getting out of hand. It's Eddie's fault really.'

'You wanker. How is this my fault?'

'Your performance to get us inside the conference inspired me to get inventive so I could get inside those lovely girls.'

'Jesus, there's a bit of creative reality. You owe me for bailing you out just now … and you can start by showing me those photos.'

'I'll show you later. It was almost too easy. They probably would have done anything I asked them, and I mean *anything*.'

Elena grabbed her other sandal and jumped on her brother, smacking him across the back and stomach, and any exposed skin she could connect with.

'You-degenerate-arsehole … imagine-what-our-mother-would-say … if-she-knew!'

Each blow was delivered like a professional beat down. Her pimp hand was strong. Anyone watching would've had cause to call the police back to the beach and cite domestic abuse. I winced at the slapping sound as sandal connected with greasy skin. And when Elena coupled it with a taunt about disappointing their mother, I reckon that must've really stung.

After the appropriate amount of punishment was served, Elena hit me once across the thigh. It was a love tap reminding me not to encourage any seedy behaviour. But she had got Mr Conroy a good one. He'd been whipped red like an instant sunburn, although, having your hide lashed by leather is hardly considered punishment when you're an irrepressible degenerate. Mr Conroy thought the whole despicable scenario was hysterical, and laughed as he dodged another thrown sandal and ran to the water to cool his injuries before Elena could pass further judgement.

# Day Two

What a magnificent feeling it was to wake up in paradise. We enjoyed a slow breakfast on the balcony and watched the surfers out on the distant breakers. It was seven-thirty and already I could feel the heat. I loved that. I wanted to grab Elena by the hand and go down for a morning swim. Cleanse the skin in salt water and renew our bodies. Sadly, that would have to wait because there were certain responsibilities to take care of first.

At roughly 9 am, the three of us walked into the conference hall for the first seminar of the day. Elena had a schedule and knew who and what she wanted to see, and organised to meet me and her brother in the Hula Grill for lunch. Then she was gone, removed from all responsibility concerning our behaviour. We were on our own, two suave gentlemen, with no obligation to see any of the conference. However, I thought it might be in our best interest to put in an appearance since we said we had paid. Sitting in the bar all day was too suspicious, some of these people were jealous cutthroats who would rat us out. So Mr Conroy and I ducked into the empty back row and sat down. He already looked glum and restless.

'Why are we here, Eddie?'

'It's Eduardo, remember? And we're here to show Elena support.'

'Show support? Are you kidding? Look at her, she's in her natural habitat. See? Already making friends. You give that girl half a chance and she'll talk the hind legs off a kangaroo and all four off a donkey.'

'That's great, but we still need to solidify our claim as journalists.'

'This is a lot of effort for free drink. Do we have to stay long?'

'I'll tell you what — you play photographer for half an hour, and after, you can drag me around Waikiki shopping. You said you wanted a hat, right? This is the high-end right here. Jewellery, extravagant clothes ... whatever you want to buy.'

'Now you're talking. So what do you want me to do?'

'Just do what you do best — mingle. Start a few conversations and take some pictures, that way we look legit. But go easy on the ladies.'

'I'm sure I don't know what you mean ...'

'You're not a European playboy here to find a wife. You're Pierre Conrad, a freelance photographer working with Eduardo Desah to cover the conference.'

'It won't be as fun ...'

'Let's try to keep the lies believable.'

'Fine. So we'll slip out during the first speaker?'

'Maybe earlier.'

'Wonderful. I'll be back soon.'

You couldn't tether that beast. It was in one ear and out the other. Mr Conroy — or Pierre Conrad — disregarded my advice and went straight for the prettiest woman he could find, and within a minute they were laughing and hanging off each other while he snapped photos. Then he moved on to his next victim, one after another — looks no longer mattered, anyone who identified as female was fair game ... What was he telling these women? I have a yacht in Monaco? A house on Lake Como? Someone with your looks should be on the cover of magazines, you know I'm a famous photographer ... It was glorious to watch, until the scene was shattered by an excited American accent. 'Hey, buddy! Mind if we have a seat?'

'Be my guest,' I said.

And so it began, time for Eduardo Desah to ingratiate himself with the local gentry. Two men with satchel bags, conference programs and cameras took a seat beside me. Journalists — real journalists — who had paid the ticket price to be here and cover the conference for their respective magazines. They removed notebooks and phones and fiddled with gear in preparation for the first speaker.

Once they'd stopped fussing, the man sitting closest said: 'That's an interesting accent you got, buddy. Where you from?'

'Australia, by way of Morocco. The name's Eduardo Desah.'

'Morocco and Australia, that's quite the combo,' the other journalist said.

'What's Morocco like?'

'Magical. The Disneyland of North Africa.'

'No shit? We're from New York and San Diego. I'm Joey Bishop and this is my good friend and long-time rival Nat Baker.'

'We write for competing magazines that produce monthly coffee-table-size monstrosities. I guess they're like the big fashion magazines of the architecture and design world.'

'Must be nice,' I said.

'It has its perks,' Joey said, 'like coming to Hawaii. But a lot of the time it's tear your hair out stressful or dead boring. You've gotta prepare for these conferences the right way, so I start each day with a café au lait laced with a double shot of vodka, and depending on who's here, a midge of cocaine — it'll kick you in the arse and make the day easier to deal with, especially in a seminar where the speaker's a robot.' And he took a long sip from his tall coffee cup and drifted into a trance.

Nat rolled his eyes and took a double shot of nasal spray deep into his nostrils. 'Joey thinks he's funny, but these work trips just allow him to lean into alcoholism.'

'You fucking hypocrite. Everyone knows you don't have allergies and the reason your eyes are always red is because that dispenser is filled with tequila.'

'It's the humidity, I swear … So, Eduardo — we don't see many international faces at these. Who do you write for?'

'*Teak and Rattan Review*. We're a small but sophisticated publication that draws a passionate and pedantic readership. It's a very specific crowd.'

'Never heard of it,' Joey said. He looked puzzled. 'So you do articles about resort furniture?'

'It's like playboy magazine for furniture. I like to write words that get our readers hot and bothered over my photographer's sexy pictures.'

'Sexy pictures?' Nat said.

'Oh yeah, man, we have amateur models use the furniture in a provocative way. Bending over to open a drawer, peeking underneath a cushion, sitting on a chair with a satisfied expression … the response has been overwhelmingly positive.'

'Sounds pretty niche, almost fetishist. That a big deal in Australia?'

'We're big in Europe. Elena Architecture and Design is what's big in Australia. Their director is at this conference doing some cross-Pacific research.'

'Who's that? Are they worth chasing for an interview?'

'Absolutely. Elena Heads is a very talented architect and designer who built her business from the ground up. Going places that girl, a rising star.'

'What does she look like?' Joey said, now fully alert and scouring the audience. 'I'm not going to sit on my hands and let Nat scoop the most interesting interview of the conference.'

'See that woman down the front? Not the one my photographer is running from, the other one ... the little blonde to the right. That's her.'

'Is she why your little rag sent you to Hawaii?' Nat asked.

'Nah, we're here on a piss-take assignment.'

Mr Conroy appeared suddenly and grabbed me by the arm. 'We have to leave. I overplayed my hand and now this pushy bitch is on the phone to her talent manager. The woman's an opportunist. She wants to decorate my yacht while I take photos ...'

'Shit ... Gotta go boys, people to burn and places to see. *Ciao ciao!*'

*

We burst onto Kalakaua Avenue and ran a block until we could hide among the tourists on the sidewalk. The comedown was slow, and Mr Conroy relaxed by sucking on a cigarillo while we worked our way through the crowd and further away from the hotel. When the adrenaline thinned in my own bloodstream, I took stock of the situation. Despite the near bungle, the morning was a success. We had infiltrated foreign territory, been accepted by the natives, spoken their language and with any luck they would make my wife their queen. But perhaps most important of all, we could eat and drink for free without anyone casting suspicion.

So as agreed, I took Mr Conroy shopping, and we strolled along the avenue and window-shopped the best of the best. There was no point taking Mr Conroy to the same ABC store where I had secured my own trilby, that label wouldn't cut it. The perfect hat would require more than a whiff of high-end snobbery, but luckily this was the red light district for posh fashionistas. Each shop that fronted Kalakaua Avenue was window-dressed to attract a certain class — elitists of discerning taste, folk who carelessly throw around money, individuals like my brother-in-law. We happened upon one of these diabolical displays and it stopped Mr Conroy dead. 'Ooh. Hello beautiful.'

The manikin in the window wore a blue sports coat, a red silk scarf, and on its head sat a bright white trilby. Mr Conroy molested the ensemble with his eyes and took a deep drag on his smoke. 'Isn't she lovely, Eddie? The craftsmanship. The way she sits jauntily on top of his head. White so crisp she is blinding me. I must have her.'

'Are you sure? I admit the hat's lovely, but if you want to show off, burning hundred dollar bills on the sidewalk will have the same effect.'

'Spoken like a true poor person. I love you Ed, but when you've never had money you learn to make do with what you can afford. Your hat is very nice, you shopped well. But this hat, she calls to me like the sirens of myth, she says *Conroy, wear the Gucci,* and I must go to her.'

So he bought the hat, the red scarf, and a shirt so eye-wateringly expensive its value baffled me. Then, to prove a point, we stood out the front of the shop and Mr Conroy handed me a hundred dollar bill. I held it up and he set it alight and we watched it burn while the hysterical Gucci staff cried in the shop window. But none of this mattered. We had killed enough time for us to safely return to the hotel, and I could get back to abusing the privilege of my press pass.

*

I sat underneath an outrigger canoe that was suspended from the ceiling, with only my notebook, a piece of pineapple upside-down cake and a Kona Longboard beer for company. The Plantation Bar was practically empty. After our little shopping expedition, Mr Conroy had gone back to his room to admire his new clothes in the mirror. Who knew how many outfits that human clothes rack would acquire before this holiday was over? He'd fill another suitcase for sure.

With the style guru occupied, I waited for Elena's seminar to end so we could have lunch together. I sipped my beer and scribbled in my notebook, dot-pointing ideas that could be expanded into a narrative worth reading. Most of it was time-wasting garbage, complete bullshit, my best ideas always came to me in the shower. On the other hand — and maybe it was beer greasing the wheels — I'd gone deep on the trials that come with negotiating the price of art on a dirt roadside in Tanzania. Focus had been difficult with goats prodding my legs while I shooed the *tsetse* flies and tried to ignore the banana salesman screaming nearby. How much *did* I spend on that painting? And to add insult to injury, the dealer took a photo of the canvas before handing it over so the artist could paint it again stroke for stroke. The cunning bastard. There was little doubt in my mind I'd been outmanoeuvred in the haggle.

My concentration was broken by a well-dressed, middle-age gentleman who approached my table and said: 'Excuse me, sir, they told me this is where I might find a free beer and a character named Eduardo Desah.'

'It appears you've struck gold and found the free beer.'

'Lucky me. Do you mind if I join you?'

'Well, that depends on who you are.'

'Don't worry, I'm not a salesman. I'm a prime mover. An instigator of exceptional opportunities. My name is William Billingsley, but most people just call me Bill.'

He extended a hand and I shook it. The grip was firm without any overexertion, Bill wasn't trying to assert dominance. I took that as a good sign. A man that tries to squeeze the life out of your hand usually has deep psychological problems. Anyway, I felt comfortable enough to introduce myself as Eduardo Desah.

'Forgive me if I butchered your surname, is it pronounced De-sa or Dee-sa?'

'It's more like the first way except you have to put more emphasis on the ending. Say it with me, De-saaaa.'

'De-saaaa.'

'There you go.'

'Excellent. It always helps to ask straight out, that way you can't make a fool of yourself. So you're a journalist for a vintage furniture magazine?'

'That's one version of the truth, but I prefer to think of myself as a storyteller, a novelist. That is the promised land.'

'How so?'

'Look around us. A warm and welcoming vibe. Sunshine at your back. Sitting here under this magical floating canoe, across from a stylish tiki bar where we can drink as much free beer as we want.'

'So the promised land is liquid *aloha*? You do realise that all the journalists are entitled to this same experience, it's one of the conference incentives.'

'And yet we're sitting here all by ourselves. It's why *every* journalist dreams of one day chucking it all in and becoming a novelist.'

'For the sunshine and the free beer?'

'Exactly. So what can I do for you, Bill?'

'Journalist or novelist, whatever you may be, you and your photographer tore a streak through the conference this morning, spoke with most of the important people, snapped some pics and took your leave. Very efficient, very mysterious. Word has been getting around that you're a man worth talking to.'

Efficient? Mysterious? All I'd done was execute an Australian half-arsed performance — you put in a quick appearance and when nobody is looking, fuck off to the pub. How had I become someone worth talking to? I wasn't sure if I liked where this was going, but I let it play out for the time being. 'Worth talking to ... Is that right? I guess it depends on what you want to talk about.'

'Are you suspicious of everyone, Mr De-saaaa?'

'Please, call me Ed — and yeah, I'm suspicious of everyone. It's nothing personal. I've discovered you can't trust a person until they've laid it all out on the table. Everyone here is pretending to be someone they're not.'

'That's fair. I can appreciate your point of view, therefore allow me to lay it all on the table. I work with some influential business people who have their fingers in many, many pies, and one of those happens to be hotel and resort development.'

'That sounds like an important gig.' I signalled the bartender for two beers.

They were brought right over and Bill thanked the bartender, gave me a grateful nod and took a sip from his beer. 'You're right, it's a position of significance. My people have been looking to invest outside of the United States market for some time. They're already established here and in the Caribbean. However, they have yet to crack the

Asian marketplace. We're aware of the enormous potential in the area but we have zero contacts on the ground. This is why I wanted a word with you. I understand you work for a magazine that is tapped right in at the source.'

Panic struck like a bolt of lightning. How the hell had this happened? Second day into this trip and I was already in over my head. I thought about excusing myself, maybe I had been overcome by a sudden stomach cramp that needed attention in the bathroom. Then I'd dump my press pass in the bin, give up this charade and escape to sunnier prospects.

For whatever reason, I stayed put. Maybe it was purely some disturbed need to find out how far I could push this farce, or maybe it was that Bill wasn't like the others. He hadn't just come to the conference for a break from real life, where he could drink and shag his way to oblivion. Bill appeared to be genuine, hardworking and interested in his work. The man was actually wearing a suit and tie — pure linen and silk, a sensible and stylish choice. I downed half the beer in one long pull and prepared to lean right into this character I had created. As a hard-hitting, feet on the ground journalist, Eduardo Desah had to see where this was going.

'So what can my little magazine tell you about the Asian hotel market?'

'We've investigated a lot of the islands in South East Asia, and Bali looks like it has the greatest potential, commercially speaking.'

'Have you been to Bali?'

'Sadly, no. Neither have any of the investors.'

That put me at ease. I had been to Bali, now the ball was in my court.

'My grandfather and I were once talking about travel. He was in the British Navy during World War Two, and sailed the world. He saw the Caribbean and travelled around the horn of Africa and crossed the Indian Ocean several times over. He'd tell me about ports through Asia, exotic locales where the sailors would buy spice and jewellery for next to nothing, and resell it for a fortune when they returned to England. But three things always stuck with me from these tales. He preferred the Caribbean, specifically Jamaica, that island just vibrated at a better frequency with him, and there was also something about good rum and gorgeous women with big round bottoms — two weaknesses I seem to have inherited through blood.'

'Your grandfather sounds like a citizen of the world.'

'He really was.'

'So what was the third thing that stuck with you about his stories?'

'A few years back my wife and I went to Bali. We'd planned a holiday where we would see most of what the island had to offer. Anyway, I told my grandfather our plans because he'd been to Bali twice. Once as a young man, when it was still dirt roads and fishing villages. The second time was more recently. And do you know what he said to me?'

'What did he say?'

'He said: "Bali. You'll go once and you'll never go back. For someone like you, Ed, once will be enough. You can't find yourself in a place like Bali, all you'll discover is a hatred for your own culture." And he was right.'

'So why didn't you want to go back? What's so wrong with the island? By all accounts it's a gorgeous escape. My nieces went last year, and if you saw the photographs from their visit … It looks a helluva good time.'

'Let me tell you something about Bali. It was once a paradise, but no more. Tourism promised so much and became the island's fatal undoing. Now it's a dump filled to the brim with drunk Australians, B-grade celebrities and desperate locals. The amount of traffic for such a small island is obscene, and you can't even see the beach from the road because it's been built out by too many resorts. The place is choking on its own success.'

'Jesus Christ, you really know how to take the wind out of a man's sails.'

'Don't get me wrong, there's still beauty, but it would take a disaster of plague proportion to reset that island. Then I might go back … Or it could be I've gone soft and reached an age where I look at the wild places of the world and no longer see adventure, but a filthy stain I'll spend years trying to wash out. I sound like a snob but that's the hard truth. You look pale, Bill, have a drink.'

Bill had a drink, regained some composure, and became very serious, 'The investors already have their eye on potential real estate. I'm now in two minds about whether I should inform them to pull the plug and look elsewhere.'

'Don't be crazy. This is a one person's opinion, one with an old-world sensibility. You're in the business of making money, and there is a ton to be made in Bali. If you plant yourself in the right location there will be no shortage of guests — ever. Especially from Australia. You'd be amazed how many people take advantage of a scenario that allows them to behave like wild animals. And truth be told, if it's not you it'll be someone else fucking up the shoreline.'

'That does make me feel better. They were right, you were worth talking to. It's always good to have an honest conversation with someone who really knows. You know?' Bill finished his beer and looked thoughtful. 'If we push ahead with this deal, would you be able to recommend someone to consult on the development? That's part of the reason I'm here, we're head-hunting architects and designers but the American sensibility won't fly in Bali, and we know the best Asian firms will bleed us like a stuck pig.'

'You got lucky. I happen to be here in co-operation with one of Australia's finest interior design and architecture firms. Maybe you've met the boss already, her name is Elena Heads, of Elena Architecture and Design?'

'The magazine boys mentioned her. Do you think we could set up a meeting?'

'Easy done. When is good for you?'

'As soon as possible. I'm only in town for the duration of the conference.' Bill stood up and slid his business card across the table. 'I'm staying at the Royal Hawaiian. Make sure you pass that on to Elena, I think this could be a tremendous opportunity. Pleasure meeting you, Ed.'

*

We were doing 55 mph in Mr Conroy's hire car — a bright white Chevrolet Camaro with the roof folded down. Our destination was up the highway, a pleasant cruise through the middle of the island to the Oahu north shore for some sightseeing. This was Jackie's idea but he was distracted. He leaned around the front seat, trying to understand my bizarre behaviour and the unusual circumstances we now found ourselves in.

'Dude, you were working at that shady travel magazine for too long. All the lying has become a bad habit, one you've managed to carry into the real world.'

'Well, that's honest. But this was a rare deal, and that's honest. Honestly. It's like being at the zoo and the exotic animals are hiding, the special ones that make the whole trip worthwhile, so you rattle the cages and wait to see what comes out. You've got to do that every now and then. Sometimes something special will show up — that's what's happening here.'

'Okay, I can appreciate that. But it still doesn't explain one thing, how the hell have you been getting away with this?'

'I'm beloved by the conference community.'

'Uh huh. I bet you've been like the cheap perv at a strip club, watching everyone make a scene while you hide in the back row with a drink and a smile because you know you'll never have to tip.'

'He knows you too well, Ed,' Mr Conroy said.

'This is just slander and bitterness because he's not involved. And we weren't drinking all day, we've been semi-social. One conference attendee even called us the curiosity of the season, although looking back, I don't think it was meant as a compliment.'

'Let them look down their noses while the other half adore us,' Mr Conroy added. 'It will throw them off the scent. And I wouldn't worry about us, Jackie, the scam was easy to pull off. Whether or not we get away with it for the entire conference ...'

'I'm not worried, I just can't believe nobody has checked your background. Maybe they really don't care about two Aussies robbing them blind.'

'He's an idiot, Jackie,' Elena said. 'I swear it's a pre-mid-life crisis.'

'It's not a pre-mid-life crisis. I'm having fun.'

'He's supposed to be figuring out whether he's a journalist or a novelist, and suddenly he's a world-class con artist. It's pure dumb luck they haven't been busted. But I suppose I can't be too upset — meeting Mr Billingsley could be worthwhile as long as Eddie doesn't talk himself into a hole beforehand.'

Jackie stroked his beard. 'Don't stress, El. It looks like Ed has found a bit of that pirate mongrel again. He'll find a way to weasel out if it all goes sideways. But you should probably ride the crazy train as far as you can while you can. All you lot have to do is keep your story straight, and if Billingsley is on the level, well, who knows what could happen?'

'It's so exciting! Even if the meeting turns out to be nothing but lattes and cake, I'll still be inside the Royal Hawaiian Hotel. You have no idea how much of a dream come true that would be. I *love* that building. We should have a drink there anyway, all of us, just for fun.'

Elena's enthusiasm was infectious, because everyone thought that sounded like a grand idea. The rest of the drive was laid-back. I inhaled the warm humid air and admired the scenery as the car drove by jungle-covered mountains, over deep mist-filled gorges, alongside vast pineapple fields, and finally onto scrubby grassland as we approached the ocean again. It was late afternoon when the Camaro cruised onto the top end of the island. We checked out the hunkered-down surf shacks, and watched the locals driving their shitty rusted-out wagons to the beach so they could hit the late swell and have a sunset surf. It was a scene not unlike Australian coastlines, except nobody in our car lived near the ocean so this was a unique novelty.

We pulled over to buy some coconut shrimp from a food truck and then sat on the warm sand to eat and watch the waves roll in. I had seen a rock pool when we first arrived on the north shore, and we drove back along our route until we found it again. There was still plenty of daylight, and the early evening remained hot and the water looked so inviting that we decided go for a swim. The enormous pool was protected on the ocean side by large rocks that acted as a natural break from the waves, however, the current inside the pool remained strong and made swimming around the razor-sharp rock and coral a challenge. But these natural obstacles didn't stop us pushing the experience further. Jackie had hired snorkel gear, so he and I went snorkelling while the twins sat on the shore and watched the sun set. We dove in and paddled around the pool for a short time, and watched little striped fish being stirred into a frenzy by the incoming tide as it swirled through the rocks and bubbled the cool clear water — now tinted gold from the drowning sun. I felt as if we were swimming in an enormous vat of champagne. And before we got cut to shreds by the coral we made our way back to the sand, where Elena and Conroy were taking photos and soaking in the fire and magnificence of it all.

*

An hour later we were back at the hotel. Elena made her phone call to Bill Billingsley and they arranged to meet for a coffee the next morning. Things were on the move.

# Day Three

The room phone rang. It was reception. Two messages had been left for us. One was for Elena from Bill Billingsley, apologising because he had to reschedule their meeting — probably to the following day, but he'd be in touch.

The second was from my brother.

'Dude, there's a place that rents Harleys only a couple of blocks away. You can book a bike for tomorrow's location scout. There's also good eating nearby, did you guys want to meet after? We can grab some food and talk some shit.'

It was a solid plan, so we collected Mr Conroy and set out for a walk to the far end of Royal Hawaiian Boulevard.

It smelt like a storm was coming, the morning muggy and overcast. I enjoyed that kind of weather, though, once we turned off Kalakaua Avenue and began walking up

Royal Hawaiian Boulevard, the scenery and smells changed dramatically. This was an Asian tourist hub; a pickup-drop-off zone for several popular Asian tour businesses. Double-decker and coach buses choked the narrow boulevard, along with taxis, scooters, parked cars and the odd Harley Davidson. It was hot and noisy and stank of diesel fumes, until we reached the other end of the block where we passed many stores operated by Korean and Japanese expats and everything opened up again.

A fold-out sign advertising a shrimp shack sat on the sidewalk. Jackie stood beside the sign flapping both arms, squawking and stomping his feet like some mutant bird of paradise. He said the bizarre dance was to get our attention. It looked more like he was trying to make polite tourists on the street uncomfortable, and when all the foot traffic crossed the road and gave the restaurant a miss, I became certain it was by design. Notice had been given, this was *his* territory.

My brother led us into the space between the two buildings where we discovered the alley wasn't an alley at all. It was an oasis from the chaos of the boulevard. A food paradise with atmosphere to match. The alley had been converted into an outdoor restaurant. The concrete ground had been built over with a wood deck, and the walls of the surrounding buildings painted in bright graffiti murals that related to Honolulu and its adopted Asian cuisine. Power and phone lines and Chinese lanterns criss-crossed overhead. Travel journalists describe multicultural cities as melting pots, a little bit of everything from all over the world, and here it was a world behaving at its finest. This was the mood in the shrimp shack — which made it easy to overlook that this fine eatery was a fire trap, one loose powerline or kitchen fire away from major disaster. You thought you were getting fried shrimp? Try chargrilled tourist instead, made from parts far and wide. It was a horrific thought that never entered anyone's mind because the place just felt *right*.

Everyone was feeling good seated around a picnic bench in the deserted alley. The wild-eyed creature flapping its wings out front had also brought beer, and he called for a bottle opener.

'I've got you covered,' the man in charge said. He reached under the counter, came over and began to crack the cap off each beer using a bottle opener attached to a foot-long wood handle that looked like it had once been a canoe paddle. 'You guys are Australian, aren't you? I can pick that accent anywhere. You guys like Midnight Oil? I love Midnight Oil. Man, what a band. I followed them on tour a few years back. Chased them right across the Pacific Ocean, from Seattle to Honolulu, Brisbane and beyond. Good times. Wild times! Especially in Australia, you bunch of half-drunk maniacs driving on the wrong side of the road. I'm from the States, so if an Aussie band comes through and you miss them, you'd better be willing to risk life and limb to catch 'em.'

It is a wonderful thing that strangers from opposite sides of the world can meet in a back alley restaurant, on an island in the middle of the Pacific, and connect over music. The chef came out of the kitchen with our sticky rice and piping hot shrimp, the steam rising toward those criss-crossed overhead wires. I knew the food was going to be fantastic because the chef was a big, happy Polynesian dude. Pacific Islanders love a feed and they know how to cook, and this dude looked well fed on his own cooking. This was a winner. The chef and the man in charge were so welcoming that Jackie offered them our last two beers and they happily accepted. Bottles clinked, food was eaten. It was a quality atmosphere.

'So, the producers have organised a photoshoot with our lead actress today,' Jackie said. 'We're doing it up north, away from prying eyes. Any of you interested?'

'Interested in seeing a photoshoot of a famous actress? As if you had to ask.'

'Good stuff. Roy is in — you can drive me in the Camaro, it'll be a lot nicer than being crammed in a van with the support staff. What about you guys?'

'Shit,' Elena said, 'I can't make it. There's a seminar before lunch I have to see. It better be rewarding if I have to miss out on this.'

'Bummer. So, bro, what do you reckon? This will be a great way to start the exposé, you won't want to miss it.'

'Whoa, I think I've been overdoing everything, it's anti-productive to a finding a stable state of mind. I need to decompress and relax on my own. Getting lost in thought feels like the way to go this morning, not getting in trouble with you pair of lunatics. I can start the article later.'

'You know these opportunities don't come along every day.'

'Nah, I'm good.'

'Suit yourself, but expect a call from me anyway. There'll be details. We better get moving, Roy. My actress is flying in mid-morning and a car is driving her straight to the location. El, good luck at the seminar. Catch you both for dinner?'

Our crew parted ways, with Mr Conroy just about skipping down the sidewalk in anticipation. It was a good thing Jackie was there to keep him in line. Mr Conroy would probably try to muscle in and declare himself the on-set stylist so he could get some face time with the starlet. And if he got that, he'd push his luck to the limit. Jackie had to know what he was in for. Maybe that was half the fun? But not for me, not today. I was looking forward to hearing about it at dinner.

\*

My alone time began with a short glass of rum in the Plantation Bar. The free beer was excellent but it suited me to actually open my wallet for once and pay for three fingers of fine golden liquor to help the creative juices flow. I could get into my writing now, expel any outside disturbances and simply be. But, as I'd come to expect, that never lasted long.

'Hard at work, I see.'

'Bill Billingsley, I didn't expect to see you today.' I took a sip of rum. 'This isn't so much work as it is putting my thoughts in order.'

'Planning your next move against the conference, am I right?'

'That's the hard truth of it, Bill. It's a game of chess out there, with a lot of obscure details to consider, like when to leave information out, what is worth sharing, and who should be involved or avoided at all cost.'

'Do you always go deep when writing about furniture? Which reminds me, everyone has been arguing about the exact nature of your publication, nobody could decide what it was. Some people thought you reviewed resort furniture, another thought it was antiques ... and someone was even under the impression it was high-class pornography for people with a furniture kink.'

'Oh, it's definitely the last one.'

'That's what I thought.' Bill gave me a sly smile. 'Well, sir, I'll leave you to unravel the complexities of the conference, but I have a question about your associate — am I correct in assuming Elena is your wife?'

'You're a perceptive man, Bill. She's still keen to meet with you by the way.'

'Good. I will meet Elena before I go back to the States, that's a promise. Work just got in the way today,' Bill sighed. 'The problem with being so good at my job is whenever

Papa leaves home and the house catches fire, nobody knows what to do!'

He tipped his hat and left. Even though the bamboozled conference crowd couldn't figure out the nature of my ridiculous magazine, I suspected Bill was sharper than your average seminar attendee and knew I wasn't writing any kind of article. But did he care? Would any of these little white lies catch up with me? Maybe ... Maybe Jackie was right and I'd worked for that deceitful travel magazine a few years too many. I hadn't even come to Hawaii for work. This was about getting our heads in the right space to move forward, but here, like at home, I was still pretending to be a journalist. Pretend to do something for long enough and you're no longer pretending, are you? Professional faker Eddie Heads ... Maybe my destiny *was* to make shit up and pass it off as actual reportage. No, I didn't like that. I wanted to write fiction, not fake news. That horrid glimpse into the future put my brain into a melt. I decided to get some fresh air and sunshine before I succumbed to this nightmare and gave up on bigger dreams.

*

Elena found me outside on the terrace. Working on my tan, a decent buzz, and the six-gun showdown to save the Arrow Head cattle ranch — the book Jackie had given me was a ripper. He'd got himself in quite the pickle had quick, slick Rick Trickle. Would he survive the unexpected return of his old gang? Would he win the heart of the cattle baron's daughter? That hot young firecracker named Belle ... You could pretty much guarantee it, but tune in next week for the exciting conclusion to *Hell is a Hot Bullet!*

Elena dropped onto the deckchair beside me and began to vent. 'What is the go with all this wannabe glitterati? Fuck you, posers!' She flipped off a cluster of aspiring models wearing metallic bikinis and so much bling they could've passed for a disco ball. 'I don't think I can take any more of these speakers. This one stood there and flapped his cheeks at the audience for an hour, just real windy. Which shouldn't be a surprise when his face looked like a smacked arse, but sometimes I think people don't even realise they're being idiotic and inappropriate.'

'Who was it this time?'

'Some swine named Trevor Avertine. The second this bastard opened his mouth I lost interest in the presentation. I mean talk about clueless arseholes, this one managed to insult half the audience and drain the life out of the room at the same time.'

'So what did this arsehole have to say?'

'The same thing as any arsehole — nothing but shit and weird noises.'

'You sound like you need a drink. I'll flag the waitress.'

'The smug little fucker kept inferring that designers wouldn't understand and we should defer to our *superior* architect brethren for guidance. But some designers *are* architects! The son of a bitch thinks all we're good for is fluffing pillows. I honestly believe he doesn't know the difference between a decorator and a designer, just like he wouldn't know his mouth from his shit-hole.'

The waitress looked beyond embarrassed and unsure where to look. I could see her trying to process the situation; how should she approach the question about our choice of drink? Could she do it without getting her head bitten off? It could have been an awkward stalemate with Elena still in the grip of some primitive jungle fury — so I took over. 'Please excuse her, she becomes a cranky little shit when her blood sugar is low and there's injustice everywhere. It's fucking lucky there's no one around with a sensitive disposition.' And then I ordered two cocktails.

The conference was clearly working like a charm, passionate anger was a good sign that Elena was finding her groove again. That made me happy, and so had her rant.

After a few stress-relieving cocktails doused any inclination toward violence, Elena returned to the conference for another seminar, and I checked my phone. There was a voicemail from Jackie, a lovely message that caused me to hold the phone away before my eardrum burst. Jesus Christ! Thirty seconds of chimpanzee-level aggression, aimed at that 'bleeding cunt-rag actress'. I could only imagine the ugly scene that led to this rage explosion, and my vibe was in serious danger of being killed by its reverberations. The best way forward — according to the chemicals altering my decision-making — was to follow Elena into the conference hall.

It soon became apparent I had made a terrible mistake.

*

How had I gotten in this situation? This was supposed to be fun, a way to screw the conference out of free food and drink, and now I was a victim of my own approachable nature and likability. Spiritualists call that karma. My phantom magazine had become such a hot topic of interest among the other journalists and conference attendees that I had landed an interview with a supposedly prominent interior designer. One of the three best on the United States west coast. Her name was Connie Petterson. She'd given me her card so I wouldn't misspell her name in the article. This would either be a monumental waste of time, or an opportunity to make more friends on foreign soil with my first genuine interview in years. I was actually nervous.

Ten minutes into our conversation I realised this was a slow train to nowhere, and after Connie had mentioned for the fourth time that her design firm was rated top three in Las Vegas, my mind began to drift. I nodded and scribbled notes and daydreamed of the beach while she went on and on … about what, I couldn't be certain. I suspected it was about how the sun shone out her arse. A typical glowing review where everything her business touched turned to gold. This was a common phenomenon. I'd heard it all before, and I realised instead of talking about the conference, she was using this interview as free advertisement to further her business. A public relations opportunity sent from the great southern land. Did this woman realise who I was? Apparently she hadn't listened to the other conference attendees about the nature of my magazine — any publicity was good publicity. But the joke was on her, the great Eduardo Desah did not tolerate a big-noting twat intent on killing his buzz.

Connie's self-congratulatory vomit continued. 'Actually, I think that's why I'm good enough to design anywhere in the world. I could even outfit a palace for royalty. Do they have palaces in Morocco? What's Morocco like?'

'Beautiful country. Spectacular. Palaces everywhere, beaches covered in gemstones — you can pick diamonds right off the sand.'

'*No*. Really? You're pulling my leg.'

Inside the conference walls, lying was as easy as breathing. I didn't need to do it and it was not my character to lie so outrageously — or was it? Maybe it was that lingering bad habit. I'd throw in the odd nugget of truth so my story didn't fall apart, but damn it was fun to see what I could get away with. Hell, I was on holiday and never going to see these people again, and the self-involved Connie was irritating the shit out of me. This *was not* the kind of work relationship I needed to cultivate, so I started laying it on thick. 'That's an honest fact, Connie. You have to wear sandals on the beach otherwise your feet are cut to shreds.

It's like walking on coloured glass. Although, damned magnificent at sunset.'

'*Holy crap*, are you for real? See, that's what happens when common people don't know what they've got. Everyone could be a millionaire. I need to go there, I'd be a queen for sure. What language do they speak in Morocco?'

'French.'

'Ooh, *tres chic*, I've always wanted to learn French. Do you speak it?'

*'Je ne parle pas bien le francais.'*

'Ooh, impressive. What did you say?'

'It's not important. So, on with the interview.'

I wanted to escape, but she was one of those frustrating people who couldn't end a conversation and would bring it back in the same direction over and over and over. These monsters would happily use up all the oxygen in the room if it meant they got to talk for forty-five minutes about the thing most important to them, namely themselves. I was stuck on that carousel. It was too painful — I had to end this thing quick. And then she gave me a perfect out. Somewhere between the words me, myself and I, came a glimmer of hope.

'So why are they even letting you foreigners into this conference? I mean, I can understand Morocco, any place where they speak French and diamonds fall out of the sand deserves my respect, but have you met the Australian designer? I bet she's come to poach clients. It's despicable. Stealing work from honest hard-working Americans ...'

'Except she hasn't come to steal anyone's clients. She came to expand her knowledge base and see how things are done around other parts of the world.'

'I doubt that. She sounded pretty full of herself, spouting how her little studio has won several national awards. Like — it's Australia, so who cares? She and those California designers have been getting on famously too, always talking about mid-century style. Like they would know. Look at them, no class, it makes me sick.'

'Surely you can't be jealous? What happened to comradery and female empowerment? I would have thought being a fellow designer you would celebrate the achievements of other women in your industry.'

'In my trade everyone is the enemy. Don't print that. They either work for me or I stamp them out. Don't print *that* either. I can't have outsiders trying to move in on my turf. How do you think I got to be top three in — actually, I'm going to need editorial approval before you publish this interview.'

'Never gonna happen. Getting back to the subject, can you really even class yourself as a designer? Aren't you just a glorified decorator? You pick the curtains and furniture — that's why we're talking, right? *Teak and Rattan Review* isn't interested in hobbyists.'

'*I'm a designer.* That's my official title, because I design *the whole interior.*'

She was getting flustered, waving her hands in the air as she talked. Her face had turned the colour of ripe watermelon and there were two distinct veins bulging at the corners of her forehead. This woman might be an aneurism waiting to happen. Did I dare push on?

'So, you have an architecture background?'

'No. Why would I need that?'

'Because interior design is more than just throwing a flattering blanket over a hand-picked sofa. It's hours of drafting blueprints for entire kitchens, bathrooms and living areas. Noting how every cupboard and drawer works, drawing the tiny details …'

'I think you're confused. We don't do that — that's architects.'

'No, that's the job. You see, I'm a close personal friend of that Australian designer and that's exactly what's required. You would be classified as a decorator. It's a common misconception, even within the industry. Many decorators call themselves designers without knowing the real depth of skill required.'

'Now you're calling me unskilled? That's just rude. You're unskilled, and I don't think you're very good at your job. *You're* a hack and *I'm* an interior designer, one of the top three in Las Vegas.' Connie stood up. 'And this interview is over.'

She stormed off and I shouted down the aisle after her, 'No one likes a pretender, Connie!' A nearby row of architects were staring. 'Can you believe some people?' I said to them and nodded toward Connie. 'Sneaking into the conference and pretending to be something they're not. Shameless.'

Brazen and unforgivable the architects agreed. I was a bastard, but thank the Hawaiian gods that was over, tonight I would sacrifice many cocktails in their honour. It might have been harsh to put Connie in her place but she needed to hear the hard truth. The other designers, architects and decorators knew their business like true professionals. I noticed every journalist in the conference hall was laughing, and they gave me a standing ovation. Joey and Nat had thrown me this interview. A prominent designer from the west coast they'd said. Top three in Las Vegas, whatever the hell that meant. The mongrels had set me up. I smiled and gave my audience the middle finger salute and went to the Plantation Bar to wipe my palate clean of that sour experience.

*

4 pm. The Plantation Bar. I'd been on this assignment for three days now. It was Friday, or maybe Monday. Who could be sure in this heat? Every day was blurring into one long sun-bleached, sepia-tone episode … and now the booze was beginning to run the show. Words had been exchanged with many unsavoury characters, but my cover remained intact — as far as I could tell. The peril of a private detective being undercover as an investigative reporter is you have to be everywhere, and everyone knows your face. So, how long before that cookie crumbles?

Things were wild and hairy. This assignment was making me weird. Or was that the rum rotting my brain? Maybe it was both. Either way, I was definitely getting weirder than I already was. I sure could go for a cigarette right now ... and then I remembered I didn't smoke. Never had.

My photographer had been slipped a twenty to get his arse down to the pool terrace and follow a new lead in the case. I wanted him to take some good pictures of the crime scene, and hoped he could keep his focus off the bikini-clad bodies long enough to operate a camera. A person of interest had jumped from a tenth floor balcony. Suicide they said. Except when he hit the water blood oozed from a dozen stab wounds in his back. A bit of digging informed me he was a journalist out on his first big assignment — now out for the count. Welcome to Honolulu old chum, at least you'll be used to the temperature when you get to Hell. So which of the conference attendees had he crossed? The eccentric Hollywood director? The man in the Panama hat that represented the movers and shakers on the mainland? Everything was a possibility now.

I was in over my head. Should I pack it in and get out of town? Give the woman back her money? *Sorry, lady, you're in too deep with this crowd and I've already made too many enemies.* That would be smart, except I wasn't smart, this broad already had her hooks in me. Maybe Honolulu did as well. I ordered three fingers of rum and told Joe to hold the ice. I swirled my glass and stared into that gold abyss.

And then she was there, a silky silhouette against the sun. Her outline resembled a ukulele melting into the floor. A real dish. The woman of my dreams. She sashayed over, swinging those hips like a hula dancer, and leaned on the counter and ordered the same drink I held in my hand.

'Don't worry about it, Joe,' I said. 'Here, doll, why don't you share mine?'

'Thank you. I'd like that.'

And I liked watching those shiny pink lips caress the glass while warm rum slid down her slender throat. She put the empty glass on the bar. It now had an impression on the rim, and I stared at that pink print and wondered what it would be like to kiss her. She noticed, and when our eyes met again she licked those sweet lips. Jesus Christ. Could I maintain composure? The temperature had gone up one hundred degrees. She gave me a crooked smile, a gangster smile. No — more like a pirate. This woman was definitely a pirate. Those piercing blue eyes held too many secrets.

She flicked blonde hair out of her face and said: 'Don't go to the conference today, Eddie. It won't be any good for your health.' She slid her room key under my hand.

More trouble, and I was too dumb to walk away. Why are the bad ones always so good? I was a goner, it would take a mighty effort to back out now. I had her money and she had me right where she wanted, between her and a crime syndicate.

One of us was going to die before this thing was over.

Then she was gone. I left a tip under the empty glass and grabbed a match-book from a basket on the bar and went outside for a smoke. Hopefully I would come to my senses before I went upstairs and let this pirate snooker me. I looked across the sand. It would be easy to go soft in a place like this with a gal like that. I flipped open the match-book, tore one off, and placed it between my teeth while I patted my chest pocket, looking for a packet of cigarettes. And I remembered that I didn't smoke, never had. Well at least I had my gun ... didn't I? It was gone, probably lifted by some shifty contractor while I was working the conference hall. Or had the dame taken it while we were in the bar? Was this a setup? I fancied that was the game. The curtains would be drawn when I opened the door, and there'd be two flashes as I stepped inside her room. Yeah, that was the game. The last thing I'd probably see was her naked, standing over me with a smoking revolver. My revolver. That'd be the worst way to go really — not being shot with my own gun, but knowing that she was there, naked, and I couldn't do a thing about it.

Who were these people? What the hell kind of conference was this anyway?

*

I closed my notebook and put the pen away. Cheesecake and cliché. No wonder pulp fiction was so hard to write well, it was too much fun. Still, the story had potential. A hardboiled noir thriller set in a fantastic version of Hawaii. No restrictions, just room to get bent. Was this the way? Maybe. There was plenty of holiday left to figure things out, but if I was going to pretend to be anything, it may as well be a novelist.

*

The conference was almost over. Short and sweet is how Elena described it, and she was right, but there was one last seminar to attend in the late afternoon. The closing ceremony.

Elena went and sat with her contemporaries from California. Clothed in dark sunglasses with my trilby pulled down tight, I took my usual seat in the back row. I'd brought a beer inside the hall and was doing my best to look unfriendly by spreading my legs and resting my arms across the back of the seats. Finally — just to hammer the point home — I'd taken a DO NOT DISTURB sign from the room and attached it to my press pass so it hung around my neck. Great sixties soul man Billy Stewart wrote a song about a man in a similar predicament. He was waiting for a woman too, except he was sitting in a park, which always felt wrong to me, I could've sworn he was sitting in a bar while he waited for that woman, and like me he was questioning his sanity. *Sha-la-la-la.* Damn right, Billy. Something told me I was a fool too, because none of this mattered in the end, they turned down the hall lights. Only the stage and the speaker remained lit.

There was a speech by the MC. He went through the usual closing statements you hear at any event. 'We'd like to thank everyone for taking the time to come out and make this a great experience. Numbers are up this year compared to last … I love the sound of my own voice … Next year we'll be in Vegas, where you can enjoy my voice again as I give my best impersonation of the Rat Pack … You know I was once slapped by Dean Martin? … We'd like to thank the hotel for having us, now watch me wank myself all over the front row … Your input has helped make this the best conference in years … Blah, blah, blah. I'm a big shiny dick.'

The beer was gone. I stuck my tongue inside the brown bottle and tried to pry out every last amber drop, but to my great regret, it was empty. I squirmed in my seat and tried not to die a slow, boredom-induced death. The situation appeared hopeless. I should have brought two beers with me … Why didn't I? In fact — why couldn't I? Who cared if it was the height of rudeness to leave right now? I'll tell you who, everyone except for the lowbrow press from *Teak and Rattan Review*. Where was Mr Conroy anyhow? Still on the road with Jackie after trying to pick up that famous actress? Or out chasing the local talent? Probably both, knowing that man.

Another speech was about to start, so I snuck out of the hall and made my way to the Plantation Bar. Before I even made my order, the smiling bartender was sliding a fresh beer across the bar. 'Enjoy, Mr Desah!' What a saint.

By the time I returned to the hall and took my seat, the speech was wrapping up and the conference master of ceremonies took to the microphone one more time.

'Okay, folks, before we close out this year's event, it's time for the lucky door prizes. First prize, as it is every year, courtesy of our sponsors, is an all-expenses-paid trip to next year's event! This includes airfare, hotel, conference passes and meals for the duration. Isn't that something? Okay, here we go, let's draw the name of our lucky winner …'

There was a cheer from somewhere within the hall. I don't recall who won. Someone popular with the regulars, because everyone clapped and shouted approvingly. Yay for that person. I was just waiting for them to hurry up so I could whisk Elena away and get back to the beach.

'Congratulations to our winner. What a marvellous trip that will be, next year in fabulous Las Vegas. Now, the time has come for our runner-up prize, and this year is a bit special. The lovely folks at the Royal Hawaiian Hotel have offered up a double pass to their amazing *luau* … and we also have this magnificent bottle of Bollinger Champagne. Fantastic. Are we ready? Let's spin that barrel! … And the winner is … Hold up a moment while I unfold this bit of paper. Okay, our winner is Mr Pierre Conrad! Congratulations sir. Where is Mr Conrad?'

It took me a few seconds to realise what had happened. Holy shit. Pierre Conrad was the name of my bogus photographer. My brother-in-law had won the door prize and was nowhere to be seen. There were confused murmurings among the crowd, was the winner here?

'Where is Mr Conrad?' the MC repeated.

I heard a voice in front excitedly mutter that they would redraw the prize if someone didn't claim it. There was only one appropriate course of action. I stood up and threw my arms in the air. 'Yes!' I shouted, and ran to the front of the room.

I walked up the stairs and realised the beer was still in my hand, so I chugged the whole thing — in front of what I now assumed was a desperately jealous audience. The room was silent as death. I think two people were clapping, but who could be sure? From behind sunglasses all I could see was a dark blur. And it did not immediately occur to me that I had further enraged this once hopeful crowd. Not only had they lost, but a beer-swilling hooligan who looked as if he'd walked straight off the beach, had swept in and stolen the door prize.

I placed the empty beer bottle on the stage and then shook the hand of the MC. He looked stunned and somewhat confused, so before the moment escaped and everyone started asking questions, I leaned on the microphone and explained that regrettably my hard-working photographer 'Pierre' was already on another assignment, shooting a spread elsewhere on Oahu. Which was probably true.

'How good is this? Next year in Vegas, folks! Yeah!'

My sunny attitude must have been contagious, because the MC didn't argue and happily handed over the prize. He threw an arm around me and smiled as we posed for a photo while I held the bottle of Bollinger aloft like I had just won the Hawaiian marathon.

Then I left the stage and ran all the way up the centre aisle and out the exit.

Of course my life was now in grave danger. How long before everyone realised they'd been cheated? I went directly to my room to avoid being set upon and beaten within an inch of my life by bitter conference attendees who knew what I'd been about since our conspicuous arrival. *Oh, he's that bum journalist who spent most of his time in the bar. He didn't even win. The son-of-a-bitch just went up there and took the prize. Why didn't anyone stop him? Where was he from again? Morocco, I believe. No, no, he said he was Australian, or maybe British? Wearing the loudest Hawaiian shirt I've ever seen ... Fucking tourists always steal the prizes. If we catch the sneaky bastard we'll club him to death with that bottle of champagne.'*

When the elevator arrived on the sixth floor I fell out in a panic, and had extreme difficulty navigating back to the room. The hallway was a lot narrower than I remember, all skewed at an angle, and somehow I was finding all the corners — a near impossible feat in an arrow-straight hallway. Damn that last beer, it had taken my legs. Where the hell was the room? I swiped at one door, and another — denied both times. Those jealous maniacs from the conference had called reception to have my room key disabled. Soon they'd catch up and hang me from the balcony as a warning to all: *This is what we do to outsiders that mess with the door prize.*

I swiped wildly at one last lock, desperate to save my skin, but mostly in a hurry to hide the Bollinger before Mr Conroy could get his grubby hands on it. There was a green light, a click, and I tumbled inside, somehow managing to slam the door shut behind me. I staggered toward the blinding light on the balcony. The rush of sea air cleared my head in an instant and all my worry vanished, because no one was searching for me on the beach or terrace. I was an idiot, but victory was sweet.

\*

It was early evening. Our little gang of four had regrouped and were walking along Kalakaua Avenue to an ABC store knock-off called Coco Grove, a name and shopfront that felt like it belonged on a Miami nightclub instead of a grocery store in Honolulu. Kalakaua Avenue at night was its own thing, a shiny plastic version of Hawaii — and maybe the worst of it. The avenue was crowded with curiosities. A man carrying a blue and yellow Macaw wandered up and down the sidewalk asking for money from foolish tourists who wanted to take photos with the poor bird. There were buskers, magicians, living statues, hip hop dance crews and shameless hawkers of useless junk — all the usual villainous scum that infect the main boulevards of any much-visited tourist destination. But I loved being on the avenue, even when it all felt as classy as strip-club neon on a hot Tuesday night.

Coco Grove was busy but our reason for visiting this specific shop was simple, the delicatessen inside specialised in Kalua Pork. Elena craved the juicy carvings for snack food. She snagged a large takeaway box of the stuff and I fell onto an exotic drop of white rum that came in a curious hexagonal-shaped bottle, and then we got out of there. But when your brother-in-law was involved, even things as simple as grocery shopping couldn't be achieved without collateral damage. Outside Coco Grove all hell had broken loose. Mr Conroy was parked in the middle of a domestic screaming match between a pirate and a mermaid.

Jackie had been watching the whole thing, and when I asked what the hell was going on, he replied, 'Roy might have mentioned, out loud, the only reason a pirate would date a mermaid was because she could suck the barnacles off a boat, they aren't good for much else.'

Apparently someone took offense to that. Which was fair, even if it was unclear who was angry with who or at what point the screaming started. But when things looked like they might turn physical with mermaid claws and a suspiciously realistic cutlass, Jackie saw an immediate need to escape a bad scene. So we grabbed Mr Conroy and swept him away moments before the cops arrived and threatened violence with 100,000 volts for anyone foolish enough to swing a sword or speak an unkind word. Luckily, we had disappeared into the crowd and were on our way back to the hotel. That was when I saw Bill Billingsley on the strip, wearing his Panama hat and another immaculate linen suit. He saw us and waved.

'Bill! Where are you headed?'

'Uncertain, Ed. I'm trying to decide where to eat.'

'We're going to Duke's. Have dinner with us.'

Bill was happy to tag along. It was like running into an old friend. I introduced him to everyone and there was no awkwardness. Bill was glad to finally meet Elena, he knew of Jackie's films, and he recognised Mr Conroy from the conference and admired his sense of style. If my brothers were peacocks they would've been spreading their tail feathers, puffing out their chests and cawing with pride. Billingsley was all class. It was seamless how he slipped right into the conversation and immediately felt like part of the family.

'By the way, Ed, congratulations on your win this afternoon. Or did your photographer really win?'

I tapped the side of my nose and Bill smiled.

'Well played. The spoils of war go to those who fight the hardest for them ... You might've heard me clapping? It was a dead crowd. Who was the other person giving you a hand?'

'If I had to guess, probably Elena.'

'Of course! What a circus that was ... hysterical to see everyone so pissed off that an international journalist won a prize. The bitching after you ran out was fantastic, you wouldn't believe all the whining. So many of them act like spoilt brats when they leave the mainland. That's why I know the prize went to the right person.'

'It's always fun to throw a cat among the pigeons.'

'Have you cracked that bottle of champagne yet?'

'The champagne's on ice but I did pick up this lovely bottle of rum.'

'Can I see? Toasted Coconut … very nice.'

'We'll have some at dinner.'

'Excellent,' Bill handed me back the bottle. 'I also heard you were lucky enough to snag an interview with the infamous Connie Petterson. The other attendees were astonished when they saw you turn her into a blustering wreck — you're now a hero. At least you were until you took off with the door prize. Still, wish I'd been there to see. It's normally impossible to get rid of that woman. She's a menace.'

'It was rough. Those design-bible bastards set me up.'

'Don't worry. Connie does this every year, corners some new journalist and tries to sell her business through non-stop jibber-jabber. She's a bully but it's a rite of passage, and you passed with flying colours.'

'Rite of passage! That might've scarred me for life.'

A short while later we were sitting around a table inside Duke's sipping cocktails in the moody light while we waited for our meals to arrive. It was crowded in the restaurant. Duke's had an interesting vibe. It looked like the kind of place Elvis Presley would have gotten in a fight. This was a scene where everything would be moving along swimmingly until somebody became pissy because they thought you cut in front of them at the bar or were looking at their girl. But we expected no trouble. There were five of us at a six-seater table, minding our own business amidst island-themed décor and laid-back music.

'So, boys,' Elena said, 'I've been dying to hear how the photoshoot went.'

'A terrible disappointment,' Mr Conroy replied.

'What happened?' Bill asked.

'I took Conroy with me to a photoshoot for my new film,' Jackie said. 'We were supposed to be doing test shots of the lead actress posing glamorously against the Hawaiian landscape — except she never showed.'

'She wasn't in the mood or she literally never arrived?'

'She literally never showed up for work, and neither did the staff van. We waited for forty minutes and nobody came. I guessed everyone got lost searching for the location. Luckily I had Roy for company, so we grabbed lunch and I gave them a call. They were still at the airport. Can you believe that? The flight had arrived but my actress wasn't on it. I thought maybe she'd been delayed, so I called the line producer and all he could tell me was she wouldn't be coming today because something had come up.' Jackie shook his head. 'The communication breakdown is frustrating.'

'Are you still going to do the shoot?' Elena asked.

'All going well, we'll be doing it tomorrow afternoon instead.'

'I realise I'm the new guy here, and I don't know a thing about the movie business, but that doesn't sound like a reasonable explanation for why time and money were wasted while you and Mr Conroy waited,' Bill said.

'That's exactly what I thought,' Elena said. 'None of it sounds professional.'

'Yeah. I thought it was piss poor,' Jackie said, 'and something felt funny. Everyone was full of weak excuses. Anyway I'm giving them the benefit of the doubt. Sometimes accidents happen, and getting out of California can be a bitch.'

They continued to speculate on what might have delayed the actress, but I heard none of it. Something was wrong. There was an evil thing looming on the horizon, circling our table like it was small boat. I had eyes on it early and was prepared, but I still hoped it would lose interest and swim away.

And then it struck with the suddenness of a great white shark. Somebody with a score to settle came at our table with teeth bared, hungry for revenge. It was the interior decorator from the conference, the one I had interviewed and driven to madness. Connie Petterson. With a few drinks under her belt and full of confidence, she dropped her arse in the empty chair beside Elena. Her intent was clear — she'd come to stir some shit.

'It's *Elly*, right?'

'Elena.'

'Uh huh ... I seen you *Elly* ... at the con ... connenerybody ... Ev-ery-body. They say you're some *great* designer from Austria.'

'Australia.'

'*Whatever.* Don-chu correct me. I don-see what's so good-bout you.' She flicked Elena's shoulder. It was a small gesture filled with violent intent. Holy shit. This fool decorator was playing with fire. And her mouth just wouldn't stop. 'Listen, little miss "I do bathrooms," should *you* even be here? This is an *American con,* for Americans. Like me. I'm an American.'

'This is an international conference in Hawaii. It's mostly Americans but anyone can attend. And the conference is over, so what's your problem?'

'You stink-en up my con is my problem. Miss no class, you need class to be international, like me, I'm classy, you're not classy so you're not international, miss no-class-euro-trash from Austria.' Connie he-hawed like a donkey but nobody else was laughing, so she continued: 'Why don-shu just leave? Let us real designers enjoy ... Pros only ... No goddamn upstarts ... in here shaking your tiddies n' battin' your lashes ... stealing our jobs — our men ... you're as bad as Mexicans, or Canadians.'

It was acceptable to watch this train wreck for a short time. I'm sure everyone was of the same opinion — that it might be funny. But it wasn't. And now it had gone on for too long. If Connie was allowed to keep running her mouth, Elena really would turn European, and things would get scary physical, so I stepped in and tried to run her off. 'No one's stealing your job. *Decorator.*'

Connie looked across the table and focused her eyes on me. To my amazement, it appeared she had come to pick a fight with Elena exclusively and hadn't noticed me until this very second.

'You!'

'Yes, me.'

'You lying bastard. There's no diamonds on the beach in Morocco! And there's no "Fortune-Six-Million Camel Scavenger Hunt," I know — *I checked*. It's like you're not even from there!'

'I never said anything about a scavenger hunt ... and even if I did, who gives a shit? Now why don't you take your drunk arse back where it belongs, out to the pool boy collecting towels — that's what you do, isn't it? You fluff pillows and pick towels.'

'Fuck you! I'm a designer. Top three in Vegas.'

The cocktail was working its magic and I felt the fire, it was time to burn this bitch to the ground. I stood up and pointed an accusing finger at her. 'You're a fucking scam artist impersonating a designer!'

Mr Conroy joined in. 'A charlatan!'

'A drunkard decorator!' Jackie yelled.

'She's taking the piss — check her pockets! I bet they're loaded with silver, someone get her out of here before she steals all the cutlery!' I kept my finger pointed at Connie.

We were attracting an audience now. Most of the surrounding tables looked in our direction and people were standing to see what the fuss was about.

'I'm no thief! I'm a designer, you ... *you fucker!*'

The waitresses had stopped serving. I noticed the manager signal the bouncer, a silent call to make his way over to our table, but the bouncer intentionally dragged his feet, he wanted to see more before he cracked skulls and ejected anyone.

'You can shove your stupid magazine right up your arse.' Connie made a lewd gesture involving her fist and a hole she made with her other hand, then disturbed us all by licking her forearm from the elbow all the way up to that fist. '*Right up your arse.*' Her arm moved up and down, pumping the air like a piston. 'Designers like me are too good for little pricks like you — *you prick ... prick journalist.*'

'But your card doesn't say how good you are.' I took a business card out of my pocket and waved it around. 'Doesn't even mention *top three in Vegas.* How do we know that's true?'

'More lies!' Jackie shouted.

'Yes, that's right,' Mr Conroy added. 'Pretending to be a designer *and* top three. Lying about your credentials is bad for business, *bella.*'

'I *am* top three! Fuck you, fuck you and fuck you.' She pointed her finger at each of us around the table. 'Especially you Bill Blinging-sley, taking sides with *foreigner arseholes ...*'

And then her eyes changed, the pupils reduced to mere black pinholes. Had we broken her? Because this was the face of insanity.

'Say another bad thing about me and I swear I'll cut her!' Connie picked up a steak knife and tried to hold it to Elena's throat. For a half-drunk lunatic her speech was surprisingly clear, but everything else was running on ethanol and she had the reflexes of a stroke victim. Before the crazy bitch knew what was happening, Elena threw a cocktail in her face. Connie screamed when the stinging liquid flew in her eyes. 'Aaahhh! Aussie bitch!'

That was the last mistake the decorator would make. The Italian blood finally rushed to the surface and Elena slapped her across the face so hard that Connie fell out of the chair. Maybe I was deep in the moment, but I swear the music stopped. The needle had jumped off the vinyl at the same moment Connie impacted the stone floor. A collective gasp sounded around the restaurant, accompanied by several whoops and someone clapping with enthusiasm. It was Bill Billingsley.

The bouncer finally rushed the scene. He made sure we were okay but had little else to do after that. The decorator didn't even try to get up again; instead she had begun the long crawl towards the bar. She was finished in Duke's. Probably finished in Honolulu. Everyone had heard Connie threaten Elena with the steak knife. The manager would have to call the cops and have her hauled off.

I left my seat to check on my wife — who was angry as hell, but otherwise fine. So I went and had a word with the manager, giving our side of the story and making a formal complaint. A complaint from a journalist, no matter how obscure, goes a long way. Nobody wants bad publicity. And the extremely apologetic manager offered to comp us for the evening. I returned to the table at the same time Mr Conroy was leaving for the bar, no doubt on a mission with suspicious motives, but he'd also been known to swing by the kitchen and make sure his meal was prepared just right. So I said: 'You better stay in the restaurant, I don't need you hassling the chef right now.'

'Relax Ed. I will go and buy our decorator friend another drink, she'll forget anything ever happened. Don't worry. There'll be no blowback.'

'Be careful, that one is mad as a cut snake.'

I sat down, had a drink, and shrugged my shoulders apologetically at Bill. It was a needless gesture. Our new friend was in great spirits.

'That woman is crazy, I've never seen anything like it. But damn, you really stitched her up!'

'I couldn't help myself. She deserved it.'

'True. I could smell the booze on her from across the table.'

'She was pretty foul,' Jackie said. 'Hilarious though; that was the loudest slap I've ever heard. Bitch went over like a bowling pin! Good thing she was already trashed or there might've been some serious damage.'

'Can you believe that brazen motherless cunt?' Elena said, and had a sip from a fresh cocktail to help calm her nerves. 'She was actually going to cut me!'

'You handled yourself well,' Bill replied. 'And think about this, the next conference will be in Vegas. You folks should come back and give Connie a rattle on her home turf. Ha! That would be excellent. I haven't been this entertained at a conference in years.'

That was an invitation to get drunk if ever I heard one, and I opened my hexagonal bottle of coconut rum and poured everyone a glass. A toast was made to 'the slap that silenced Duke's' and Bill's best conference in years. Then the food arrived. It was a good meal and the manager was true to his word — we didn't pay a cent.

# Day Four

Elena wanted to meet me downstairs. She said it was too early to wrap her head around whatever ridiculousness her brother might be involved in, so the job fell on me to rouse her twin from his beauty sleep. Today we were going on an adventure, and Mr Conroy was meant to drive Jackie in the Camaro while I piggybacked Elena on a Harley Davidson.

I knocked on his door and waited. There was silence. Mr Conroy had disappeared early last night and I wondered if he was currently locked in the embrace of some gorgeous young thing picked up on his travels. I knocked again and this time the door was opened by a dishevelled-looking woman wearing last night's clothes. Makeup smeared all over and mouth agape, doing a perfect impersonation of a parrot's arsehole, she wiped drool from the corner of her mouth. Bloody hell. What kind of bedraggled monster had Mr Conroy been shacking up with? The worst kind. It was Connie Petterson. Her eyes almost popped from their sockets when she realised it was me at the door. She pushed past me and ran down the hallway as quick as she could toward the elevator. That was the last I ever saw of Connie.

Mr Conroy shouted from somewhere inside the room, 'Is that you, Eddie? I'm just in the bathroom, come in, *bello.*'

The room was dark and reeked of an overabundance of women's perfume, alcohol, body odour and sex. I opened the curtains and the glass doors to allow some fresh air to blow away the pungent remnants of a shameful night. Mr Conroy swaggered out of the bathroom in his underwear and looked exceptionally pleased with himself. 'Good morning, my brother … Ah, it looks glorious out there.'

'Dear god, man, what happened to your pride? When you said you were going to smooth things over with Connie, I didn't think you were actually going to give her the rough with the smooth.'

'She needed Mr Conroy.'

'Hmm, all over the room apparently. I hope you used protection.'

'You look like you need Mr Conroy too. Come give me a hug, Eddie.'

'Stay right there — I'm not giving you a hug in that state. Jesus, those undies leave nothing to the imagination. You didn't have a follow up session this morning?'

'We might have if you hadn't shown up.'

'By the state of her I did you a favour. Pull yourself together, we're going out.'

'Give me half an hour.'

'We'll be in the Hula Grill.'

We had finished in the restaurant and were waiting in the lobby for Mr Conroy to get his Gucci-encased backside downstairs, when things took a nasty turn. Wendy, the lovely woman from the first day of the conference, had recognised me and was heading straight for us. 'Eduardo! Eduardo!' She waved in a frantic manner, her face full of concern as she half skipped, half ran to catch us.

This was a long way from the bright and cheery woman sitting behind that check-in table a few days ago. My instinct to flee was strong. I should've kept my head down, played dumb, tried to do a runner — this was not a social call. Wendy displayed all the telltale signs of a bill collector. All she was missing was a baseball bat.

'Eduardo! I'm so glad I ran into *you*.'

I smiled. No need to panic — yet. 'Good morning, Wendy!' Everything will be fine. Remain calm. 'What can I do for you?'

'It's not a big thing. We're just having trouble tracking down the payment for you and Mr Conrad. We checked the billing records and can't find anything from your magazine. Forgive me, I know you're a professional so this is embarrassing to ask, but do you think they just forgot? It would explain your absence from our guest list.'

I saw the colour drain from Elena's face. However, I had prepared for this.

'Wendy ... it's the most awful thing, the magazine has gone bankrupt. I have no idea when the payment will come through. It may not come at all ... I'd cover it myself except my money is tied up in rental cars and hotel bookings.'

'Oh, that is just *awful*.' Wendy put a hand to her mouth and took a moment to fully appreciate my unfortunate circumstance. 'Will we be able to reach your editor?'

'I could give you his number but I doubt he'll answer. I was on the phone with our office last night, the whole thing is a shambles. Turns out the editor packed a bag, left his wife and ran away to Thailand with his secretary.'

'Oh my god! That bastard, leaving you all high and dry like that.'

'Oh, it gets worse, he'd been dipping his hand in the till for years, siphoning money from the magazine to furnish an elaborate second life — a flash apartment, fancy car, clothes and jewellery for his secretary. It's disgraceful, years of hard work down the toilet, but we should've seen this coming. The signs had been there for months, years even. Missing equipment, bullshit assignments, general disinterest ...'

'So why send you to Hawaii if your editor was about to jump ship?'

'To throw us off the scent that we'd be jobless before we got home.'

'What will you boys do now?'

'I couldn't say. It'll be a struggle for a while, but we'll get by. Pierre and I are good like that. We're resourceful.'

'Oh, Eduardo!' Wendy embraced me, and I'm pretty sure Elena rolled her eyes while Wendy poured her heart out. 'This is all so wrong. It's unfair to put honest, hardworking people like yourself through such an ordeal. Look, I don't want you to worry about the money. I'll take care of everything. The conference will just write it off. We often have no-shows anyhow, so there are allowances for these kinds of situations.'

'Really? Thank you so much, Wendy. You're one of the good ones.'

'You take care, okay? Maybe Miss Elena will give you a job? Good luck.'

Wendy left us and ran into Mr Conroy coming out of the elevator. She gave him a hug and they exchanged a few words, and after they had taken a photo together, she kissed him on the cheek and walked away.

Mr Conroy came over to us. 'What the hell was that about? Wendy said she was so sorry to hear about the magazine and hoped I wouldn't have any trouble finding work. She gave me her phone number.'

'*C'mon*, I didn't get a phone number.'

'That's because Wendy assumed you were with me and she didn't have a chance,' Elena said. 'Which is true. Plus, she may like photographers better than writers and that's why she went for Roy.'

'Also I'm sorry to say, Ed, as handsome as you are, I am utterly irresistible.'

'You're both funny. I thought she was offering him a job.'

'A blowjob maybe.'

'Oh my god, I was about to say the same thing,' Elena said.

Twin-sense: the supernatural ability to read your twin's mind for the purpose of a unified explosion of inappropriate thought or behaviour, with often hilarious results ... and I would've joined in, except for some reason we were still in the hotel lobby drawing attention to ourselves. This was no good; I feared Wendy would reconsider and come back to claim the debt. But the reality was that none of that mattered. We now held an ace bargaining position and could offer her one romantic evening with Pierre Conrad if she'd quietly forget the whole ordeal ... A blowjob maybe?

*

Elena checked her phone as we walked along the avenue. She was excited. Bill Billingsley had promised to call and organise a time to meet for drinks in the afternoon — a proper sit down to finally discuss Elena's architecture and design business. With all the excitement the previous night they hadn't gotten around to doing it in person. And the days of a prime mover tended to become chaotic, so Bill wanted to wait and see what happened before committing to a morning tea.

We met Jackie at the corner of Kalakaua Avenue and Royal Hawaiian Boulevard and walked to the top end of the boulevard. Not long after, we were standing out the front of a white plantation-style building with a turquoise shop sign. Jackie hovered around while Elena and I received our orientation. He didn't need to be there, but as an enthusiast, he wanted to check out the custom Harley Davidson Sportster I had hired.

'Okay, guys. Are you familiar with this type of bike?'

'Yeah,' I said to the mechanic. 'I ride a Harley back home.'

'Good to know, good to know. So, make sure you fill up the tank before you return it, otherwise we'll charge the difference to your credit card. It won't be much, depending how far you ride. Five bucks max. Do you have a route picked out?'

Jackie held out the map and indicated the loop we intended to take. 'We're doing some location scouting for my film. We're gonna cruise the south-east section of the island. Follow the coast road and stop at the lookouts, hit the mountain crossing, go through the tunnel and come back to Honolulu on the Pali Highway.'

'Okay, that's cool, that's cool. It's some good riding out that side of the island. Just make sure you don't take any pork with you.'

'Why would we take pork?' Elena said.

'You're going to be riding for a while, you'll no doubt stop for food or take snacks. I only mentioned pork because you guys want to come back on the Pali; there's an old superstition about that area. Legend says that the great Pele, the vengeful volcano goddess ... well, she was shacking up with a demi-god, this half-man, half-pig dude named Kamapua'a. It didn't last and they broke up.'

'Half-man, half-pig? That dude was punching above his weight the day he snagged the volcano goddess. How did he manage that?' Jackie said.

'Maybe he was good in bed?' Elena said.

'No doubt, no doubt. But their breakup was not a good one, she told him to get lost and never come back. So, if anything made from pig comes from the windward side of the island to this side, Pele gets real shitty. Cars break down, people get stranded, the weather turns on them ... and sometimes worse happens.'

'Worse — what do you mean worse?' Elena asked.

'Last year a dude was driving a rental car with the top down. He came out of the Pali Tunnel and splat! Dead. Crushed by a boulder that fell off the mountain. They checked the car afterward and he had a pork bun stashed in the glove compartment.'

'Bullshit,' Jackie said. 'That can't be real. It's just superstitious hokum, right?'

'Believe what you want, man. But me — I wouldn't take any chances.'

'We'll make sure to err on the side of caution,' I said. 'We won't even take bacon-flavoured snacks with us … There's no ham on those wraps is there, El?'

'We are hog free. I got Tandoori chicken and tuna.'

'Right on, right on. It sounds like you folks are all set. Remember, drop-off is five-thirty, but if you do happen to go north make sure you get back to Honolulu before four-thirty because the traffic gets hectic — like really jammed up. I wouldn't want you guys getting stung with a late fee. Otherwise, have fun and stay loose.'

The dude waved us a *shaka* hand sign and we rode onto the boulevard where Mr Conroy waited for us in the Camaro. The electric roof was down so he could wave as we rode by. Jackie jumped into the passenger seat and they pulled in behind us.

There is nothing like tearing down a tight street between tall buildings on a Harley Davidson with a custom exhaust. People with an unrefined ear cringe, but those of us in the know hear sweet music that the primal brain believes is Mozart. This is often followed with a nod of appreciation and the inability to stop smiling.

We cruised through town, passing the ever welcoming bronze statue of Duke Kahanamoku on Waikiki. I revelled in the spectacle as all those faces on the beach and sidewalk looked our way when the motorcycle rumbled past — Yes, it's me, Eddie Heads. I'm a famous writer …

We entered the shaded road around the edge of Kapi'olani Park and weaved up through the posh suburbs, and along the cliffside road around Diamond Head. Then we rode back inland to the Kalaniana'ole Highway — the main artery road of south Oahu. People say the islands are laid back, relaxed and life moves at a slower pace. This is true, until you hit that particular stretch of road and mix with the locals across four lanes of traffic that rockets and zigzags in and out of each other like some high-stakes game of tag. My goal was to stay as far from that madness as possible, ride the outside lane and not get wiped out by waves of maniacal vehicles.

Soon enough, we passed the last exit to suburbia and the city traffic thinned. For me this was always when a ride got exciting, because the safety net was gone and it was just you and the bike and the road; and the thing about Harleys — they are unreliable monsters. They vibrate, inexplicably break down, or if you're lucky, catch fire. And when the road opens up and you can really twist the screw, everything shakes, and it takes a moment or two to adjust, and there is worry, *Will I survive this?* But the bike holds together and suddenly you're flying, so you let go — that tension you felt becomes adrenaline, which becomes pure bliss. And when this is experienced with little-to-no protection, shirt flapping in the breeze, wind in your face, there is no sensation like it … and riding in the tropics is a sensation all on its own.

Our little convoy began a climb toward the scenic south-east coastline. The famous Hanauma Bay marine conservation area lay on our right. A police car had blocked the entrance and waved us along because it was filled to capacity. Not that we were hoping to gain access anyway — the road ahead called. Out here was the adventure, and the sea breeze rushed to meet us as we wound along the cliffside road with endless views of the deep blue Pacific.

We stopped at a lookout and Jackie jumped over the safety rail to join the other reckless tourists who thought it necessary to stand on the rock shelf to get that one special picture. A few quick snapshots of the coast and we were on the move again, roaring down the hill to a flat straight of hot blacktop beside a desolate beach, with nobody to slow us down and destroy the rush. The road curved inland again and climbed uphill to the next lookout. Makapu'u Point. We stopped here to gaze up the east coast of the island and take more photos. From this vantage point you could see the lush green mountains from their summit all the way down to where they reclined away from the white sand that bordered the ocean. Directly below the lookout, Manana Island and its smaller twin, Kaohikaipu, poked their heads above the water and tried to distract from the view, but it was hard to ignore those mountains towering over the glistening ocean.

A small crowd was at the lookout with us, and they all took photos — including a newlywed couple in full wedding attire. Their photographer had instructed them to do as

Jackie had done at the previous location — jump over the safety barrier so they could climb the rocks and get that one perfect shot. A kiss framed by the Oahu coastline. How the hell had she managed to get over the barrier in that massive gown? And why here? Why not be like the Japanese tourists and do wedding photos on Waikiki Beach? At least that was safe. This was life-risking madness for the sake of the sentimental. I began to imagine out loud what might happen if things went sideways for the newlyweds: 'A strong wind swept in unexpectedly. The gust scooped her up under the dress and carried her away like a white lace umbrella in a tropical cyclone.'

'Eddie! You shouldn't make up stories like that,' Elena said.

'Yeah that's sick, bro ... wait, does she survive?'

'And is she wearing underwear?'

'Only her husband knows if she was bare-arsed. He jumped off the cliff and grabbed onto her ankles in a desperate attempt to save her. It's okay, they floated down to that stretch of beach over there and were so caught up in the moment that their firstborn was conceived on the sand five minutes later.'

Elena swatted my arse. I sniggered like a villain. And we got back on the road. We cruised down the hill to a stretch of flat road at sea level — Waimanalo Beach. The water was dead calm and the sun shone bright here. Only the day before I had told a tall tale about the beaches in Morocco being covered in gemstones, but here in Hawaii that was not so far from the truth. Except, instead of the beach, it was the ocean that sparkled under the sunlight and looked as if it were made of diamonds scattered across sapphires.

At the backside of the mountains, we rode a jungle-fringed freeway that snaked up the slopes to a huge intersection where we were forced to stop. I was keen to get going again; the sun had disappeared behind an ominous grey cloud that looked ready to spill its guts down our side of the island. But that was only a mild worry compared to the Harley. Even though the engine was idling as it should, the bike felt unhappy. It was fighting me like it was uncomfortable moving onto the mountain crossing. My hand began to cramp holding down a misbehaving clutch lever, and as the light transitioned from red to green, I released all that clutch tension and throttled forward. The bike had other plans and coughed and died beneath us, holding up the traffic. Elena was practiced at this kind of mishap and jumped off the back and began to wave the traffic around us, while I wheeled the dead machine off the road. Mr Conroy pulled over behind the bike.

Jackie jumped out to check our situation. 'Dude! Did you *stall?*'

'No. I did not fucking *stall.*'

'You totally stalled …'

'Fuck off. The bike did something weird … Hang on, I'll try and start it again.'

It took three attempts going through all the motions — neutral, kill switch, ignition — and finally the Harley came to life and we were able to get on again.

We crossed the intersection without further incident and cruised up the slope and into the tunnel that would take us through the mountain and back out toward the coast. Riding through the tunnel beneath Konahuanui Mountain was a buzz, and I throttled hard just to hear the reverb in the tight concrete tube. I was looking forward to the next part — the climax. Bursting out of the tunnel into the sunlight, followed by a downhill run between the trees at high speed. The moment approached and I buried the throttle. Elena squealed and pressed her breasts against me. Her thighs squeezed my hips, and I erupted into the white light. The vibration. The thunder. The glory. The sudden complete lack of power ... my bike had died again.

I pulled over to the shoulder and signalled for the Camaro to do the same.

'Are we okay?' Elena asked, although she wasn't overly concerned, this kind of thing was a regular occurrence at home. Sometimes old bikes just stop working. Except we weren't on an old bike — not even close. This was exactly the kind of scenario that makes you question value for money. Maybe it was the mechanics fault? We dismounted and I gave the Sportster a quick once-over.

'We're okay baby, but I'm not sure what happened. Nothing looks out of place.'

'Ah, shit. Same again?' Jackie said, after he and Mr Conroy had exited the car.

'Not sure, man.'

'Did you hear anything fall off?'

'This is a brand new Sportster, it shouldn't be dropping parts. It felt like we've run out of gas ...'

I'll be the first to admit it had happened before. Sometimes you get reckless because you're in such a hurry to go for a ride you don't bother to check the fuel level. Other times your bike runs like a pig, and a carefree blast turns into a mid-stride cough and splutter where you're suddenly limping to the nearest gas station, dangerously low on reserve fuel and hoping to hell you make it ... and sometimes those cheap bastards at the rental agency short-change you and everyone is confused and your wife wants answers ... 'We can't be out of gas, right, Eddie?'

'There's no way. They gave us the bike with a full tank, and look, this one has a fuel gauge. The needle hasn't even dropped to half-way.' I unscrewed the fuel cap just to be sure and the fuel gauge had told the truth, the tank was three-quarters full.

'See. We've hardly used a drop.'

'Where are we right now?' Jackie asked. 'If we can't get your bike started I'll have to call the rental place so they can send a truck to pick it up.'

'I'll check my GPS,' Mr Conroy said. He jumped back in the Camaro and pressed the ignition button. The headlights blinked once and nothing happened. 'That's weird ... the car won't start.'

'What do you mean it won't start?' I said and went to check on the car.

'I've got the paper map here,' Elena said. 'We just went through this tunnel, which puts us on the Pali Highway, Jackie you better call the office and tell them we're on the Pali Highway ... You don't think we've done something wrong?'

'The only thing we weren't supposed to do was bring pig up here,' I said.

'I don't get it,' Mr Conroy said, 'I have ham. Is that a bad thing?'

'*Yeah,*' Elena replied. 'The locals say it's bad luck. How come you have ham?'

'I had a craving for Kalua pork after you bought that tub last night. So I swung by Coco Grove while you guys were doing the safety briefing. They'd already sold out, so I grabbed a ham roll for the drive. You just never know when the hunger will set in. It's in the cooler bag behind the passenger seat.'

'Get rid of it!'

'Why? I want to eat it.'

'This doesn't look good. I've got no signal, I'll wander down the road and try for a few more bars.' Jackie walked about a hundred metres down the hill and I kept a close eye on him.

The sky had grown dark, like the gun-metal colour of the navy ships in Pearl Harbor. This was becoming grimmer by the second. The wind picked up and thunder rumbled across the mountain top. I could feel the ground tremor beneath my feet, a steady vibration that was powerful and full of warning. Something felt terribly wrong. I feared we had angered the vengeful goddess Pele, but Jackie returned and his words filled me with confidence and sunny optimism. 'This is fucked. Now the phone isn't working. What the hell is going on?'

'It's the ham. We have to get rid of it right now. Throw it away, Roy!'

'Don't throw it! That will make things worse,' I said. 'We need to dispose of it another way. Roy you need to start eating. Do it now before this gets bad.'

'You've both gone mental, or you're having me on … I'm not throwing this roll away. I'll eat it when I want to and not before. I refuse to be rushed because of superstitious rubbish. Look at the size of this thing. This is a sandwich that has to be enjoyed at length, and I'm not even close to hungry.' He looked stressed, and his exasperation was about to be compounded further. It started to rain. A sudden and vicious downpour accompanied by cracking thunder and lightning. 'Shit, the leather! I've got to get the roof up!'

Mr Conroy pressed the ignition with the wild desperation of a man who knew ruined leather upholstery would bring hideous financial blowback. But it was hopeless. There was no life in the machine and no manual option to get the roof on. Everything was electric. He gave up the fight and stepped out of the car in near hysterics, with the cursed ham roll still firmly in his grip.

*Whoop! Whoop!* A siren indicated the arrival of yet more good news. Blue and red lights flashed behind the Camaro. The police had pulled over to investigate why this group of idiots was standing on the side of the highway in the middle of an electrical storm. Nobody stepped out of the patrol car for a minute or two, but that was okay, it wasn't like we could feel impending doom crawling down the mountain to claim us. I actually preferred playing chicken with a vengeful goddess while these good officers took their sweet time putting on rain ponchos. And good on them, they even made sure to pull a hood over their head before they exited the vehicle.

'You folks alright?' the first cop asked.

Elena was experiencing a micro-meltdown and launched straight into our story. '*He* brought ham over the mountain.' She pointed at Mr Conroy. 'And our bike broke down, and *his* car won't start, and the phone doesn't work, and now it's fucking raining!'

'You brought ham on *this* highway?' the first cop said. 'Are you crazy?'

'I didn't know! I wasn't at the safety briefing … I didn't know!' Mr Conroy shouted, waving the ham roll in the air. The drama was coming thick and fast now.

The first cop motioned to his partner with a pointed finger. 'Quick, bro, grab that tin bucket from the trunk and the lighter fluid.'

They looked like frightened children expecting the arrival of the bogey man — exactly the kind of comfort you look for in law enforcement. The second cop was inside the trunk faster than we could ask what the bucket was for.

'We're going to have to burn it,' the first cop said. 'That's the quickest way to appease her.'

'No! I paid for this sandwich and I'm damn well going to eat it.'

'The ham is on a sandwich?' the first cop asked.

'The stupid twit hasn't eaten it yet because he's not hungry,' I said.

'You better get to eating, sir, or we're going to light it up,' the second cop said. He had returned with a metal bucket and a bottle of lighter fluid. 'Pele is *pissed*.'

'I have a lighter. Let's get this shit done,' Jackie said.

'Back off, Jackie.' Mr Conroy clutched the ham roll to his chest. 'It's such a waste of talent! Pay off the greedy bitch some other way.'

'*Sir*, we only need to get rid of the meat.'

'For fuck's sake, Roy! *Give them the meat*,' Elena shouted.

'Never. Why should I care about this Pele?'

'She's the mother of the islands. Would you disrespect *our* mother?'

That did the trick. Mr Conroy was powerless against Italian guilt. He opened the roll and started shovelling ham into his mouth like his mother was about to smack him black and blue if he didn't. It was an American serving — a ton of ham on a six inch roll. The situation was desperate. No more time could be wasted, so I stepped up to help and grabbed a fistful of lunch meat and stuffed it in Mr Conroy's gob. Flaps of slimy pink flesh hung out the sides of his mouth as he tried in desperation to chew while he dropped to his knees and begged the wrathful goddess for mercy *'I'm sorry, Pele ... Please forgive me ... urgh ... Mother ... forgive ... meee!'* I continued to force feed him but he was having a difficult time breathing and had to suck air through his nose in short snorts while he choked wads of half-chewed ham down his throat. The gagging was horrendous, a mess of saliva, pig meat and snot bubbles.

It was terrible but we had no choice.

Elena wrestled the remainder of the ham roll away from her brother and dumped it inside the tin bucket. The lighter fluid went in next, and Jackie put it to flame. The sandwich went up like a miniature bonfire and was a charred pile of goo in a matter of moments. Mr Conroy swallowed the last of the ham not long after. Was Pele pacified? Our answer arrived as quickly as our luck had turned. The rain stopped, the sky cleared, and the Camaro roared to life again, catching the police officers by surprise.

Then the roof mechanism activated and put the soft-top back over the soaked leather interior.

'Whoa. That was spooky,' Jackie said.

'You folks got lucky,' the first cop said. 'This could have been much worse — last year a guy driving a convertible got flattened by a boulder. It's a good thing you didn't come through the mountain at night. I'm Hawaiian-born and raised, and the legends you hear about our islands are true. Don't let anyone tell you different.'

'That's facts. This stuff ain't no bullshit, bro,' the second cop said. 'You guys are tourists, yeah? Are you going to another island after this?'

'We're doing Kauai in a couple of days,' Jackie said.

The second cop looked thoughtful but I could see his unease, and Jackie latched onto that vibe straight away, no doubt imagining a nightmare scenario once we reached Kauai. Cursed films were often legendary in the scope of their disaster. I knew my brother had dreams of a smooth shoot and no wish to join that infamous club, so we paid close attention to what the second cop had to say next.

'Study the local superstitions. Most people breeze by, too dumb to recognise what they're into, but you've encountered the biggest and baddest lady on these islands. And you can bet she told the other gods you're coming.'

'Now you're just fucking with us,' Jackie said.

'Not even a bit,' the first cop said. 'We'll escort you down the mountain just to be safe … And *you* that brought the ham. If you see an old lady walking beside the highway and she waves you down, you better give her a ride wherever she wants to go.'

'*Why* would I do that?'

'Because it might be Pele, and it's the right thing to do. Be safe out there, folks.'

We thanked the cops and got back on the Harley. It started without a problem.

Minus one ham roll and looking rough as guts, poor miserable Mr Conroy climbed inside his waterlogged Camaro and put the roof down again. Jackie jumped in beside him. Now it was stinking hot, sticky and humid. The sooner we got back to the ocean the better. We hit the road slowly and once everything felt right with the machines, we gave the cops a thumbs up and they took off.

We rolled into Honolulu ready to refuel and regroup after all the drama on Konahuanui. We drove to Beach Walk and parked halfway up the street. This place was special, a haven from the bustle of Waikiki, although from outside appearances the location was merely a wall of small trucks wedged end to end on a vacant lot between a coffee shop and The Breakers Hotel. But this was a magic trick. The enclosed space was an outdoor food court serviced by food trucks. Screened from view was a carpet of fake grass covered in long picnic tables and colourful umbrellas. A string of coloured lights at one corner of the lot signalled the point of entry and we went inside.

Ten minutes later, Mr Conroy was waving a French fry in my face while he got all philosophical about why he would never look at a ham roll the same way again. 'It's a peculiar thing, I never would have guessed the dangers that come with eating high-end lunch meat. And you know, there's a valuable lesson here ...'

'Which is?' I asked.

'One should never take a sandwich at face value — it might try to kill you.'

'I already apologised for being a bit rough, but Pele wanted your blood. It had to be you that ate the pig because you committed the taboo.'

'True enough. I've always known my end would come at the hands of a woman. And someone of my lineage deserves no lesser death than murder by goddess. However, like all women, Pele will have to wait her turn.'

After lunch we lined the interior of the Camaro with beach towels to soak up any lingering moisture. Jackie's re-scheduled photoshoot was only a couple of hours away and the boys were eager to hit the road again. This time we were all going to watch the shoot on the north shore. We had plenty of time. The rental agreement required we return the Harley by 5.30 pm, no later, or incur a fee. But the mechanic had flat-out lied about the fee, which was actually a hefty financial penalty. If we arrived after closing we'd have to pay for another full day's hire. But 5.30 pm was a long way off, and Elena might need to peel out early anyway. Her meeting with Bill Billingsley was only a phone call away, even though there had been no word all day.

There is no better way to explore a foreign city, island or country, than getting hopelessly and confusingly lost in it. I have an excellent sense of direction, and although I thought I knew Oahu pretty well, the island was about to prove me wrong.

I don't invite drama, but it seemed determined to find me. We got into trouble again when I became overconfident with the traffic on the main highway. I'd been all smiles, easygoing, thrilled to be blasting on a 1200cc rocket, but somehow I lost sight of Mr Conroy and Jackie. I blamed the weather and scenery, it was too good, too distracting, because no more than a minute earlier we'd been behind the bright white beast. Then it was gone. I looked for another road that would send us on a course north, and the next exit proved to be another mistake. We were now headed south west. I pulled over to check the map while Elena made a phone call.

'Jackie, we're lost. Where are you guys?'

'Right where we're supposed to be, on the Kamehameha Highway going north. Where the hell did you two end up? Is everything okay?'

'Your speed demon brother is trying to figure that out … Where are we, Eddie?'

'Sorry, beautiful, haven't got a clue. Better tell them to do the north shore without us, we'll meet at the pineapple plantation after the photoshoot.'

'Mm-hmm. Did you hear that, Jackie? ... Yeah, bugger ... Okay, we'll meet you at the pineapple plantation after.'

'I can't believe I lost them. Where are they?'

'They went the right way, headed north on Kamehameha. So where are we?'

'Way off course. I don't know how it could be so hard to find our way ... must be all this roadwork. I'm going to get us on the highway and we'll work backwards.'

'Sounds good. Let's rock and roll.'

Except I couldn't find the highway again. I started looking for signs to the international airport, my choice of landmark to start over, but streets were blocked everywhere, and we deviated over and over, passing the Aloha Stadium twice, stuck in some hellish perpetual loop of perplexing roadwork. What should have been a straightforward venture was becoming an exercise in pure frustration. Where the hell was the airport? Why couldn't I get back to the highway? It was like the geography of the island was working against us, rearranging itself every time I thought we were on the right track. And then Elena was tapping me on the arm and waving wildly at a sign for the airport. Finally! I followed it and got us back on the highway and immediately saw our salvation. An exit to Pearl Harbor. We could get to the harbour and work our way back to familiar territory. In hindsight I should have stayed the course — instead I panicked and took the exit.

The bike cruised down the exit ramp and I began to feel better. But it was a short-lived sensation. What followed was something like, *You miserable fucking road, where the hell have you led us now?* I'm aware it was my fault, but when things go bad on the road it's always easier to blame everything else, including the road. Example: *Shitty concrete highways! The front wheel tracked in the road seam and forced me onto the shoulder ... that palm tree jumped right out in front of me — bike's a complete write-off. Fuck this road.* Or the current scenario. *Restricted access! Is it aliens? ... Then get the fuck out of here. Garbage-arse-piece-of ...*

There was a roadblock ahead, and not because of more municipal works constructing new superhighways. I'd taken the exit, expecting the historic Pearl Harbor visitor centre. This was not it. We had stumbled onto the actual working military base. We had no business being here. The road split into six lanes with a guard box at the end of each lane. In the far-right lane, a long row of cars waited patiently to be processed and granted access to the base. This was all wrong. We did not *want* to be here, and no way was I going to waste an hour waiting in line to be told I *shouldn't* be here.

Elena agreed with me. 'We stuffed up again, didn't we?'

'Thank you for saying *we*. I need to find a way back on the highway.'

'How?'

'Just make sure you smile when we get to the guard box ... and if things go bad it might help if you flash them. Man, woman, we don't discriminate, everyone loves boobs.'

'Oh, god.'

With my instinct for survival and talent for bullshit in readiness, I pulled us into the far-left lane — as far from the other cars as possible — and slowly approached the guard standing outside his box. A serious man behind a pair of dark sunglasses. He said something into a walkie-talkie and then put it away and stood with one hand on his hip — where the gun was. The other hand was raised in front of his chest, the universal gesture for STOP. Despite the temperature, I maintained a sense of cool and stopped the Harley in front of him. He walked around the side of the bike ...

A helicopter hovered somewhere overhead. I could hear the steady beat of its blades in the air, and I waited for the heat to descend, the moment a dozen Navy Seals with assault rifles jumped out of that chopper or burst from the bushes to surround us in a rush. I swear I could see their camouflaged faces staring at me from cover, waiting for the go signal — take the girl prisoner but shoot the rider. Common sense said that would only happen if I was a jackass. *Don't cock it up, dude.* I felt a single bead of sweat roll down my back and settle in my crack. My interaction with the guard would require tact, charm, and sophistication. So in my thickest Australian accent I said: 'How's it going?'

There was a moment where the guard appeared confused. Maybe it was the accent that threw him. Maybe Elena had gotten her tits out. I bet he was seeing stars, and not because of a magnificent pair of flesh melons, most likely he was dazzled by a classy-as-hell gentleman who had bothered to ask how his day was going. The guard studied my appearance — a crooked smile, bright orange Aloha shirt, ripped black jeans and cowboy boots. Society's upper crust, without a doubt. After inspecting me, he looked at Elena and the Harley. Finally, he waved a hand at the air in a circular motion. I couldn't hear the helicopter anymore. Was it ever a threat? Had he called it off? Or was he just waving his mate over from the guard box? Goddamn, I could murder an ice-cold beer in this baking heat. But all these thoughts quickly evaporated when the guard said: 'Can I help you folks?'

'Sorry about this, man — we took a wrong turn. Could you help us out? We just want to get back on the highway and head north.'

Never underestimate the appeal of an Aloha shirt and an American motorcycle with a hot blonde on the pillion seat. The guard laughed, and he and his buddy escorted us into the compound until we reached a section of road where we could turn around and ride back onto the highway. They also gave us directions to reach the north shore.

I said: 'Can we interest you boys in a beer?' Elena removed two cans of Kona from her backpack.

We were saving them for the north shore, but we needed to make an offering to the island in exchange for good fortune. It was a heavy sacrifice, but those boys bloody well deserved it, and they downed those beers safely out of sight behind the guard box while Elena blew them a kiss and the Sportster powered away.

The directions were good. We'd finally managed to shake whatever gremlin was keeping us from finding our way, and half an hour later we arrived at the pineapple plantation. Our timing was excellent, Jackie and Mr Conroy were parking the Camaro when we pulled into the grounds. At first glance, the plantation was a charming reminder of the way things were ... then you dug a little deeper and discovered a second-rate theme park that forced you to pay a premium for every experience. But having come all that way, who would back out? Nobody. It was a brilliant scam.

I wandered over to the Camaro with the weariness of a cowboy after a long day on the trail, while Elena practically ran to meet Jackie and Mr Conroy.

'Hey, boys! What happened? We thought you'd still be at the photoshoot.'

'It was a non-event,' Mr Conroy replied.

'*No*. You don't mean it happened again?'

'Yep. The lousy bitch was a no-show,' Jackie said. 'And nobody could tell me why. I swear something's up ... there's no loyalty on this production, it smells like a mutiny. I should have the lot of 'em strapped to the beach while the tide comes in. Maybe then I'd get some answers.'

To cure those blues we rode the rails on the Pineapple Express. Chugging along through burnt-orange scenery, air thick with cigarillo smoke, enjoying the good life on a miniature steam train tour of the pineapple fields. This cocktail provided the unexpected sensation of instant happiness, and to further improve the vibe Jackie passed around a small medicinal bottle of white rum he'd purchased from a gas station after being stood up. I smelt the rum fumes and was tempted but kept my distance — not while I was riding. Our mood was good, all things considered, and after we staggered from the train Elena and I tested our blood sugar tolerance with a pineapple float. I could feel the fluid in my veins turning to thick syrup with each mouthful, and by the time we finished I predicted a heart attack was in my immediate future. But before that eventuated, it was time for us to get back to Honolulu and return the Harley.

Elena checked her phone before we hit the road. No missed calls.

This time the Camaro followed behind us and the return trip was excellent. Oh yeah, man, a sweet ride. As far as the locals were concerned there was no designated speed limit, so *be like water, my friend* — go with the flow. If the speed signs read 55 mph you goddamn better be doing 90 mph. Adapt to survive. That's what I did, and everything was going to plan, the exact opposite of the debacle on our way to the plantation. Things were looking good; we had left our run a bit late in the day but all signs pointed to an easy ride into Honolulu. I don't know what the mechanic had been worried about. We left the plantation at roughly 4.30 pm and there was only light traffic. I suspected his speech was all a ploy to scare people into returning the bikes early so the staff could catch the late afternoon surf. Fair enough, I suppose, but when you only had the bike for a day you were determined to get your money's worth. It was a lot of money in Australian dollars, and a dollar meant that much more when you were out of work.

Tall buildings began to appear on the horizon and the signs for Honolulu became more frequent. It had been a blast and completely made up for the earlier disaster. Elena's bright smile appeared in the side mirror. I felt the same way, and I was certain the boys in the Camaro were feeling it too. This had been a good run. One of the best. Sun, uninterrupted speed, and a smooth ride … Then the traffic began to thicken. I thought nothing of it because we were closing in on Honolulu. I should have been more suspicious. If this day had taught me anything, it was to never get too comfortable on Oahu roads.

The traffic ground to a halt. All four lanes jammed bumper to bumper and going nowhere fast. It was a car park on the highway. I remained upbeat — this was nothing to worry about. We were probably wedged in the bottleneck of a popular exit, soon the traffic would thin again and we could get back into a rhythm and cruise to Waikiki. Except ten minutes later we had barely crawled more than a few miles. Well played, Oahu. I began to wonder if this was all a knock-on effect from our faux pas with the ham. Was Pele still upset with us? Even if she was, I refused to be beaten and began to weave in and out of cars and split lanes where I could. But our progress was still slow. We stopped beside another Harley and the rider gave us a nod in shared despair.

Elena's phone rang while we were at a standstill. It was Jackie. She put him on speaker.

'Can you believe it? First no photoshoot and now this bullshit! There's no way you're returning that bike on time. *Fuck*, that's another three hundred bucks!'

'I know. I know … Hey, did you call me before? … No? I thought I felt the phone vibrate … Plenty of petrol? I hope so.'

I was full of nervous tension — a need to move, to throw caution to the wind. My skin tingled all over and my head felt like it was being fed a constant stream of electricity.

'What time is it, babe?'

'Jackie, I better go. Keep an eye on us … *Shit*. It's ten past five, we're never going to make it back in time.'

The human standard in situations like this is to freak out or break down crying. Oahu presented me with a third option. Reassurance came to me on the wind, like a moment of clarity at the high point of a particularly great acid fantasy, this one a purple sky filled with flocks of flying sea turtles, and one of them said: *Things will only get better.* And they did …

A siren blared in the distance. It came from behind us and was growing in volume. Then, as if it had been perfectly rehearsed for a Hollywood musical, all four lanes of traffic split down the middle and created a wide channel for the ambulance to pass through. I manoeuvred the bike out of the way and watched the emergency vehicle fly by. The other Harley rider was nearby. He looked over his shoulder and signalled for me to follow. There was never a moment in my mind where I considered there might be a body in the back of that ambulance, or that it was on its way to save a life, or that taking advantage of this situation was bad taste. Those were the worries of people who weren't trying to stay ahead of a three hundred dollar bill. Fortune favours the bold, so I waved for the Camaro to get behind us and we chased the ambulance along the highway like it was our own presidential escort.

The other cars had squeezed themselves into awkward positions all along the highway and every vehicle in front was still clearing a path for the ambulance. It was unbelievable how much of an easy ride we were having, and in almost no time the exit for Honolulu appeared. We waved to the other rider, got off the highway, and it was down to business. Honolulu would be easier; the traffic was lighter and I knew my way around. But time was running out. We were lucky if we had ten minutes.

Buzzed on peak adrenaline and a violent dose of pineapple sugar, I weaved the Sportster in and out of the chaotic late afternoon commuters. We were like slow motion lightening, avoiding traffic snarls and zombified drivers of an unpredictable nature, leaving no evidence but the pop and crackle of thunder spewing from the Sportster exhaust pipe. We surged onto Ala Moana Boulevard. I throttled like our life depended on it and we got lucky with the lights onto Kalakaua Avenue, but there was more to do. I cut across three lanes and ran one red light, and another, leaving frantic car horns and abuse in my wake. Then we scared the shit out of fifty tourists on the sidewalk as the bike screeched into the one-way street after Royal Hawaiian Boulevard. I was pushing hard. Really screwing it on. Elena dialled in and kept her head down while the Sportster shot up the narrow side street ... So close now ... Tighter and tighter. An amber light blocked our way, but I could see our destination and would not be denied. Amber became red and I expertly ignored a third traffic signal and triumphantly skidded into the driveway of the rental agency ...

But what should've been victory quickly became panic, and I came within a breath of that heart attack when Elena clutched my shoulders and brought the world to my attention. A police cruiser was parked out front, red and blue lights flashing, and two officers on the sidewalk were having a serious discussion with the owner of the rental agency. Were we busted? Had the fuzz been alerted to our antics on the highway and through Honolulu and somehow traced the license plate here and sent a patrol car to net us on arrival? More importantly — had I beaten the time limit for drop-off?

One of the bike mechanics rushed over, took a hold of the handlebars and shooed us away. The cops never looked our way, and nothing was said about the drop-off time. We checked the clock: 5.28 pm. Two minutes to spare. Whatever was going on — and it didn't look good — we were being given a free pass to get the hell out of there before anyone started asking uncomfortable questions. The Camaro rolled into the street a moment later, with Jackie and Mr Conroy doing their worst to look inconspicuous. So we jumped in the car and drove away. Jackie high-fived me and I sunk into the back seat. Somehow we'd gotten away with everything. I couldn't figure it. There had been a lot of drinking on this holiday, except for today where I was stone-cold sober, and yet, it had been an emotional roller-coaster. Run-ins with Hawaiian gods, the police and the military, another missed photoshoot, and we should never have made it back to the rental agency in time. But we did. Was there *mana* involved? Had the sea turtle really been looking out for me? All I could be certain of, was in between all the drama, there had been some really great riding — swings and roundabouts, but what did it all mean? Maybe the universe was showing me that no matter the obstacles, I was the master of my own destiny, and if you were fortunate enough to see an opening, a chance to move forward, you should grab it and hang on tight ... or maybe it all meant nothing and it was just a weird day.

Elena finally had a spare minute to check her phone. There was one missed call, which was about right for today. The kettle never boils until you step away.

She dialled the voicemail and listened: 'Elena! It's Bill Billingsley. My apologies for the extremely late notice, I know you've been waiting all day for this, but sadly I have to postpone our meeting again. Work has been a complete bastard ... I know, I know. Full of excuses. But you know how it is when you're dealing with panicky clients that need rescuing any time the wind changes ... Anyway, if you're available tomorrow we should get together. Mid-morning if you can make it. Give me a call first thing and I'll make sure we get it done. Hope to hear from you soon. Cheers.'

# Day Five

Bill Billingsley folded his newspaper, put it aside and waved us over to the table. The time was 10 am, and we were inside the Royal Hawaiian Hotel, standing on the elaborate black and white café terrace.

Bill kissed Elena on the cheek, shook my hand, and invited us to sit. 'I love it here in the morning. Another exciting day in paradise, am I right?'

'It is wonderful here in the morning, although I don't know if talking about work could be classed as exciting,' Elena said.

'Now, Elena, never underestimate the power of good company, good coffee and a good piece of chocolate cake to infinitely improve a dull topic of conversation.'

'I should leave you to it,' I said. 'Call me when you're done, beautiful.'

'What are your plans, Ed?' Bill asked.

'It's a slow morning for me, the comedown from yesterday has been heavy.'

'What happened?'

'We had an interesting day on a Harley, and Jackie's actress bailed again for no reason. He was pretty pissed; I imagine someone's head is gonna roll.'

'That's a rough situation. How is Jackie handling things? Have you spoken?'

'Not today. Last night he got blind drunk and I haven't been able to reach him all morning, the phone kept sending me to voicemail. He's either sleeping off a hangover or giving someone on the mainland a horrendous blast.'

'Well, that explains a lot. You obviously haven't seen the news today.'

'Oh god, what news?' Elena said.

'It was one of those entertainment news channels. No more than an hour ago, they had a photo of Jackie holding a bottle of Jack Daniels and giving the finger to the paparazzi from the hotel balcony. The story goes, the press was tipped off by a room service attendant. Jackie was holed up in his room with a pile of cocaine and when the kid came to deliver breakfast your brother pulled a .44 magnum on him. Not sure if there's any truth to that but I can only imagine the press will be camped in the lobby of the Modern by now.'

'Jesus Christ! I know an exit when I hear one.' I kissed my wife, tipped my hat to Bill, and ran down the beach to the Modern.

\*

An hour later Elena called. She said all business talk had finished and if I felt like being social I was invited back to the café. I wandered over to the Royal Hawaiian, looking forward to collapsing in a chair at the café and being surrounded by pink arches and tranquil tropical gardens. I wanted to close the loop on our earlier conversation with Bill, and I *needed* some of that thick rich chocolate mud cake. Or a very large, very colourful cocktail. Some kind of sugar boost to pick me up after Billingsley's information had been spot on ...

The vultures were already circling when I arrived at the Modern.

'Out of my way, you savages,' I had said, pushing through the crowd of scumbag journos camped in the lobby.

Already so many, and all of them waiting to collect a cold-blooded bounty for the juiciest piece of trash they could dig up. Worse still, they didn't even have to work for it, the dirt was being served on a platter — literally. The dickhead from room service was peddling a photo opportunity with the cocaine remnants on Jackie's breakfast tray, and several interested parties were already bidding. Entertainment journalists are the worst, even the shadiest travel writer can't compete with the loose morals of those bastards. They can print any vicious rumour they want and present it as a possible truth until the subject or their publicist shoots down the story as a fabrication. But it's hard to stay ahead of a lie, news travels too fast these days, and this was a developing story where the subject had no idea he was circling the drain.

It could've been ugly for Jackie. Thankfully his fixer had arrived on the scene. I'd been pissed off seeing the exhibition in the lobby, but by the time I stepped from the elevator onto the tenth floor I was smiling — this was, after all, my area of expertise.

Police and hotel management were already in the suite and my brother was being wrestled to the floor for reasons beyond his comprehension. That's when I stormed in, looking sweaty, wild-eyed and agitated — my appearance made the bullshit that came out next all the more believable.

'Oi! What the bloody hell is this? No search warrant, excessive force, invasion of privacy … I'm Mr Heads' lawyer, and I think you'll find this is a classic setup by a fame-whore looking for their fifteen minutes.'

'We received a tip about illegal drugs and an unlicensed firearm.'

'If you're referring to the .44 in the news report, I was just in the lobby where that crooked room service attendant is posing for photos with a Dirty Harry replica and a tray of baking powder. It's a scam, the punk is telling every reporter a different story. That's fraud, officers — and not a good look for the Modern. I'm also a travel journalist, how would it look if, say, *Lonely Planet* got wind that guests of this hotel were being pimped to the press for fast cash?'

The police didn't want this kind of big-time drama. It would be a hard sell charging Jackie with anything when the incriminating evidence was downstairs, and they'd look ridiculous trying to explain how a scared-out-of-his-wits room service attendant disarmed a well-built man who was out of his mind on cocaine … Yes, a small-time collar on a dishonest hotel worker was a much better scene. So, they released Jackie, and hurried downstairs to slap handcuffs on the room service attendant — and what started as a terrorist auction was elevated to an arrest, and then made a public execution by the irate hotel manager, who dropped the axe on his employee as the cops were stuffing him in the patrol car. This all unfolded in front of that pack of ravenous hyenas called the entertainment press, which meant the scandal made every news outlet before lunch. And the most satisfying part? Jackie Heads — Film Director, was later issued a formal apology from hotel management and refunded the entire cost of his stay.

We escaped while everyone's attention was diverted. I made Jackie pack his bag and check out of the room remotely. I used his lighter to trigger the smoke alarm, and we snuck down the fire stairs to the pool deck and used the connecting walkway between the Modern and the marina to run away. Nobody got wise to our scheme, confusion reigned supreme, and I stashed my brother in our room at the Outrigger.

'So, Jackie is in our room right now?' Elena asked.

'It's the best I could do in the moment. He can share with Mr Conroy tonight.'

'That's a good job. But if I may, I have a far better solution,' Bill said.

'What's on your mind?'

'I was just explaining to Elena that I've been called back to the mainland early. The wheels are always spinning, I'm afraid. So, if you're interested, the two of you can have my suite here at the Royal. You already have tickets to tonight's *luau*, why not have the whole experience? Enjoy yourselves and leave Jackie in the Outrigger.'

'Wow … and what do we owe for this lavish accommodation?'

'Not a thing. It's my experience that some things are just meant to be. A bad situation can often lead to something better. I think you'll like the suite; it faces the ocean and is very plush. Stop by the front desk after lunch, I'll make sure there is a key waiting and everything is arranged.'

Neither of us were sure what to say, so we just said thank you.

'It's my pleasure.' Bill was careful not to spill on his ivory linen suit as he spooned a chunk of dense chocolate cake into his mouth. For a moment he looked lost in the bliss of the dessert, and when he returned from the land of cocoa and butter, he focused his attention once again on me and Elena. 'And where are you two headed next? After Honolulu that is ...'

'Kauai,' Elena said. 'We're doing the back half of our holiday over there. Should be very relaxing. The only planned activity is a little bit of location scouting for Jackie's film. He booked a place in Poipu.'

'Poipu? Lovely spot. I've stayed on the south coast plenty of times.'

'It's going to be so much fun.'

'You can tell me all about it the next time we get together.'

'The next time?'

'Oh, I have a feeling we'll run into each other again. We'll need to have a follow-up meeting after everything I learned today,' Bill said, savouring another mouthful of cake. 'Sweet perfection.'

\*

That afternoon we were back inside the Royal Hawaiian Hotel, travelling to the top floor in a shiny gold box. We exited the lift and stepped into a long hallway decorated with colonial patterned carpet and matching wallpaper — a drab letdown compared to the glorious lobby, but after following the long winding corridor to the very end, we opened a door and were reintroduced to luxury.

Elena ran around like a hyperactive child with sticky fingers — she had to touch everything. Feel the texture of that pink floral wallpaper, the bright upholstered furnishings, those plush towels. Above us was a double-height ceiling, thankfully out of Elena's grasp or she would've put hands on that too. Truth be told, because it was a historic building the bathroom was a little snug — a small gripe when the room was a hell of a lot nicer than anywhere I'd ever stayed. This was a hotel for people who wore rose-coloured glasses. Romantic nostalgia was what the Royal Hawaiian was all about. Once upon a time you could walk onto the Juliet balcony, now you could only open the window and lean out. I imagined modern safety standards required this because at some point an idiot had toppled off the balcony and broken their back on the metal roof below. Or maybe some kid wandered onto it and tried to squeeze through the railing and got wedged in between those narrow bars: '*Hello front desk? This is the corner suite — we need help! Our son is stuck in the bars of the balcony railing.*'

*Jesus Christ. Not another one … Can't you people control your children? It's all about upbringing you know — nothing a few swift smacks across the backside won't fix. Goddamn. Sit tight and make sure he doesn't dislodge while you're not looking. I'll send maintenance around with a ladder and a bucket of bacon grease.*'

Even without balcony access, the corner suite had a direct view of Diamond Head, and you could look, uninhibited, down onto the beach. This room was famous. You could pick it out on any postcard photograph or painting of this unique hotel, and now Elena and I were standing in it. That was special.

\*

'*Ciao.* You have reached the bed chambers of Mr Conroy. State your business.'

'Roy, you dirty bastard, I'm taking Elena to the *luau* tonight. She has requested your stylistic skill set. Put some clothes on and come over.'

'Finally! I have been summoned to work my magic.'

'Indeed, sir. You are required.'

'I'll grab my gear and be right up.'

'We're not in the room. We're spending the night over at the Royal Hawaiian.'

'Excuse me?'

'I'll explain when you get here. Meet me in the lobby of the Royal in twenty.'

'Will do. By the way, how did you know I was naked?'

'Goodbye Roy.'

Twenty minutes later Mr Conroy strode into the palatial lobby. The Royal was a cut above the modern stacks that crowded around her, a fact obvious to Mr Conroy before he even walked inside. He had employed a small team of hotel porters in pressed white uniforms to valet one oversize tan leather handbag. He handed another his new white trilby and a pair of white gloves, and one of these lads was even going to be tasked with pressing the buttons for the elevator. Then he clapped his hands to bring all the porters into line behind him. Our stylist belonged in a place like this. I could see him sniffing the air for quality, glazed eyes lusting after every beautifully crafted inch — if opulence was a golden blood that oozed from the walls, Mr Conroy was the snob vampire that sucked it dry. Maybe too much exposure to this elitist had turned me into a snob as well, because I was suspiciously comfortable here, although, I preferred to think of myself as adaptable and open to all cultural experiences.

I waved from the elevator lobby. 'You think you have enough porters, Roy?'

'One can never have too many footmen when there is an event to prepare for. Especially in a place like this. It's unbelievable. What's your room like?'

'Absolutely gorgeous.'

Upstairs, Mr Conroy placed the oversize handbag on the bed and removed a black case from inside. This was his tool kit, his professional primp and preen equipment. And he would spend the next two hours giving his sister a complete hair and makeup overhaul and help dress her for the *luau*. Mr Conroy — *stylist*, was now in session.

\*

Elena and I stared at our reflection in the elevator doors, and gave an approving nod. We looked stunning. The doors opened and we walked through the warmly lit lobby to a line of brass bollards draped with a gold rope. A hostess stood beside the seating plan with a guest list, and I gave her our names. She smiled and said: 'Welcome to the *luau*.'

Beyond the rope was an arch leading outside to a grass terrace facing the ocean. Four round tables were placed in an arc at the rear, these were for people who had only paid for the *luau* and complimentary cocktails. We had one of these tables all to ourselves. In front of us were three long rectangular tables filled with people who had paid for an extravagant seafood dinner and the show, and in front of those long tables was the stage. I reflected on our position here at the back of the terrace and decided it was the best seat in the house. Not bad, considering I'd scammed the conference out of these two tickets. Two tickets meant for Mr Conroy. Two tickets that could be better used by me and my wife. Two tickets to paradise? Maybe.

We were served cocktails as the sun got low and the sky darkened. A young man with a ukulele took the stage. We expected a few charming Hawaiian folk songs strummed on his miniature guitar, but that didn't happen. There is something magic about finding live music that vibrates on your frequency. It charges every cell in your body with ethereal energy. Sometimes you can recreate the experience with an amazing album and a chemical stimulant, but its power is lessened with every play through — you'll never reach the same high as a transcendent live performance. This young man plugged his weapon into an amplifier, and zapped me in the head. I was jolted out of reality as I knew it. This was all new — I had to rewire my brain to accept what it heard because all sense of time and space was lost when the music sent me soaring star bound on high-speed electric dazzlement. And it was pure. Like hearing Eddie Van Halen shred through *Eruption* for the first time — a sonic revelation you could almost see ... more drinks arrived. Sippy sippy.

When I looked up again we had travelled through time — what the hell were they putting in these cocktails? Our world darkened at the edges, looked softer, and light glowed around a woman in a grass skirt. The world swirled around her, and she bent and swivelled and swayed and cast a spell on us. Black magic woman. Hypnotising me with the deliberate and balanced wave of her hands and shake of her hips. Suddenly there were six of her, all dancing, all different colours ... all powerful. It controlled your soul to watch that rhythm — slow and steady, gradually building in tempo and heat, faster and faster, until finally they were a frenzy that sent my eyes spinning and heart racing to the frantic beat of bongo drums. A kaleidoscope of hula dancing perfection. The spell was broken when some drunk idiot couldn't handle the heat and tried to jump on the goddess, only to spontaneously combust in a flash of fire.

I sipped from my cocktail, wondering what had happened. Who had killed him? Was I still conscious and sitting beside Elena? Hail Satan, she was there, drowning in Blue Hawaii — who could keep up? We were barely hanging on. Overstimulation was a real danger here ... and then a god appeared with a giant flaming stick in each hand. A god covered in the artwork of his people. He heralded an ancient war cry to the heavens and twirled those sticks like deadly weapons, flung them in the air and beat them against his naked chest and thighs, over and over, in a powerful and frightening display of strength and reflex. This was a cyclone of fire, a yellow and orange light trail that whirled through the air and sucked us into its vortex until this master of sparks released us when he stabbed the sky and ignited it in flaming glory. Fire *Aloha*.

Blinding white light followed and we were dropped back into our seats at the rear of the terrace. The crash was sudden. The comedown to reality, sobering. There was applause all around, and I felt my hand being squeezed by my wife. Elena had tears streaming down her cheeks and a bright smile on her face. She had loved every second of the performance, and that was the greatest feeling in the world.

# Day Six: Part One

Before we went to the *luau*, I'd given Mr Conroy our room key for the Outrigger and asked him to make sure we hadn't left anything behind, and, when the time came, to check us all out of the hotel. He was also responsible for Jackie, or vice versa, whoever was having the better morning. If they were both on their drama it would be a disaster that could mean missing our flight, which put my stomach in a knot during the short taxi ride from the Royal Hawaiian around the corner to the Outrigger.

Mr Conroy and Jackie Heads were waiting on the curb side, well-dressed, sober, and without any strays sniffing around hoping for a good time or a free ride. I was relieved everything had gone smoothly and my body relaxed without destroying my shorts.

We went straight to the airport, where the driver dropped us at the domestic terminal and we collected our tickets for the next leg of the adventure. The flight was due to depart in forty-five minutes, so we waited at the gate and told Mr Conroy all about the *luau*. He was only half interested, which confirmed I'd made a wise move keeping those tickets for myself. Mr Conroy was more excited about how well his sister had cleaned up — not that it took much with Elena, he was just exceptionally proud of his work. For a few minutes we were pleased with his enthusiasm, and then he ruined it by reverting to his overblown Italian machismo. 'So, did you get lucky after the *luau*?'

'Come on. You're not supposed to ask that of your own sister.'

'But I *can* ask it of my brother. So ... did you?'

'A gentleman never tells.'

'You did! A twin can always sense when something like that goes down.'

'No, you can't, you lying peacock,' Elena said.

'I swear it's true, otherwise how would I know you got it twice?'

Elena looked like she was unsure whether she should smack her degenerate brother or be impressed by his twin sense. I raised an eyebrow at Mr Conroy and smirked. How the hell did he know that? The filthy pervert was probably spying on us.

We all turned our attention to Jackie. My brother paced back and forward with his phone pressed against his ear. This was a heated exchange. It held all the tell-tale signs that something of great importance had gone awry. Jackie was not impressed. Colourful expletives made their way out of my brother's mouth in frequent and quick succession, and loud enough that the uptight family behind us were outraged and their baby was bawling its lungs out. I felt a tug at the back of my shirt. It was the wife of the uptight family. 'Excuse me. *Excuse me* ... I find that man's language *extremely* offensive and he's disturbed my poor baby.'

'Ma'am, I'm not his keeper. What do you expect me to do about it?'

'Well, he should apologise. And ask the good lord to rid him of that foul mouth.'

She was probably right about the apology, how many people had been traumatised or frightened by this gangly, hairy swear-bear as it raged back and forward beside the line? I was mildly sympathetic until she kept talking.

'And I don't think much of the inappropriate conversation regarding your sex life either. You all need to find Jesus and rethink your behaviour.'

'Rethink *our* behaviour? I don't think it's appropriate you eavesdropping on our conversation. What does your lord and saviour have to say about nosey busybodies? That's bad behaviour. A bit like this screaming baby.'

'Hey pal, we're just good honest Americans on vacation. We don't need to be hearing that kind of talk.'

'That's right, George, that's right! You all listen to my husband.'

Mr Conroy stepped in at this point. 'Excuse me, my brother-in-law is correct. You should both mind your business, but I also sense you're repressed, could it be jealousy? Madam, you have an ample bosom, maybe if you allowed your husband and child a suckle on those sweet teats more often we wouldn't have to listen to all this screaming.'

Holy shit. We were going to get kicked off the flight. Why couldn't people mind their own goddamn business? Shit … did I say that out loud or just think it? Was her husband nodding in agreement with Mr Conroy? I tried to maintain a serious expression. As far as I could tell we still held the moral high ground, but the urge to burst out laughing was strong.

Jackie became vocal again. 'Listen to me, you filthy mongrel, I'll have your nut sack for a coin purse!'

'Oh my lord, is he serious? Must be some kind of bizarre satanic fashion trend. That can't be a real thing. Is that even possible?'

To my amazement this indignant woman was now looking to me for answers. Oh dear. We were dealing with a couple of poor sheltered innocents. And if they weren't scarred enough already, I was about to ruin them further. I couldn't help it. She had handed me an invitation to be ludicrous. Welcome to the world, folks, this is your initiation.

'Yeah, it's real *and* very possible. If you ever find yourself invited on a missionary expedition to Papua New Guinea, think twice — your husband's bits and pieces might end up a three-dollar souvenir at the Port Moresby craft markets. Sailors love that kind of keepsake.'

'Eddie, you're ridiculous.' Elena broke into a fit of laughter. She had lost all composure, and it was catching, because I failed to keep it together after that and Mr Conroy soon joined me. Today we were the arseholes.

The unfortunate family behind us didn't know what to think, and by some miracle our argument had been forgotten, probably because they were trying to wrap their heads around so much shocking new information. All of it was half-truths and lies of course, but I'd managed to put out the fire. Or was that dumb luck? Whatever the case, our flight was called before things spiralled out of control again.

Jackie hung up the phone and stepped into line as if everything was normal. 'Jeez, that baby is loud as hell. What set it off? They better not be sitting behind us on the flight.'

He'd obviously had an unpleasant conversation about work, so I didn't bother to point out the string of bewildered faces stretching through the terminal behind us. It was incredible we'd only upset one family and hadn't been run out of the airport by a violent mob. Life is funny. Sometimes you follow the rules and everything goes to shit. Other times you behave like an arse and it all works out. And there are situations like this one, where control is an illusion, everyone is a maniac, and fate is balanced on a knife edge — things could fall one way or another, or split you up the middle in the ugliest way imaginable. But you play the cards you're dealt, and today we scraped by. Apparently my hand was full of aces and jokers.

A few minutes later we tumbled into our seats. Premium class. The front two rows of a domestic inter-island flight. It's a bigger seat and free drinks for the duration. We'd barely been on the plane and I already had a mai tai in my hand. So did Elena and Mr Conroy. They were sitting beside each other for once, and I watched them swish their cocktail with the colourful plastic stirrer and lift the drink to their mouth, the same little finger extended on their right hand. In perfect harmony. And they displayed the same satisfied smile when they finished.

I took a gulp of my own drink and leaned in to talk to Jackie about his situation. 'Dude, you're not making the most of this privileged position. You should have a beer in your hand by now, especially after whatever went down in the terminal. That was a bit intense. You made a baby cry and offended all of the Americans — a risky move after you were almost arrested. You wanna talk about it?'

'Nah. I'm too frustrated right now. And who was offended? You can't do or say anything anymore without someone getting offended or trying to throw you in jail. People are too bloody soft these days. You're right, I need a

beer. Stewardess!' Jackie waved his enormous paw in the air.
'Bring me a tall glass of your finest ale!'

She brought him a can of their cheapest beer.

I ordered two mai tais and had them sent to the husband
and wife we'd almost come to blows with in the terminal. A
small peace offering to set my karma right with the universe.
I twisted my moustache and wondered if that was going
to stir up more trouble. Do good Christians drink alcohol?
You're goddamn right they do — and if not, well, the folks
in seats B and C of row fifteen were about to get their first
taste of Hawaiian fire. Honestly, I was doing them a favour.
That would loosen them up good and proper.

As far as I was concerned, everything was as it should be.
Soon we would be on another island and could put all this
absurd bullshit behind us. No more Hollywood drama or
police investigations, no Hawaiian gods trying to kill us, and
no alter-egos. This was a new island and a new vibe. Now
was the time to step back, slow the pace, to really wind down
and relax. I could switch off the brain and allow myself to
finally get my head right. I figured I could manage that —
*we* could manage that. Unless the hand of doom was just
over the horizon, waiting to smack us down again. Yeah —
Nah. Probably not. Another mai tai quickly sorted out the
*what ifs* and forty minutes later we touched down on Kauai.

# Kauai – Day Six: Part Two

Lihue might be the nicest airport terminal in the world. A building that is simple and unpretentious, it encapsulates the Hawaiian sensibility. It was upgraded in 1987 to its current size, although for the uninformed it might have been unchanged since the 1950 inauguration. The building was all exposed wood beams, open-air courtyards and breezeways. Classic mid-century-modern architecture with that traditional Hawaiian flavour infused. Aside from the main atrium where you could grab a coffee or sit at the bar, the remainder was like walking through a museum. Indigenous artwork and historical exhibits decorated the walls throughout the terminal, and it even held that old-world musk in the air — a certain combination of ancient wood, old carpet and damp. I felt at home here. Welcome and comfortable. There was none of that invasive dread you encounter walking through a large-scale international airport — that inescapable feeling that Big Brother is watching — so acting on pure instinct you begin to tread carefully, because one misstep or word out of place could spell disaster, like a trip to a small windowless room accompanied by a rubber glove-wearing bull dyke named Bobby. I recalled the incident at Oahu immigration and knew that Lihue would never be that experience. It was all *Aloha*.

We bypassed the luggage carousels and stepped outside, then wandered across the road to the open-air car park and shuttle service that would take everyone to the car rental facilities. Elena and Mr Conroy took one look at the crowd waiting for the shuttle and rolled their eyes. There was no shade, it was sticky hot, and waiting in line with all the same people we had pissed off barely an hour ago would be torture. Jackie would have no problems with a trek, and the others could be convinced of anything if it was a better alternative, so I suggested we walk to the rental car agency. Fresh air is always welcome after a flight. It's a hateful situation getting off a plane and having to squish into another small metal container beside more stank, soggy humans who have no control over their brain—mouth function. *Hey. We're not friends. You ever hear the AC/DC song Highway to Hell? It was about this bus. Don't talk to me...*

Thank the gods we walked. It was exactly what we needed. We dodged around the odd wild chicken in the car park — the first sure sign this was Kauai — and trekked toward the service road. Sprinklers watered the airport grounds, and the water overspray and smell of wet grass was refreshing. That helped energise the group.

We beat the shuttle bus to the rental agency by a good ten minutes, and by the time the first sweaty, red-faced tourist staggered into the air-conditioned office we had already secured our vehicle. Jackie booked the car for Kauai, and strangely it was another white V8 convertible. This time a Jeep Wrangler. A vehicle that, despite only having two doors, still dwarfed the ride I would have chosen — any modest four-cylinder. A compact car with automatic transmission is always a sensible option on foreign terrain. There's less to think about and the handling of a small Japanese car is always top shelf. But I wasn't in charge of the vehicle and Jackie wanted a soft-top Jeep. The counter clerk had tried her damnedest to upsell him on the vehicle and the insurance, but he had pre-paid, knew exactly what he wanted and would not be swayed. We weren't there to impress anyone, our crew knew exactly who we were and where we were going. And right now that was the north of the island for some sightseeing and more location scouting for my brother's film.

Elena fell in love with the little Jeep and christened it the baby elephant. We set out with the soft top and windows down, and the music turned up. Our brothers sat up front while I shared the back seat with my girl. I threw an arm around Elena, and my other hand dangled out the rear window so that sweet tropical Kauai could breeze through my fingertips. Welcome to the garden island.

*

It's officially listed as two highways, but the reality is one main road runs top to bottom and around Kauai in a crescent-moon shape. It's impossible to get lost. Our accommodation was on the south coast, but first came Jackie Heads' private guided tour. We were driving north to the famous Hanalei Bay.

This island held a different atmosphere. Everything felt older and more relaxed. Tourist towns like Lihue and Kapa'a were streamlined and simple compared to the complexities of Oahu. Further up the island we passed waterlogged fields of a type that could easily be mistaken for rice crops. This was where they farmed taro, a starchy root vegetable that was used to make *poi* — a meal sacred in traditional Hawaiian culture. And beyond these expanses of flat greenery were grass fields that would come to a sudden end and shoot straight up to form enormous mountains that reached for the sky at severe angles. Jagged peaks dense with tropical forest, untouched by the hand of man, and dictators of multiple weather formations on the island. We experienced them all as we drove — sunshine to black clouded sky and rain. Thankfully, it was easy to anticipate the downpour, and Jackie would pull over so we could quickly throw the roof over our heads and save us all a soak. Then ten minutes up the highway we'd be basking in glorious sun again.

At some points, the highway was the only hint of civilisation, until you drove through a populated area and the buildings would crowd the road like leeches around a life-giving artery, feeding on the energy of the tourist dollar. But its hard to ignore that Hawaiian allure; it beckons you to pull over, look around, and somehow charms you into leaving money behind. Everything was built beside the main road, the downside being severe traffic jams in these towns at certain times of day. But the flipside was Kauai felt almost untouched when you ventured away from the highway, and it was during these back-route explorations that I came to understand the value of a four-wheel drive vehicle. The driving surfaces were unpredictable and rough, and some roads were so harsh they looked like they'd been used for artillery practice, so if you tried to drive through using the wrong vehicle there was real danger of losing your car to a pothole or a merciless bog.

Jackie took us as far north-west as we could go, the last town on the map — Hanalei. The Jeep wound through the backstreets, passing houses perched on sturdy log stilts, ready for that rare occasion when the great ocean goddess *Namaka* would unleash her anger on the island in the form of a devastating tsunami.

Jackie parked the car near the long Hanalei Pier. The bay was calm and the beach almost empty along its entire stretch, most likely because of dull skies and light rain. But damp sand felt soothing under bare feet, and we walked to the western end of the beach, stripped down to our swimwear and ran into the waves. It was strange, almost too good to be true. I couldn't believe we had the place to ourselves. Sure, the weather was below average, but when the sea is always warm and the view is this good, why wouldn't you be in the water? All four of us originated from dry mountainous areas with too much wind, so we were only too happy to make the most of the circumstances.

It was probably a natural trick of light that made everything here look green. The sky, the mountains, the trees, the ocean, the familiar turtle that poked its head above the waves and slipped from view a moment later. I stood in chest-deep water with Elena cradled in my arms, her hands clasped around my neck, and we looked back toward the beach and marvelled at the emerald mountains beyond. These giants of Kauai that reached all the way to the coast and closed in around the bay like a protective arm. In the upper atmosphere the rain came down with more force and cascaded down the sides of these mountains and separated into many white torrents. Waterfalls. So many waterfalls.

'I've needed this,' Elena whispered in my ear, 'We've finally escaped, haven't we?'

'We must have, unless this is all a dream.'

She kissed me just to make sure we were awake.

After Jackie took his location photos, we began the long drive south.

\*

'*Aloha*, folks! Welcome to the Poipu Plantation Resort. My name is Gemma, how can I help you today?'

The young woman who greeted us from behind the counter was an absolute stunner, with wavy dark hair and flawless brown skin. Mr Conroy didn't waste a second and was on her as hard and fast as a convict who hadn't seen a woman in years.

'*Aloha Gemma.* You must be the loveliest thing I've set eyes on since we arrived.' He grabbed her hand, kissed it, and leaned on the counter. 'You can help us by having dinner with me. Wine, dancing, maybe a beach rendezvous. *La dolce vita* … What do you say?'

Elena shoved her brother off the counter. 'My apologies, Gemma, this one's defective. Sometimes all the neurons don't connect and he just blurts out rubbish.'

'Rubbish? I meant everything I said — oof!'

I put my foot on Mr Conroy's back and posed like he was a big game trophy while Jackie took our picture. Gemma ignored us and stuck to the script like a professional, 'Umm, so how may I help you?'

'We're checking in. My name's Jackie Heads, I've booked two garden-view apartments and already finalised the payment.'

'Great. Let me see … Jackie Heads … Yes, here you are.' Gemma handed my brother a pamphlet explaining all of the resort facilities and then launched into a well-rehearsed monologue about this magnificent plantation house, the property, the gardens, 'and through those double doors is the restaurant and bar. There are a couple of entrances into the restaurant, so it doesn't matter which way you come to the house through the gardens. And if you eat on the veranda the views are beautiful.'

Gemma was friendly, intelligent, and her well-being was going to require attention because Mr Conroy was a dog with a bone that needed to be buried. Elena may have shut down her twin for the moment, but for how long? Gemma was in the danger zone until we could protect her from this tornado of romantic thirst. Mr Conroy needed distracting with a more immediate offering. Normally a dirty magazine and a handful of coconut oil would be enough, but my brother-in-law would only turn his nose up. *Why would I settle for less than the best?* he would say. And one look at Gemma made it hard to argue against this point of view. But I knew another way to damp down his fire. Wine. Lots and lots of wine.

This place wasn't a typical resort. Our accommodations were self-contained apartments, set in blocks dressed up to look like *ye olde* sugar plantation houses, and Jackie had rented a pair of them, stacked one on top of the other. Single bedroom, kitchenette, living room with teak and rattan furniture — ripe for a sexy magazine photoshoot.

Everyone was pleased with our location at the top of the hill, where it didn't matter if we behaved like perverts and scallywags. It was perfect for a pirate crew of unconventional taste. Nobody bothered to unpack. Bags were tossed in the bedrooms and we explored our new living arrangements. I opened the sliding door at the rear of our apartment and wandered across the small terrace and onto the grassy slope beyond. You could see the ocean from here, and we were surrounded by enormous banyan trees, frangipani and every variety of hibiscus flower. On a bright day there was enough colour here to make your eyes bleed.

'Ahoy, Eduardo!' It was Jackie. He and Mr Conroy were leaning over the balcony of the upstairs apartment. 'What a view, eh? I can almost see the beach from here.'

'Did you know,' Mr Conroy said, 'we can see clear into the apartments on the lower slope when they have their shutters open? Maybe we'll catch a free show.'

'That just means they can see you too, so no funny business on the balcony.'

'I'm sure we'll behave … probably.'

We regrouped and went across the road to a general store called Whalers. Booze, smokes and food were required. The onsite restaurant operated as a separate entity to the resort, which meant no meals were included. It was pay to play every time. We were fending for ourselves again. But I preferred it like that. Buffets by the pool were for the polo

shirt crowd, and the plantation didn't have a pool anyway —
there was no need when it was right on the beach.

\*

AN EDITORIAL NOTE, COURTESY OF MR CONROY AND JACKIE
HEADS: 'I'd like to take this opportunity to make it clear that
I am not cheap. See, we went to buy groceries before dinner
… And the specifics of the argument escape me, but there
was much name-calling and threats of physical violence. All
I can confirm was an overreaction by my sister in regard to
the amount of wine purchased from the store. That was all
Eddie's fault. For some reason he insisted I have it, and as far
as I'm concerned it was a perfectly acceptable amount. Six
or seven bottles is not overkill, and it was low alcohol merlot
and sangria, so bad behaviour would be at a minimum and
there would be none of these after-effects, like an axe splitting
your head open … I suspect Elena was simply shitty because
she went shopping under the impression it was for food, and
there was none in my bag. But that's what the restaurant was
for! What I needed was cigarillos after exhausting my supply
in Oahu. This was of little concern to my brat sister, who
said my priorities were up my arse, which was harsh, but
looking back was probably fair … and I love her to death, so
to uphold the family honour, and save myself from a situation
that made me look like a peasant, I offered to cover the bar
tab and buy everyone dinner — which meant a medium-

rare steak for that carnivorous twin of mine. Juicy meat is all she ever puts in her mouth. It can't be helped I suppose, oral fixation runs in the family. I recently had an evening rendezvous with this woman named Connie and she really put my tongue to work ... there's nothing like parking your face in a woman's soft folds to create warm drippings. It's breathtaking. Don't you agree, Jackie?'

'Jesus, dude. Boundaries ... Anyway, after everything was smoothed over, we eased into a relaxed and enjoyable evening. At least, that's what was supposed to happen. After a good feed and couple of whiskeys I was feeling great, everyone was. Nobody ever expected shit to go sideways. Nobody saw it coming except Eddie; he seems tuned into that kind of thing. But by then it was already too late.'

\*

We ate dinner on the veranda of the Plantation Restaurant. The meal was good. Not great but good. And Mr Conroy did buy Elena her steak dinner, and paid for everyone else as well. He was worried that after his faux pas with the wine, everyone would start to think of him as a tight-arse and his reputation as a cultured provocateur would be ruined. We enjoyed seeing the degenerate snob humbled every once in a while, although, we would never ruin the poor guy's reputation. He was our brother, and after the amount he paid for that dinner, we might even give him a pass the next time his ruinous behaviour became a problem.

We had the veranda to ourselves, and the mood was relaxed. It was quiet too, except for the birds, cicadas and pleasant conversation. A man who had been drinking at the bar came outside and asked if he could join us. I was reluctant. I don't take well to strangers in my downtime, especially those who invite themselves to dinner or drinks. Given my occupation as a journalist and sometimes fitness guru, anyone would think I was a real people person, and I am ... except when I'm not working. Then I hate everyone.

On this occasion I was overruled by the group. Everyone was in such good spirits that they were happy to include this stranger. His name was Papa Benjamin. That's how he introduced himself. Papa Benjamin was middle-aged, and a local of the island. Half Hawaiian, half Samoan. And in an extraordinary feat he could list ten generations going back on both sides of his family heritage. His was a line filled with brave warriors and sea-going explorers. Tough people, unafraid of death. 'The Pacific Ocean is streaked crimson with my ancestors' blood. Paid in full to a great many kings and queens across many, many lands,' he said. 'For this reason, the gods favour me.'

Why did he tell us that? I don't remember anyone asking for this information. It was creepy. But things lightened when we got to talking about why we were in Kauai and what we all did for a living. Papa Benjamin was a tour guide. He was a nice enough dude, but something was off about him — I just couldn't put my finger on it.

Was it his shifty eyes? The cheeky smile? Being able to list ten generations almost effortlessly? Shit, anyone can lie on the spot and claim to be something they're not. How hard could it be to fake a heritage? Not hard. And the longer we talked, the more that distinct off-ness lingered, and yet the exact reason remained elusive. It was unsettling. Not enough to ruin my evening, but sometimes you just know *something is up*. More and more often the bartender would stick his head outside for a peek, give Papa Benjamin the stink eye, and ask us if everything was okay. Everyone would reply that they were 'Good. Fine. Great ... Can we get another round?' The bartender would smile and slink away again. This odd behaviour didn't go unnoticed. Something about Papa Benjamin was mischievous, and the bartender knew it.

When nothing unpleasant occurred, I finally left it alone and settled into a happier groove. I sipped my rum and basked in the warm glow of the house lights. Elena wanted to go for a walk before the steak began to sit too heavy. I said I would wait for her here, and then she disappeared to the bathroom and afterward went back to the apartment to change clothes. Papa Benjamin left the table a moment later and said: 'I'm bringing back a special treat for my new friends who have been so welcoming.'

Nobody bothered to ask what the special treat might be, we were too comfortable. I leaned back in my chair while we waited, and sipped from crystal filled with sweet spiced liquor, and expressed my fondness for the drink. 'You fellas need to get yourself a glass of this rum. It's like washing your tongue with a sunbeam.' I held up the glass and was mesmerised by the light dancing through the golden liquid.

'A sunbeam?' Jackie said. 'Brother, what you need is to start drinking whiskey and get off the rum. You know that shit makes people weird and angries up the blood.'

'Not my blood. And I'm already weird … there's nothing wrong with rum, it was acceptable currency throughout the world for centuries. And if I'm not mistaken, that's a beer in your hand, not fine Canadian whiskey.'

'You're both drinking peasant water. This glass of red has to be the smoothest, full-bodied cherry I've had slide across my tongue in an age,' Mr Conroy said.

I smirked about that, and Jackie said: 'Nobody believes that, Roy. I'm sure you've had plenty of smooth, full-bodied cherries slide across your tongue recently.'

Papa Benjamin returned with a jug of Hawaiian punch in one hand and an already full glass in the other. He insisted that everyone fill their glass and have a drink with him. We toasted to a great evening, took a sip of the punch, and like synchronised swimmers fell out with our arms in the air. Eyes watered. We coughed and choked, breathed fire. You could see the vapours in the air. It looked and smelt like fruit salad but was adequate for use as rocket fuel.

'That'll strip your insides like paint thinner,' I said. 'How much rum is in this?'

'Enough. It's a secret recipe passed down by dark kahunas.'

'Fucking hell,' Jackie said. 'You might be finishing that on your own, Papa. I don't know if I'm ready to have that kind of night. I can already feel a case of the squirts coming on.'

Five minutes passed and everyone filled their small glass again. Everyone except for our new friend, Papa Benjamin, who had a strange look on his face, a seriousness like he was about to invite us to commit murder or rob the bar — maybe both. His eyes were bloodshot and wide and searched the veranda in a strained and wild way, like he was afraid somebody was watching us ... listening to our conversation. What did this man know that we didn't? He waved us in close and said in a low voice that was dead serious: 'Can you hear them closing in? See them moving out the corner of your eye?'

I knew it. All evening I'd had suspicions and now they were confirmed — this man was a lunatic ready to horrify. Where was Elena? Why the hell couldn't I stop drinking this punch? And Papa Benjamin ... He continued to disturb.

'Do you boys know about the Menehune?'

'Menehune?' Mr Conroy repeated. 'What's that?'

'Not what. Who. Ancient Hawaiian little people filled with powerful *mana*. They're everywhere around these parts, always watching ... waiting for a chance to use their advanced technology on lower life forms ... Shhh.' He held a finger to his mouth. 'Can you hear them? That creaking in the rafters? I've already seen some tonight. They're here right now, watching from the shadows ...'

'Get the fuck out of here,' Jackie said. 'You're drunk, Papa B.'

This was a worry. Papa Benjamin had started down a seriously dark trail, and judging by what came out of his mouth next, would not be led back to the light any time soon. 'Okay, boys. Let's cut the shit. How much do you know about your ancestors?'

My buzz had changed to something else, a kind of tension, something uncomfortable and closer to adrenaline. My heart raced. I'd been in this situation before, when I smoked some bush-weed with a Māori who had asked the same thing, with that same intense look on his face. I knew the only way back to Aloha was to give a sensible account of our heritage, to show that we weren't disrespectful Westerners and had at least some idea of how we came into being — the alternative was to tear arse into the jungle, naked and screaming, with only a cow fibula to use as a billy club. Jackie knew the drill — Mr Conroy would have to be initiated.

'We're Australian and British, probably more, I have suspicions about North Africa. Our ancestors were adventurers,' I said and motioned to Jackie, who was nodding in agreement.

Papa Benjamin laughed, 'Ah-ha! And like Captain Cook you've journeyed to Hawaii. Hopefully no one mistakes you for Lono, we all know how that turned out.'

'Things appear to have twisted darkly,' Jackie said.

I gripped the sides of the table, looking for some stability in a situation that was quickly unwinding in punch-fuelled madness, 'No. We're already in the hurricane.'

'Holy shit,' Jackie said, 'you're right. I can feel it too.'

Mr Conroy either ignored this darkness, or its meaning flew over his head. He remained happy and upbeat and eagerly explained his Italian heritage: 'My family is full-blooded Italian. Elena and I are twins, we share a strong bond. We're the first generation born in Australia, but our parents and grandparents and their grandparents are all Italian. From the northern villages ...'

Mr Conroy was really into it and had begun to talk about Milan. And somewhere between Milan and a sudden shift sideways into a conversation about the benefit of Italian leather over its poor Australian cousin, I realised that Papa Benjamin had left the table ... Where did he go? *When* did he go? Did he ever exist?

'Where did this frog come from?' Jackie said, staring at the tablecloth in a manner I found disconcerting.

'What frog?' Mr Conroy asked.

'This frog. Look at it. Yellow and black and giving me the eye ... I do believe this frog has sinister intentions.'

'Don't touch it!' I said. 'That's a poison arrow. Very deadly.'

'*What frog?*'

Jackie nodded at the table. 'This one. It's definitely unhappy.'

'Oh my god, I can see it. Flick it away Jackie *before it kills us all.*'

A whining buzz split the air and raised in volume inside my ear canal until it was unbearable. I flinched violently and shooed it off. It happened two or three more times. 'These mosquitos are a pain in the fucking arse. It's like Africa all over again. Look at the size of that bastard! Bloody thing's the size of a kookaburra — *watch out, Jackie, it's on your shoulder!*'

'*Did I get it? Did I get it, Ed? Tell me I got it …*'

'This is not good, gentlemen. My wine has been stolen.'

'Did you drink it?' Jackie said.

'No. It was definitely stolen. Probably by that jealous frog.'

'Frogs and prehistoric mosquitos — the jungle is closing in. Only strong alcohol will ward off the creatures that have come for blood. We need more drinks.'

'Bartender!' Mr Conroy shouted. 'Three more drinks!'

'What about the punch?' Jackie asked.

'Leave it,' I said. 'The punch is a jug of darkness; we need to get light again.'

'I wish there was some way to record these phenomena … Bloody hell, the frogs are multiplying. Red and yellow … They're all over the table.'

'*Dear god, there's a purple one,*' Mr Conroy said.

'Shut up both of you … can you hear that? Drums, and chanting, we've stumbled into native territory — we need to arm ourselves.' Then we were inside the lodge where it was safe. I adjusted my pith helmet and had another swig of rum. 'These natives will come for us. They'll mistake us for their gods and try to kill us and harvest our body parts to gain power.'

'It's true,' Professor Jackie said. 'The same thing happened to Captain Cook. They thought he was the returned god Lono — murdered him *right there on the beach.*'

'*Murder.* What can we do? The jungle is turning against us and now we're going to be hunted like common swine. I'm too well-liked to be butchered!'

'Calm yourself, Pierre. Evil spirits haunt these parts, but this lodge has all we require.'

I removed a pair of spears from the wall and handed one to Pierre Conrad. Professor Jackie armed himself with a war club, and not a moment too soon. The lodge was suddenly invaded by a gang of withered grey zombie creatures who shrieked like howler monkeys. And then there was a naked red-skinned demon shouting at us. A female demon with a body built for sex, and yellow hair that stood up like fire — a succubus — and I was to be her human sacrifice. If we hung about, this cunning demon would have her way and suck my soul out through my cock.

The command was given to move forward, and our expedition fought through the zombie-like creatures with our spears. We had to escape their pawing, and some annoying talky gentleman who kept insisting we owed him money, despite my esteemed companion's word that everything was already taken care of by our good friend Pierre Conrad and it was a despicable act to even ask if we could afford to cover it, when he, Professor Jackie, a well-respected doctor of film, had a tab at the lodge anyway.

We ran along a twisting jungle path lit by torch fire. Somehow we got lost. Everything was against us. We doubled back like ZZ Top, and now tall huts were everywhere. Violent screeches in the darkness … what madness had we stumbled into? A large red beast with glowing yellow eyes menaced us as we crossed a stone clearing, and it was only by the might and daring of our intrepid crew swinging spears and roaring with rage that we managed to escape with our lives.

At camp I rushed around, gathering provisions while Pierre Conrad raved from the edge of the cliff, cursing the jungle and its savage inhabitants. He swore there would be no Italian blood spilt on this hillside, for his beauty would conquer all, and he poured sweet red sangria into the abyss as a symbol of defiance.

Professor Jackie stormed inside the cabin from the opposite direction, '*Quick.* I've secured an elephant. If we move now we can escape this nightmare.'

We rushed through the vegetation, hacking at the bush with machetes until we reached the pachyderm. We climbed on its back and the professor took the reins. The beast trumpeted and moved swiftly through the jungle, but our mood remained tense.

This venture appeared doomed. There were screams in the night. Bright lights. I tried to focus on a point straight

ahead and ignore the voices calling my name. I knew it was
a trap. Could we escape this darkest and wildest of jungles?
Only a supreme effort of bravery would do. More drums
echoed in the darkness, their source unknown.

Pierre was in a wild manner, shaking his spear, and
swearing blue murder at the shadows along our path. I
could've smacked his fool head. It was the ancient night
marchers of Hawaii. They had come for our souls — to
force us to serve the old gods and march with them for an
eternity, and there was no hope of escape by laying prostrate
on the ground while we waited for their passing ... not atop
this great white elephant. I closed my eyes but feared I would
be able to see beyond the veil of reality and have my spirit
snatched anyway.

We were now on a straight. Free and clear — once more
under stars. And another swing of the universe struck us
with luck most foul. We had taken a bad turn and somehow
landed inside a native village. How had we been captured?
The professor was speaking to one of them — the chief,
negotiating a truce ... or was it a distraction? My god, what
if he failed? Was there ever a more desperate situation? I
was inclined to think not. But salvation came in the form
of a cache, left behind by other explorers that had trod the
deep jungle and failed to escape. I held up one of their skulls
and examined the poor blighter. A victim of headhunting.
Jesus, they had even placed a price on this one. *Five dollars*.
The skull market must be flooded for such a bargain to exist.

Pierre was distraught. Tears streamed down his cheeks as he swatted the skull out of my hand and insisted we were too valuable a commodity to stay here much longer. I took several bottles of rum from the cache and my companions helped themselves to what they needed. And then the natives turned on us. The professor had failed, apparently his expertise did not extend to negotiation. Shouting and all manner of violence occurred. We barely made it out alive.

The elephant trundled along a hardened river of lava while the succubus and a lust-crazed Hawaiian woman pursued our troop. Persistent buggers. If they somehow captured us I would bravely sacrifice myself and breed with them. It was my duty, whatever it took to save the lives of my beloved comrades … The world came to an end. The sky was on fire. Red and orange. Shooting toward the stars like a bloody hand reaching for the moon.

'What devilry is this?' the professor shouted. 'We'll be scorched to ash!'

'It's Pele!' I replied. 'She's come back for us!'

'Not again. Not again!'

'What did you do, Pierre?'

'I didn't do anything. She hates me!'

'You left the old woman on the side of the road, didn't you? You swine!'

'It was only one time. She had a dog and I didn't want it to scratch the leather.'

The professor shouted over his shoulder in a matter-of-fact manner, 'I told you we should've given her a ride. Now she thinks you're a former lover. If she catches us she'll have your manhood for a trophy.'

Disaster struck while he was distracted. Our elephant came unstuck, crashed into the bush and broke a leg. The professor did what was right and put it to sleep. It was a sorry situation.

Pierre was of no help. He knelt on the ground and begged the goddess for forgiveness, except she was not in the mood. 'I'm too beautiful to die so young! To hell with you, Pele.' Pierre shook his fist at the fireballs. 'To hell with you — *you temptress. Hag! Bush pig!*'

'Quiet, fool, you're making it worse!' the professor shouted.

We stumbled into the jungle and were immediately surrounded by cockerels ridden by miniature Polynesians with spears. The Menehune. We had been warned they would come for us. There was a tremendous squawk and their kahuna medicine man rode in on the back of a giant nene. Their magic would curse us forever if we crossed their people, so we ran for the coast. We ran for days. Through villages, across bridges and a sea of grass, until we discovered an enormous staircase down to the beach. After much life-threatening struggle on that rickety passage, we navigated our way to the sand and staggered toward the moonlit ocean. Pierre collapsed on the shore, threw his arms in the air, and cried and blubbered and drowned his sorrow in sweet wine. Professor Jackie ran further along the beach, armed with a spear and intent on securing our position should the Menehune track us down, or the Hawaiians — we could see their fire dance in the distance, hear the drums of doom, followed by the chilling bellow of a conch shell. They knew we were here. Would they drag our severed limbs away for worship? It was the bones … the bones were valuable. My universe imploded and then exploded — reformed, and when I opened my eyes, I was lying on the beach with a golden goddess floating above me. She lifted me away from all the fear and aggression of the night. We flew at tremendous speed to her palace of light, and she placed me on a bed of palm leaves, where I drifted peacefully into the never never.

*

AUTHOR'S NOTE: At this critical juncture, the story will be handed over to my wife, whose interpretation of events may vary slightly to my own.

AS WRITTEN BY ELENA HEADS:
Those idiots. Let me tell you what actually happened — what I witnessed that night. I'll try my best to describe it in a writerly way, but anyone reading can be assured this is a factual account.

So, we were at The Plantation Restaurant having a wonderful dinner, and we were joined for a drink by a new friend — we should probably reclassify this person after what happened. I think *the Devil* is more appropriate, but his name was Papa Benjamin.

The trouble started when I excused myself to use the bathroom. Papa Benjamin was right behind me and went straight to the bar and ordered a jug of Hawaiian punch — I know this because I heard him make the order. Who knows why he ordered the jug, maybe he'd convinced Jackie and my brother to kick on? But Eddie was supposed to be going for a walk with me, that's why I went back to the apartment to change clothes.

I was tying my shoes when the phone began to ring. I really didn't feel like answering it either. Reception always calls at the most inconvenient moment, usually while you're asleep, or just getting out of the shower, so you answer, and your depraved husband decides to strip your towel from your body and pin you in a compromising position, and you're so delirious with lust you barely register what the voice on the phone is saying ... Sorry, Oahu flashback. Anyway, the timing of this call was unusual for several reasons, so I could only assume it was important and answered, 'Hello?'

'Is he trying to do a magic trick? *I don't know*, it's your fucking bar, you do something about it ... Sorry. Hello? Is this Elena?'

'Yes, this is Elena.'

'Thank god I managed to find you. It's Gemma from reception. You better get back to the restaurant as soon as you can.'

'Is everything okay? What's wrong?'

'It's your family. They're acting strange and scaring the other guests.'

'I've barely been gone. How are they already drunk off their arses?'

'Not just drunk, I've been to enough parties to know what drunk guys are like. Something is wrong with them. They're freaking about things that aren't there and speaking in a weird accent, like they're trying to be British — Oh shit, your husband just removed the antique spears from the wall …'

My stomach lurched. I was so pissed off. How *the fuck* did they get so drunk and rowdy in such a short amount of time? I'd been gone thirty minutes, tops. That wasn't nearly long enough for those boys to get out of control, but Gemma sounded pretty wound up, her last words before she hung up the phone were, *'Please hurry.'*

I heard the disaster before I could see how bad it really was. Something crashed inside the restaurant as I ran across the car park, and a group of guests spilled out of the front door, yelling and screaming. 'Goddamn freaks! Maniacs! Don't go in there, lady, *they'll murder you.*' I've got to tell you; I began to wonder if we had adequate travel insurance.

Gemma stood in reception, helpless to do anything but watch the bizarre scene in the next room. I went straight to her side. 'Elena! Great — are they on medication? I checked the drink order and you guys haven't had that much. What's going on?'

I said I was going to find out and stormed into the restaurant, fuelled by adrenaline and rage, and feeling unreasonable enough to take on this nightmare by myself. The bartender was hiding behind the counter, carrying on about not being paid. 'It's the worst kind of mistreatment, after all I've done for them ... Look at this mess! And they refuse to tip!' There's nothing worse than a whiner. The bartender claimed he was looking out for us the whole time, but in this moment, he behaved like a total wanker.

Anyway, all his bitching fell on deaf ears. Eddie and my brother were standing near the entrance, holding spears with the sharp tips pointed forward. Jackie stood behind them, with one hand on Roy's shoulder and his other hand waved a ukulele like a club at a group of terrified guests — poor retirees who had come for a quiet dinner during their vacation and had been confronted by these maniacs just inside the doors.

An older gentleman was having none of it and yelled abuse at them.

'You're a damn disgrace! How dare you terrify my wife like this.'

It was pretty bad, I felt for him. And where in the world did Eddie get a pith helmet? This farce had to end.

'Oi! You three need to stop! *Now.*' That got their attention but not one of them seemed to recognise me. Eddie looked at me in a way I've seen countless times before — he was mentally undressing me — and the other two looked spooked, so they grabbed Eddie and all three ran from the restaurant.

Papa Benjamin was laughing his arse off. I stalked over and demanded to know what happened.

'Relax, Elena. They'll be okay, I swear. How is your husband supposed to find himself if he hasn't looked properly?'

We all had a few drinks with dinner, and nobody was anywhere near drunk except Papa Benjamin, so what surprised *me* was him being almost coherent when my boys were out of control. Something suspect had happened, and there was no doubt in my mind Papa Benjamin was the cause. He could see that too, and for a moment showed the appropriate amount of fear, because this was a personal betrayal, and I was a volcano ready to erupt — that's what Eddie would say.

'Elena, I swear it's gonna be okay. It really is okay … They're just on a quest to learn about their ancestors. They might even meet the Menehune on the way.'

'Ancestors? Menehune? What *the fuck* happened to them?'

'They drank too much punch.'

He started laughing again, and I no longer liked Papa Benjamin. I'm not a violent or angry person, but I don't tolerate bullies and idiots, and I have a tendency to act out … I swung an underhand fist into Papa B's groin that connected like a sledgehammer on a pair of grapes. The shady bastard deserved it; nobody messes with my family. Sadly, I didn't stick around to watch him crumple because Gemma grabbed my wrist and dragged me after the boys, all I heard was a deep groan and some moaning about 'right in the coconuts'.

We arrived outside just in time to hear a car horn blaring. A red Jeep was flashing headlights at three deranged lunatics waving spears and behaving like they were being attacked by a wild animal. I was so embarrassed. Then they ran off again, this time in the direction of the apartment. I could deal with them in the apartment. I'd just lock them inside and let them ride out whatever alcohol-induced affliction this was. There'd be no more drama.

It looked like a crime scene. There was a massive red puddle on the terrace, the sliding door was open, the lights were on, and there was nobody home. Thankfully nobody had been murdered. But something bad had happened, and something was missing. Something important. And the front door was wide open. I checked the countertop and my fear was confirmed.

'Gemma, they've taken the car keys.'

'Oh shit. I'll call security and the grounds staff. They patrol the car park on buggies.' Gemma dialled her personal phone. 'Security ... This is Gemma from reception ... Not so great, I need you to radio everyone and tell them to watch out for three drunk men ... Elena, what do you drive?'

'A white Jeep. It's a two-door soft-top.'

'They could be driving a white Jeep … Yeah. Try not to use force but be careful, they have spears ... *Spears* … No, that's not a joke … Great. Thank you.'

*

The baby elephant was being driven with none of the spastic urgency I saw in the restaurant. A tortoise could have outrun them, and it was impossible to lose the Jeep with its high beams turned on and roof folded down. Two men were standing in the back — it looked like Eddie and Roy — holding those stupid spears like they were on a hunting expedition … I never did figure out how they found time to put the roof down.

We jogged beside them and were soon joined by a security buggy and a couple of grounds staff on foot. Everyone shouted for them to stop, which somehow only created more panic. When I think back, we must have looked like creepy shadows to the boys, just weird threatening voices coming out of the dark. And I recall hearing someone yell *night marchers*. It's no wonder they began to carry-on like they were in extreme danger, but really, the only danger was a possible low-speed collision with a parked car.

I believe my anxiety reached its peak when they managed to navigate outside the resort. Using the rear exit, they drove onto the main road, crossed to the far lane, and continued to drive well below the appropriate speed limit. Fortunately, they were on the shoulder, which was okay, it was a much safer situation … unless they decided to throw those spears at passing traffic. God, can you imagine? Some poor local driving along, minding their business, and suddenly a spear flies through the window and impales their chest! Who would go to prison for that, I wonder? It could be a group effort at this point, the list of people involved in this event was getting long.

So, where was I? Oh yeah … The situation took another bad turn when the baby elephant jerked to a stop, and they ran inside the shopping village. Drunk antics inside the resort could be contained, or at the very least, managed. Drunk antics in a public space was a disaster, the police might get involved. One of the security guards offered to help but I asked him to wait just in case the boys came back. And let's be honest, being accompanied by someone dressed like a police officer would only escalate the situation while the boys were off their face.

By the time we made it inside the shopping village there was no sign of them. We couldn't hear anything horrible happening at the eateries, so we approached the only shop still open, Whalers General Store. That's when the screaming started — first a woman, and then … 'Sir. Sir you can't do that, if you're going to open that you have to pay for it … *Sir! Put that bottle down … I'll call the police!*'

The store manager was trying to stop Jackie from eating straight off the shelf. Eddie had armfuls of liquor and was singing: 'Black and red and gold and white and spiced, that's nice …' Several skull-shaped tiki mugs had been smashed on the ground. Roy stood on the remains and guzzled a bottle of red wine like a greedy vampire, spilling it down the sides of his mouth and all over his shirt. If there were any other customers they were either hiding or had run at the sight of spears. So, the store was now under the sole protection of the manager, because the pathetic girl behind the cash register was in hysterics and no help at all. She was too busy waving around a can of mosquito repellent like it was pepper spray. These goons stalked around like loose cattle, not the monsters she was making out they were. Sure, they had spears … I'll admit the situation was beyond our control. And their chatter was flat out bizarre.

'These bloody chips have gone bad! Bloody stale, I say. Like sawdust, eh!'

'How much for the screaming concubine? I'm in the market for a loud one …'

'That's a poor investment, Pierre, just like human heads. Damned skull trade is in the toilet. Professor! If they want our heads, we won't take any less than fifty each. Pounds not dollars!'

'You hear that, chief? Fifty, that's *pound sterling*. Now, bring me a canoe! Do you realise there's a river of lava out there? I don't wanna hear any guff about fireproof costing extra … I believe I have a tab here.'

*'Oil. Where's the Oil. I need to glisten!'*

'That'll attract like Captain Cook, you kook! We need food to stop jungle rot.'

'Pineapple is good for that. Better get a Pina Colada.'

'I say, I say, I say, chief … Are we both speaking English? Why can't you understand me? Must be my posh accent … Fucking rough as guts these villagers.'

'The natives are getting restless, Pierre. *Look out*, lusty purple head-hunters!'

'Quick — save the rum and your virtue!'

The boys ran from the store. But not before Jackie removed his leather belt, slapped the red-faced manager across his backside and shouted: 'Giddy up!'

If I've learned anything from Eddie, no matter how bad a situation you are in, even if you're the guilty party, if you are polite, plead ignorance and are extremely apologetic, you can get away with just about anything. And that's what happened. With Gemma's help I explained our situation, paid for everything on the spot, and the pissed-off manager kindly decided *not* to ban us from the store. That was lucky, I didn't think he would be so understanding. Money really does heal all wounds. Smashed mugs and food all over the floor was not a pretty sight. But, you know, there was no real damage done and no need to call the cops. And you know what else? All that cleaning probably helped the poor shop assistant forget her life-threatening ordeal. Moron — young girls can be such over-dramatic idiots … I'm being too harsh, aren't I? To be fair, my lovely family had traumatised her —

in the same way young children are traumatised by strange farm animals. I bet she'll never work the night shift again.

But I've gotten off topic again. Where was I?

There was some kind of celebration nearby, with their own music and fireworks display. It would have been really nice to watch if I wasn't chasing a carload of irrational lunatics who got distracted by the light show, swung off the shoulder, and crashed into the bushes at the rear entrance of the plantation. That might be the slowest single vehicle accident ever, like a parked car had rolled into the garden because of a failed handbrake — except there happened to be a drunk film director behind the wheel. Thank God there were no paparazzi on location to capture the moment.

Roy was straight into his dramatics, doing a repeat performance of his show on the Pali Highway — begging the goddess Pele for forgiveness while the other two stroked facial hair and assessed the damage. Then I swear Eddie said: 'Put the beast out of its misery,' like the car was a crippled animal. And I watched Jackie *euthanise* the Jeep by stabbing it in the gap between the front tyre and fender. Complete nonsense.

Now the worst appeared to be over, I should've been able to relax a little, except there was a sudden urgency to their movements and they ran into the resort shouting: *'To safety!'* But really, how safe had anyone been that night? It was pure luck we were all in one piece, although, I wondered about psychological scars … Somewhere a voice yelled *'Menehune!'* and a whole family of chooks ran out of the bushes, followed by a security guard who said: 'They've run down the hill toward the beach.'

I didn't care as long as they stayed inside the plantation.

By some miracle there was zero damage done to the car, Jackie had only stalled, so I parked it properly inside the resort. Gemma needed to get back and clear up whatever mess was left behind at the restaurant. I thanked her for all the help and said we'd pay for any property destruction. Well, Jackie or Roy would pay.

The security guard followed me down the hill, through the villas and across the bridges, to the grass clearing in front of the ocean. The boys were nowhere to be seen. But a trail of dropped liquor bottles indicated they'd gone down to the beach. I found Eddie lying on the sand drinking rum. Jackie was halfway along the beach, running toward the Sheraton Hotel where they were having a *luau*. You could see the fire and light show and hear their drums from all the way over here. Jackie's motives were a concern, but Roy was a more immediate problem. My brother had stripped down to his underwear and waded into the water up to his knees, where he now stood, drinking a bottle of wine and crying out to the gods. I wasn't sure if that was disrespectful to the Hawaiians ... his behaviour has always been regrettable.

Even though the night had been one long shit-storm, I caught a break and avoided having to perform a sea rescue in the dark when Roy stepped away from the water, crossed the sand and disappeared up the stairs. I knew he might wander aimlessly for a couple of hours, but he would end up in a comfortable bed and sleep it off. He's my twin, he'd be fine without the other two egging him on … which reminded me that Jackie had vanished. With some luck he would do like Roy and simply make his way back to the apartment. But it's always a good idea to cover yourself when drunk people are involved — don't take your eye off the ball — and I asked the security guard to follow his tracks. Just in case. There was every chance Jackie would end up at the *luau* and try to kill someone with that silly spear. That would end his film career fast, and the last thing I needed tonight was another disturbing phone call — this time from the police: 'Yes, Mrs Heads, your brother-in-law has been jailed for drunk and disorderly conduct, with intent to commit grievous bodily harm … He kept raving about how '*skewering them*' was the only way for a professor of film to keep his audience in their seat.'

Men. They grow old but they still act like boys when they drink, the only difference is there's more weight to drag around when they can't walk straight. No wonder so many wives leave their intoxicated husbands to find their own way home. That being said, I wasn't ready to ditch mine just yet. Eddie had passed out, and I rolled him on his side so he didn't choke on any vomit. No rock star death for this one. I was determined he live a long life. And for fifteen minutes I sat on the sand with my husband. In the moonlight. Listening to the soft break of the waves. It would've been very romantic under most circumstances.

I woke Eddie with a gentle kick in the bum. He groaned and our eyes met and he smiled — mumbled something about being rescued by a goddess ... I hate that those words made me blush. Have you heard this one today? Fuck you, Eddie — for putting me through such an ordeal, *and* for being such a sweet man that I instantly forgave you. How shit was that? I couldn't even be angry with him. Because when you broke it down, the only fault of the boys was sharing a drink with a stranger who appeared generous and trustworthy. But even the friendliest people can be two-faced monsters with sick fantasies.

I was ready to call it a night. I gripped Eddie's leg with both hands and dragged him along the sand until we reached the stairs. Somehow, I managed to get him standing and up to the grass. It was slow going, there's nothing harder than trying to navigate someone that is hopelessly drunk. It's a good thing it wasn't all uphill to our apartment, because that would've been *really hard*. If I ever see Papa Benjamin again I'll break his fucking legs and force him to do the same walk. We did eventually make it back, and I dumped Eddie on a deckchair and left him outside to sleep and recover.

Exhausted, but knowing there was more to do, I went back to the restaurant to calculate the damage. I was so relieved, it really wasn't that awful, and what amazed me was the staff were happy to sweep the whole affair under the rug. It turned out my boys caused almost no destruction to the restaurant, only a few smashed glasses and plates and spilled cutlery from a tablecloth that had been dragged off during the fiasco. The few disgruntled customers caught in the crossfire had also been pacified, and our account was settled by charging any damage to Jackie's room — he wasn't even upset and wrote it all off as a work expense. Two antique spears and a ukulele for film props, plus a dinner party that got a little too wild.

After the bartender got over himself, he had called the cops. Unfortunately by the time they arrived, Papa Benjamin had disappeared and the tainted Hawaiian punch had been disposed of. The police took my statement and Gemma backed up everything I told them. She was a complete sweetheart, and the following day I bought her a bunch of flowers as a thank you gift. The police were very sympathetic and pleased nobody was hurt, although, at that point in time I only knew the location of *one* out of the *three* deranged victims. Jackie and my brother were in the wind, so I returned to the apartment. Eddie remained passed out on the terrace, face down in the plastic slats of the deckchair. I left him that way and went inside, had a shower, and went to bed.

We were going to be okay.

I woke up the next day ready to continue our Hawaiian holiday as if the night before had been a bad dream and nothing more. And that is what really happened. Except — and this is frustrating because there were witnesses — I still don't know where my husband got that ridiculous pith helmet. Eddie reckons he was never wearing one, the resort staff never mentioned it among the missing inventory, and the stupid thing had disappeared by morning. Someone or some *thing* had spirited it away.

# Day Seven

I found myself confused. Had it all been a wild dream? I woke up feeling like I'd been dragged through sand, and I needed water because there was severe dry mouth. No hangover to speak of. A little rough around the edges but otherwise fine. I tried to wrap my head around that for a moment ... although we hadn't really drunk that much, it still verged on the impossible. This would take some time to consider ... and my brain ... it was working in slow motion. Why was I outside, drooling through the gaps of this uncomfortable deckchair? Elena must've brought me back from the restaurant and left me to pass out. Except something didn't add up, there was a large portion of the night missing, and I could only fill the hole with strange visions too bizarre to be real.

I unstuck myself from the chair. There was a body lying on the grass halfway down the slope from our little terrace. I staggered down to investigate. It was breathing — that was important. It was also face down and completely naked. There were rooster feathers sticking out of its bum crack in a neat little line.

I rolled this unfortunate individual over and gave him a poke in the ribs.

'Mr Conroy. *Roy*, wake up.'

'Ugh. What time is it ... are we still on Kauai?'

'Not sure. We need food, and electrolytes. Need to clear the air. Get some clothes on, we'll have breakfast then go for a swim.'

While he pulled himself together, I went to find my wife and face the music.

It was a miracle Elena wasn't pissed off. Not even a little. How was that possible? She seemed more concerned I wasn't brain-damaged after our Hawaiian punch had been spiked. Spiked punch. That explained *a lot*. You don't always get lucky in life, but the love of a good woman — not just a good woman, one that will have your back and drag herself through hell to protect you — is a gift you never stop appreciating. Elena was a goddess, and I loved her even more after she told me what happened. Then she gently informed me that I had better go and clean up.

I went into the bathroom and stared at the twisted creature in the mirror. I looked a wreck. I mean, really shit.

The deckchair impression across my face would take hours to go away. A dip in the ocean would cure all, but for the moment a splash of ice-cold water, mouthwash and dark sunglasses had me feeling halfway back to human again. Once I'd freshened up, Elena hit me with some information that might've been better delivered in the afternoon, after the fog over my brain had lifted.

'I've just got to tell you this quickly. Before I went to sleep last night I did some research. The police told me that Papa Benjamin — aka Benjamin Kane — is a drifter and known to mess with tourists in local bars. He doesn't normally work the resorts; we were unlucky to cross paths with him.'

'Well, shit. Did they catch that dodgy old lush?'

'Unfortunately, no. By the time the cops showed, he'd already done a runner.'

'Too bad. I doubt he'll come back this way.'

'Maybe, but addicts and repeat offenders can't help themselves. I mean, who drugs people for kicks? Honestly. Maybe he has mental health issues? He was friendly enough, but there was definitely something about him that wasn't quite right.'

'I got that feeling too.'

'Here's another thing that will spin you out. It was probably just the weirdness of the night, but for whatever reason, I started researching Hawaiian gods. *Papa* is the name of the earth goddess, kind of Mother Nature on the islands. And *Kane* is the creator god, he separated the earth and the sky to create Hawaii. It made me think, is *Papa Benjamin Kane* the gods in human form coming to play games with us?'

'That is a fascinating theory ... and creepy as hell.'

'Did any of you insult Papa Benjamin, or say anything kind of dumb? When I bailed him up at the restaurant he said you were on a quest to discover your ancestors.'

'He did mention ancestors, right before everything came unstuck.'

'Mhmm. Well, it reminded me what the cops on Oahu said, that the gods knew we were coming. Weird coincidence, right?'

It was weird. A very strange and unnerving coincidence, although, still *only* a coincidence. Benjamin Kane was probably just some island nut who disliked outsiders and wanted to fuck with people on holiday. But something about that triggered flashbacks from the previous night. Disturbing images haunted me — got me thinking. What if Papa Benjamin wasn't a nut? Had I invited Kane's wrath because I was reluctant to invite him to sit with us? Had we made contact with our ancestors? How deep into the volcano could I go? And was it too early to start drinking again? Because this was heavy. My mind had sailed away on a trade wind, now lost in the maelstrom ...

'Ground control to space cadet, are you there? Come in, Eddie.' Elena could tell it was too early and I needed a distraction. 'You can relax babe. If the gods were playing with you, I think they've had their fun. Let's get you to the beach for a swim. The fresh air will do you wonders.'

Elena was right. I felt better the moment we stepped outside. The day was muggy and overcast. Barely any people around. While the other two sorted themselves out, we got a head start and walked down to the surf shack at the edge of the grass clearing, where there were a handful of people setting up on the recliners, though, these folks didn't stay for long. And it looked deserted down on the sand and out across the ocean.

We asked for two towels from the attendant in the surf shack. The dude manning the shack was named Dale, and he was a *dude*. Dale looked to be in his early forties. A mop of blond hair and a pair of black, thick-rimmed spectacles decorated his head. I suspected they were for reading — we would soon discover his long-distance eyesight was fine. He also wore a bright yellow aloha shirt. His entire persona was ripped straight from the seventies California surf scene. And that may very well be where Dale originated, maybe Malibu or Newport Beach, but the era he adored had long since moved on. I figured at some point he grew tired of the new scene and the direction that wave was headed, so he packed his board, stuffed a duffel full of wax, aloha shirts, and his stash of vintage porno magazines, and hopped a plane for the islands. Maybe he'd spent a few years exploring which Hawaii best suited his taste, and that eventually led Dale to Kauai — where today he was manning this Poipu surf shack. Probably as a favour for a friend — *Cool cool? It's only for a week, man. Twenty-five bucks an hour man, and you can eat all the icy poles you want … Sound good?*

I bet it did — to start with anyway. Until out of the blue that friend took off, and a favour for one summer had somehow turned into a full-time gig that had lasted years. Too many years … dealing with noisy, inconsiderate, sunburnt arseholes from places far and wide. Whatever zest he might've had for the job was long gone, and this morning Dale looked less than enthusiastic about being in the shack. He was hardly dressed in any kind of official capacity either, except maybe as resident surfer dude. I sympathised with Dale, his story might've been a spooky vision of my possible future — what I would become if I hadn't been saved by fate and forced into action.

We left our towels near a palm tree on the lawn, and we went down to the beach. The water was calm and warm, and despite the cloud cover, amazingly clear. Nothing about the scene looked threatening in the slightest. Elena and I waded out beyond the waves and happily swum around and floated and talked, just drifting on that warm current and enjoying that we were the only two humans in the middle of this tropical wonder. For twenty uninterrupted minutes we enjoyed the good life before the first signs of other humanity made themselves present on the sand — a trio of happy-go-lucky Japanese tourists. One guy and two girls, with beach towels draped around their necks. The guy carried a day bag, and all three of them held a big bright inflatable rubber ring, the same pool toys that were selling by the boatload on Waikiki Beach.

Roughly five minutes passed and the Japanese tourists had settled on the sand and were applying sunscreen. It was at this time Elena and I decided to get out of the water. We gave the trio a friendly wave, and crossed the sand, climbing the stairs to the plantation. Then we rinsed under the beach shower and dried off under our palm tree. Curiosity soon got the better of us, and we wandered to the edge of the grass and stood by the verge. The ocean looked beautiful. The two girls from the trio we'd left on the beach were venturing into the water with their inflatables, while their boyfriend stood on the sand and took photos. Elena purchased two icy poles from the surf shack, and we sucked on them and watched these two girls floating on the slow waves. It was almost hypnotic, the ebb and flow of the tide and these pink and purple rings bobbing up and down on the surface of the water like bubbles in a lava lamp. The girls were having a blast, laughing and chattering loudly. Elena thought it was cute, and it was — for a time. But one does not simply slide into a giant inflatable ring and expect to conquer the ocean. I could sense imminent disaster.

Elena and I were used to the tricks of the ocean because we grew up in Australia, where it doesn't matter if you're country or coast-bred, as a child you get taught to be aware of certain things when you go swimming at the beach. Things like rip tides. And even though this was some of the calmest ocean we'd ever swam in, these girls had not been paying attention to the current and were being swept down the beach away from their boyfriend. The tide was also dragging them further out, into the same deep water where Elena and I had been happily floating, and it became apparent very quickly that the girls were not competent swimmers.

We watched in horror as one of them slowly lost her grip on the ring and her head sank deeper and deeper inside the giant doughnut. In the end, her arms were sticking straight up in the air, pressed against the insides of her inflatable, and the only part of her head we could see was the top of her hair. She floated like that for a few minutes, while Elena and I slurped our refreshing icy poles and watched and waited. Eventually her friend paddled over and managed to drag her back up and onto the ring. But whatever cheer they had been experiencing was long gone ... replaced by the sound of the ocean, and creeping dread. Two girls, looking like a couple of doe-eyed cows who had wandered onto a wood raft for fun — confused because they were now being carried out to sea. The girls knew they had stuffed up big time and could no longer swim back to shore. Elena and I stood at the verge dumbfounded. We understood that we were witnessing something awful, and yet we couldn't look away.

*Warning: rip tide. Do not enter the water if you are a weak swimmer.*

These large signs were everywhere to prevent a situation exactly like this one. And it wasn't a case of an impenetrable language barrier. These warnings were written in English, Japanese and Korean, accompanied by idiot-proof (or so the signmaker thought) pictures showing the dangers. If a warning sign exists anywhere, you can be damn sure incidents of a similar nature have occurred there on more than one occasion. Obviously these tourists had ignored the great big warning sign, which was right beside the surf shack where they had collected their towels.

More absurd behaviour followed. Instead of going for help, the girl's boyfriend grabbed his own inflatable ring, ran into the surf and began to swim out to the girls. He was going to save them. He wanted to be a hero. Hell, if he was successful maybe they'd reward him with a threesome when they made it back to dry land? Sex on the beach. That must be what he was thinking, or why risk going at all? I couldn't stand the stupidity and went to the surf shack.

'Hey, Dale man — there's three people in the surf and they're in trouble.'

'Shit. Really?'

Dale ambled out of the shack and followed me to where Elena kept watch in stunned, open-mouthed, suspended animation. Icy pole syrup had dribbled over her fingers and down her arm. All that remained was a colourful stick in her hand. She was as immersed in the scene as that girl had been in her inflatable ring — completely sucked in.

The boyfriend had caught up with the two girls. They were lunging for his arms, trying to grab at him in a desperate attempt to save themselves, and in the process pushed the helpless fool under the water and only worsened their situation. By the time he recovered and remounted his tube, any energy he might have reserved to get them back to shore was gone. Now all three were slaves to the tide. The right equipment can be a fantastic aid when you're swimming through the ocean, but if your gear is shit and you can't paddle a stroke, why the hell are you dipping your feet in the water?

I considered the scene, 'This is grotesque. How long can anyone stand to watch? Do we let them drown? Where are the lifeguards?'

'We should be calling someone to help them,' Elena said.

'Nah ... I wouldn't worry about it,' Dale said, and sucked on his own icy pole. We were shocked by his blasé attitude, but he was not taking the piss. It was obvious Dale had seen this kind of calamity before. 'The current will take them down the other end of the beach where it shallows out before the point, they'll be swept back into shore up there.'

'Are you sure we don't need to call anyone?' Elena said.

'Nope. And you guys shouldn't worry. It'll only ruin your day. Trust me, this shit happens all the time. A few weeks ago we had a guy get swept right out the back.' Dale waved his hand in the direction beyond where Elena and I had been swimming, where the water became dark and the illusion of safety was no more. 'It took him forty-five minutes to reach the beach again, but everyone gets back. Eventually.'

'Ha. Looks like you called it right,' I said.

The three inflatables and their passengers were drifting further and further to the far end of the beach, and in the process moving closer to the sand. They would be rattled by their misadventure, but they were going to be safe.

'The lifeguard at the next hotel will already have an eye on them. They have a jet ski over there and keep watch from their own tower. Nobody ever drowns, but sometimes it's better to put these tourists through an ordeal so they don't ignore the surf warnings in future.'

Elena nodded in approval. 'So you're essentially thinning the herd.'

'Ha. Yeah that's right. Every year it's the same story. All these tourists show up that can't swim and get themselves in trouble. You would think they'd go home and tell their friends; warn them, you know? Maybe they're too embarrassed to say anything, it was "such a great time" … So their friends come to Hawaii, buy those same dumb-arse pool toys and get stuck in the exact same situation.'

'Fucking tourists,' we said.

Dale agreed. 'Fucking tourists.'

*

I didn't like the look of them. This pair had been loitering around the car for the last ten minutes and now they were staring at me. You could just tell they were full of sinister intentions, and we had ignored all the warning signs. Lock your car. Keep your windows rolled up and roof canvas pulled across if you know what's good for ya — inexperienced travellers might be surprised to find they have been robbed, or worse, acquired a stowaway or two.

Bonnie: I don't know about this, Clyde.

Clyde: Trust me, baby, it's gonna be so much fun. You'll love it.

Bonnie: Really? I've never killed anyone before.

Clyde: The first time is always scary. But once you've spilled blood, no other thrill comes close … except having your feathers ruffled in public.

Bonnie: Ooh, can we do that too?

Clyde: Sure, baby. Let's rub one out on the hood of this car.

Bonnie: Right here? What if someone sees us?

Clyde: That's what makes it exciting, my sweet chickee.

Bonnie: No, I mean what if someone sees us doing the other thing … that guy has been watching us for a while. I'm worried he might be onto us.

Clyde: Relax, baby, look at him — head cocked sideways, vacant expression … looks like a dummy to me. Nothin' but a pervo. C'mon, baby, dontchu wanna get *wild?*

Bonnie: Okay. Let's do it … I love you, baby.

Clyde: I love you too, baby. Follow me!

I watched the two chickens jump the windshield and land in the back seat of the Jeep. What a pain in the fucking arse. They'd have to be booted out of the car before they shat on everything and made themselves at home, or worse. There were always stories about careless drivers who met with unfortunate ends because of homicidal poultry …

'What have we got this time, Sergeant?'

'Another rental Jeep rolled off the highway. Driver got surprised by a bush chicken hidden under the seat. Started pecking at his ankles while he was doing seventy miles an hour.'

'Those warning signs aren't out for decoration. Damn *haole* never learn.'

'Yep. Them bush chickens is a ruthless lot too, ambush you then get away without a scratch — that gamey meat makes 'em all rubbery and flexible … would you look at that? Little bastard who caused the wreck just strutted out from under the Jeep like it was only passing through.'

'Quick! Shoot that pop-eyed motherfucker!'

\*

Jackie and Conroy resurfaced after eating a sturdy breakfast and drinking a high-end dose of Hawaiian caffeine from the outdoor coffee shop across the road from the resort. They'd spent an hour trying to put together the pieces of a fractured night, and agreed it was probably best forgotten because both had upstanding reputations to think about.

Elena and I were relieved to see our brothers weren't too much the worse for wear. None of us had been turned into a drooling vegetable, but after all the previous night's action, it felt like a good idea to get away from Poipu for a few hours and explore. There was supposed to be a coffee plantation down this end of the island, and Jackie wanted to do more location scouting for the film, so we threw our supplies in the Jeep and kicked the stowaway chooks to the curb. Then we hit the road.

If you travelled north-east, the road wound its way through a valley where vast fields of tall grass were scattered with acacia trees. The area could've passed for African savannah, until you hit the top of the hill and entered a mile-long tunnel of eucalyptus trees. It was like being transported home in an instant. There was a good reason Jackie was scouting Kauai for his film — one island could pass for a great many countries from all around the world. But we were headed south-west. This area was grubby tropical suburbia, ugly new housing developments, and the ultimate fools' paradise — the golf course estate.

The sun managed to break through the clouds as we turned onto the Kaumuali'i Highway and headed west in the direction of Waimea Canyon. Out here, beyond the jungle-covered mountains, the land was baked red, the grass was dry, and the houses were humble. It was a good thing we woke up in Poipu and not out here in the country towns — a fuzzy and somewhat confused head could've been fooled into thinking this was outback Australia. You're on a different Kauai out here, one completely opposite in look and feel to the lush north. This was wild country.

The agreed approach was to drive and get lost out here. And from what I could see it wasn't going to be hard to drift mentally either, this was a day made for dreams.

\*

11 am. Old Hanapepe Town. It was Tuesday ... or maybe Thursday. Who could really tell anymore? Hell, it felt like six weeks had passed since I'd taken on this assignment. Time on this island was even slower than it was on Oahu, and I'd been out here baking my head in the sun, trying to figure out what the devil was going on. Every evening was spent drinking to oil the gears. Thinking.

They were watching me. Everywhere I went — suspicious, sideways glances. Word had spread and people knew I was digging ... for what, they weren't sure. It was a nuisance. On an island this small, everyone knows everyone else's business, and they keep that information close to the chest, because on an island everyone has dirt under their feet they don't want others to see. It's all about leverage. Life on Kauai works on the barter system, and I'd used that to acquire a lead. Anyone can be convinced to part with valuable information when you use the right motivational tools. Sometimes it's a fresh pineapple. Sometimes it's cold hard cash. And sometimes it's the business end of a revolver.

I needed an edge. A fresh perspective on things. I had it in my head to buy a detective novel. Art imitating life, imitating art ... was I through the looking glass? Not yet. But I'd been through the bottom of the rum glass several times over, so I was getting close. This assignment was getting hairy again.

I walked out of the bookstore with a four-dollar paperback in my hand. Stylised pulp. It was a steal that had snagged me with the bright artwork on the cover, but I'm shallow like that, I like a good cover. Especially on something with some substance behind it ... although, this kind of reading material was dishonest, you couldn't trust what might lie under the surface. A bit like this case, or the woman that put me on it. Or this town, or life in general. Even the classy art deco cinema next door was a good-looking fraud — glitzy on the outside, you would never guess they showed dirty movies in there. Adult entertainment. I couldn't get in the mindset. Who would want to sit in a public space with a room full of perverts, knowing that every one of them had a handful of crab meat while they watched an oyster get shucked on the big screen. A live show was always better. Apparently, some nights you could watch a good old-fashioned kick line in there, and afterwards meet the girls behind the building to organise a tumble by the river. For a fee of course — sailors can be such filthy bastards.

I checked my pockets for a packet of cigarettes, and remembered I didn't smoke, never have. A car pulled up in the street. The Hollywood film director — my new contact — sat behind the wheel. My photographer, Pierre Conrad was with him. Both men slid sunglasses down their nose to get a better look at the dirty movie theatre. The Italian bird in the back seat did the same and smiled. I stepped off the curb and climbed into the back seat with her. There was a lot of leg on display. She caught me looking and smirked. Christ, it was hot out. Why did these Hollywood types always drive convertibles? I looked at that sun-browned leg beside me and stopped caring. She dragged the skirt all the way to the hip and revealed a white garter with a pistol tucked under it. But the gun didn't hold my attention for long. I shifted awkwardly in the seat when I caught sight of that little crease where the top of the thigh meets the hips. If I didn't keep my head on straight I was going to get slapped or shot. It still felt like this was all some kind of game to her. Did this fox really fear for her life? Her demeanour seemed too easygoing for the stakes we were playing. She flipped her blonde hair to the side and offered me a cigarette from a gold case, and I told her I didn't smoke, never have. Maybe it was time to change that habit ... then again, maybe not.

We took off up the wide main street. Port Allen was just around the corner, and nefarious dealings were sure to follow. The film director's financial backers operated from a warehouse out there. The same people who had their fingers in the dodgy real estate racket. The same ones who had that sap thrown over the balcony in Waikiki. And the same crooks were involved with pineapple and dirt cheap coffee ... an honest trade, too good to be true.

So what else was going on here? It was beginning to feel big. Maybe too big for a lowbrow like me. I should've asked for more money. Scratch that, I *would* ask for more money, this very afternoon, as long as I wasn't decorating a pine box with my bullet-riddled remains.

I had one thing going for me, and that was nobody liked foreigners taking a slice of the local pie. There would be hell to pay if the plantation owners discovered they were being undermined by a scheme based offshore. Because the mentality is, you're nobody on this island if you're not in the plantation game. Except here, in Old Hanapepe, where they play things fast and loose. Where you can get three fingers of whiskey and a hula girl lap dance for the price of the daily newspaper. Where you can trade fresh fish and pawpaw for a new set of white walls on your shiny Buick. There's a lot of charm out here on America's last coast. Folks could make good on these streets if they were willing to get a little dirty. But not me ... not yet anyway.

*

'Eddie? *Eddie.*'

'Sorry, beautiful, what were you saying?'

'You were daydreaming, weren't you?'

'I was — has anyone ever smuggled drugs in hollowed-out pineapple?'

'I ... don't know. What made you think that?'

'Just playing with ideas. I'm thinking about writing a detective novel.'

'You're a shit, now I need to know if anyone has ever smuggled drugs in a pineapple.'

We passed by a secluded property near the beach. It accommodated a handful of plantation-style cabins hidden among palm, banyan and acacia trees. I recognised the location. This area was part of greater Waimea. At one time I'd researched this place and thought what a wonderful thing it would be to take a month off from life and hide out here, just to read and write and swim and soak in all this cleansing sun. Burn away all the negative bullshit people carry around with them these days. That sounded like a good time, almost perfect, just me and the birds and the sea turtles — isolated from the rest of humanity. There was just one vital element missing, and it would be lonely without her.

The Jeep approached a seaside community called Kekaha. We skirted around the houses and followed the coastline highway where it became a flat straight stretch of road at sea level. It was a quiet day on the road with only the odd bit of local traffic, and there hadn't been another vehicle for miles. We passed the last houses of Kekaha. Here it was just the highway, with scrubland on one side, and the sand and relaxed ocean on the other. The water shimmered under the midmorning sun. I insisted we stop the car, and Jackie pulled onto the sand on the ocean side and we all jumped out. I removed my thongs and Elena did the same, and we walked into the water together. Jackie used the opportunity to take more photos and Mr Conroy snapped some pictures of his own. Then they both joined us in the ocean, and we stood up to our knees in the water. I enjoyed the feeling of it lapping at my skin, and the warmth of the sun on my face. Elena held my hand and we stared at the endless horizon, feeling like we must be the last four people on the face of the earth ... and what a feeling that was.

\*

2 pm. South-west Kauai. Another episode so soon? I must be having a rough day at the office, finding it hard to stay focused on things that were real. Many factors competed to destroy my resolve. The little devil on my shoulder suggested I chuck in the case, take the money and run ... This afternoon heat sizzled my brain, as did the woman sitting beside me, melting my morals, trying to choke me with lust. Weird and getting weirder. I almost caught a bullet at Port Allen earlier and the post-adrenaline crash was severe. I hadn't had a rum for hours because I was trapped in this absurd car with this absurd Hollywood director. I needed something to liven me up and straighten me out.

Caffeine was the choice. The Kauai Coffee Company to be precise. I never drink the stuff, it goes out the way it comes in, like nasty black sludge. That's why they started flavouring the shit with vanilla and caramel, or essence of toasted banana. But coffee people won't cop that. They'll turn up their nose, look at you like a leper and call you an uneducated, uncultured redneck. A bogan tourist on the café scene. A bum. You ordered a cup of tea? Sacrilege. What would a private dick know anyhow? Aren't you all supposed to drink coffee? Don't believe everything you read or see in the movies. I know what I like, and it ain't coffee. Although, it does smell pretty good.

I convinced the Hollywood director that we needed to stop at the coffee plantation, and he was only too happy to oblige. Artists love coffee. The dame was into it, and my photographer loved it, although, as long as there was a wad of green at the end, he was just happy to be. The big convertible swung into a big dirt car park. The plantation was massive. All of this used to be sugar — now it's four million coffee plants growing cherry worth a fortune. They spread from the road all the way down to the sea. I could smell the salt in the air, followed by the aroma of coffee. The pungent tang of dirty money.

They were serious inside the old McBryde estate. You could do a tasting here, and a little woman worked the room with a silver tray covered in macadamia nut cookies. Not for me. If it ain't an Anzac biscuit or a ginger snap that'll break your teeth, I don't wanna know. But she forced my hand and suggested I wash it down with a coffee. Paradise, one cup at a time … apparently. You can do a tasting for anything these days. I'd rather be doing a rum tasting up in Koloa, or having a burger and a cold beer back in the comfort of the Hula Grill, watching events unfold in that snake pit soaked in coconut oil that they call Honolulu.

The bean boys were into the tip and grind — professional roasters kept behind glass to show the tourist types how it's done, with the exception of the Italian actress leaning on me. She insisted they were *doing it wrong* and whispered in my ear that they weren't giving it enough cream and sugar.

'Italians add a dash of grappa for fire. Goes down smooth, just like me.'

She was killing me. If I was *actually* killed on this case, they'd probably fly out my coroner friend to identify me: 'Heart attack? On a coffee plantation, you say. Eddie never did like the stuff ... Because of a woman? Ah, rigor mortis of the crotch area, makes sense. A stiff with a stiff — at least he died happy.'

Jesus, it was hot in there. We went outside. A giant novelty coffee mug sat on the lawn. They knew how to work you here. I took notes.

'You boys mind if we do a publicity spread?' the Hollywood director said. 'Getting a few choice shots of my starlet will sell a bundle of tickets when the film releases.'

'Pierre, you'd better handle this. I'll do the write up tonight.'

'A bit posh for the *Star Bulletin* don't you think, Ed?'

'You might be right. We can aim a little higher, given the right enticement.'

'Which papers will you sell to? I'd prefer big ones. I can offer a generous cash incentive ...' and the Hollywood director opened a wallet stuffed with bills.

'Three hundred bucks and we have a deal. I'll see to it all the big papers with *Times* in the header get a taste. LA, New York, London. Maybe Canberra, definitely *Singapore Straits*.'

'Singapore is interesting, that would open the doors to a whole new market of cinema-goer. Speaking of new markets, where the hell is Canberra?'

'Canberra — the capital of Australia? You never heard of it? I'm not surprised. That one is for me, my local haunt. I like a chance to thumb my nose at Sydney and Melbourne.'

'That doesn't sound like good practice, turning the big city papers against you.'

'I'm freelance. I have no loyalty to anyone but the highest bidder. And I wouldn't be doing my job right if I wasn't making 'em squirm. If I can turn the big papers into a needy wreck that's good. If I can do it to an entire city, or two cities, well … that's leverage.'

Pierre went to work with his camera, and the starlet went to work on the coffee mug. She was a professional. The camera loved her, she could pin-up model with the best of them. Leaning, bending and arching all over that enormous mug like she was the hot steamy jitter juice ready to slide on in. She might make a man change his stance on coffee.

While they got artistic, I investigated. Port Allen had been an eye-opener and presented a surprising lead … what was in the greenhouses and the mill at the coffee plantation? Product of a different kind. Foil packages dumped inside charming little brown paper bags and covered over with

Kauai's finest blend. Ten bucks? Only until it hit the mainland where the price went up a thousand-fold if you didn't know how to keep your nose clean.

And then it was raining horizontally for the second time that day, and the raindrops were made of lead. Someone had ratted me out. The actress? Her director? Had Pierre been bought? Don't be crazy, Eddie. My feet burned in these leather boots, but that's the price you pay when you want to look good. At least they weren't Cuban-heeled. Running in boots is an art form — one that I've perfected, and now put to use, running for my life through endless rows of sour berry bush. One hand on my hat, the other on my gat, but no time to stop and shoot back.

Somehow my luck held. The others had heard the wild scene and the car was already running. I dove into the back seat and landed on something soft that smelt like orange blossom and sweet spice. My face had been cushioned by the lap of the actress. I didn't want to leave but she growled at me. No — that was the car. V8 torque sent the rear wheels into a spin and rust-coloured dust flew into the air as the car peeled out of Kauai Coffee Company and rushed like a spearhead for Highway Fifty and Poipu. This assignment might work out after all if I could stay alive long enough to put all the pieces together. Man, I needed a drink.

# Day Eight

I stood on the downstairs terrace and stared across the beautiful gardens, contemplating my plan of attack for the day. The phone was ringing in the upstairs apartment — had been for a while. It was an unpleasant and far-too-loud intrusion on an otherwise ideal morning. Hotel phones always have the volume dialled up to the limit, and this one rang and rang … and rang some more. Jackie had gone down to the beach for an early swim, which meant the phone was the responsibility of Mr Conroy.

I guessed he was most likely up to his eyeballs in drool, fast asleep after another night of hard drinking. Mr Conroy had gone all-in on a high-stakes gamble and tried his luck with Gemma one last time. It didn't pay off. And sadly we didn't see it. Jackie filled me in after he caught me standing

on the terrace wearing nothing but my hat and a smile ...
Elena and I had taken an afternoon siesta on the living-
room floor, and I found myself in trouble when I woke up
and stumbled outside, half-dazed, looking for fresh air and
a life-affirming conversation with a strange bird wearing
a red mohawk. The family at the barbeque down the hill
were not impressed. And that was the trouble — I had lost
my sarong. Thank god I didn't wake up with wood — that
would've really put them off their food. Jackie wasn't so sure;
he reckoned their teenage daughter looked very hungry.

But that was yesterday. This was now, and the phone had
stopped ringing. Whoever was calling had given up and would
no doubt try again later, or if it was urgent, they would send a
member of staff to confront the devil in the upstairs apartment.

It was unexpected when Mr Conroy appeared on the
balcony.

'Eddie. Hey, Eddie! Are we having breakfast?'

I looked up at this dishevelled creature, naked as the day
he was born except for a bath towel wrapped around his
head. In less than an hour this greasy-looking hobo would
scrub up to resemble a stylist of high class and snobbery
— a contradiction in an inconsistent universe. He had no
business being out here on the islands, and yet, our trip
wouldn't be the same without him.

'We've already eaten,' I said.

'How about second breakfast? Or elevenses?'

'Come for a swim first, we'll do brunch after.'

'Spectacular.' He gripped the rail with both hands and ripped the loudest belch I'd ever heard, losing his towel in the process. A flock of birds in a nearby tree spooked and took to the air. The lord of wind and wine had risen to welcome a new day on the island paradise of Kauai. I could almost see Jackie emerging from the surf and looking back up the hill, a disturbed expression on his face, and mouthing the words, '*What the fuck was that?*'

'Oi, once you've finished destroying the ozone layer, get some shorts on and we'll head down to the beach,' I said.

'Righto.' He disappeared, but a second later his shaggy head hung over the railing again. 'Oh yeah, front desk called ... said something about a bill for a Singapore sling?'

'A Singapore sling? You're the only one that's been in the restaurant ordering expensive drinks. I don't know what kind of cocktails you've been throwing back.'

'No wait, that's not right — it was a bill for slinging ill. Did we abuse someone last night? I'm not known for slander.'

'Nah. A drunk couple in the parking lot were abusing each other, she beat the shit out of him while we laughed our arses off on the front porch.'

'We did get a bit happy ... You let me drink too much wine again, Eddie.'

'Your weakness for the grape would've tempted you no matter what. Now, do we need to go to reception or not?'

'Wait a sec ... It's on the tip of my tongue ... I know it will come to me.'

Elena came outside, dressed and ready for a day that involved little more than soaking up rays on a large beach towel. She took one look at her brother and asked me, 'What's going on? Is he still drunk?'

'Without smelling him it's hard to tell ... *Conroy*, what did reception say?'

'I remember! It was a bill for being ill and sly ... Which is obviously a secret code meant for me. I knew the girl at reception was playing hard to get, she wants me bad, man ... Elena! They're billing me for being ill and sly.'

'That makes no sense, you're delusional. Gemma already told you *no*.'

Elena was right about that, so I was trying to read between the lines. There was a pattern to his words that I was beginning to put together — a definite path through the drunk-ish talk. Ill and sly ... They're billing me ... Half asleep when he picked up the phone ... And everything clicked into place. 'Holy shit. It was Bill Billingsley.'

'Yes, Billingsley! Wow — I was way off. Too much wine will do that to you.'

'You horrendous drunk!' I removed the rubber thong from my foot and threw it at the idiot on the balcony.

'Watch out! Looks like I'm not the only one who's ill and sly.'

Elena looked confused by the abstract conversation that led to this revelation but understood the nuts and bolts enough to realise the importance of what was said.

'There's a message from Bill Billingsley? Unbelievable. I better get to reception, sunbathing can wait.'

\*

There was a briefcase attached to the desperate-looking man who hurried through the plantation gardens ahead of Bill Billingsley. You could pick Bill from a mile away because of the Panama hat and expensive linen suit — this time with a jacket slung over his arm to accommodate the heat. All class and easy manner, unlike his travelling companion … If you've seen it enough times, you can tell when someone is on the cusp of death, and Bill's companion was teetering. Possibly because of his suit, an impractical ensemble about two sizes too snug and made from a cheap fabric that would strangle him in this humidity. But cocaine is a hell of a drug, and judging by the rapid, twitchy demeanour, and constant brow wiping, the real issue may not have been a dangerous miscalculation of the weather, but a man in serious need of a bump. Either way, his future looked bleak. He had an almost certain bubble on the brain. He could only hope the worst he suffered was severe chaffing. I felt uncomfortable just looking at him.

I waved them up to our terrace and tried not to laugh at the poor bugger.

'Good morning! How's it going, Bill?'

'I'm well, sir. Beautiful day. Nice resort. Very pretty in an old-world sort of way, and quiet. I hope that's kept you out of trouble.'

'Sure.'

'Very good. And this is Mr Johnstone. He's a lawyer. Do you mind if he sets up in your apartment? I'm afraid he's not accustomed to equatorial conditions and requires air-conditioning.'

'No problem, you can set up on the dining table. The ceiling fan is already running. Do you need anything else, Mr Johnstone? Ice water? Baby powder?'

'Water would be appreciated,' Mr Johnstone said, and hurried inside.

'No worries, there's ice in the freezer — don't touch the rum ... That suit is a disaster. Mr Johnstone did not dress appropriately for the islands. Did you boys leave the mainland in a hurry?'

'No quicker than usual. I told him he chose poorly, but what do you expect from a lawyer who watches his wallet? He refused to buy a linen suit before we left California, even though I told him he'd need something that breathes. You know what he said? Why spend the money when I'm only going to be there for a couple of days? Backwards commonsense if you ask me.'

'Maybe he spends all his money on bad habits and party favours?'

'You mean drugs and hookers. Airport security thought that too. Johnstone was already sweating buckets in that suit and got all agitated when the dogs didn't like his stink. But he's straight as an arrow and good at his job. He just has zero street smarts. I even suggested he bring shorts and keep it casual for Kauai, but some people just can't be told. It would've made life a hell of a lot easier for him during the strip search.' Bill shook his head and sighed. 'Anyway, where's that lovely wife of yours?'

'Sunbathing. Walk with me and we'll go grab her.'

'So, now that we're clear of Oahu, what does the future hold for Eddie Heads?'

'Oh dear, how long have you known?'

'Since the day we met, but after our first conversation. You've got balls — or you're completely mad. I know that there was never a *Teak and Rattan Review* and you were taking the conference for a ride while you're out of work…'

I went to interrupt but Bill stopped me.

'Relax, Ed, I'm not going to rat you out. You made yourself a little too interesting, and it's my job to know all about the people I'm dealing with. For instance, I also know you were a travel writer and the story you told me was mostly true. With that kind of quick thinking imagination you should consider a career in politics. Unless you were serious about being a novelist?'

'I was always honest about writing novels. That's where I want to be.'

'Good. That sounds promising.'

'I had a suspicion nothing got by you. Thanks for being cool about it. The truth is I'm at a crossroads and trying to figure out the next step. I'm here to get my head straight.'

'I get it. It happens to everyone. But until you have the next step figured, I have something that should hold your undivided attention. Your wife is going to need your support, we're very interested in her work.' We stopped in the shade of a palm opposite the surf shack and surveyed the scene. 'Now, where's Elena? There's important business to discuss.'

Bill waited while I retrieved Elena. She had managed to snag one of the popular beach recliners that faced the ocean. The view was fantastic, but I didn't like using them. The setup felt almost oppressive because the chairs were pushed right up to the verge, and only a single white chain served as a fence to safeguard where the grass dropped away to bushes and then the beach below. Guests were expected to employ commonsense and not walk straight off the edge, a worrying prospect considering the hand-holding most people needed. Elena lay face up on the recliner with a large beach towel spread out underneath her. A wide-brimmed sun hat shaded her face so she could read her adventure novel without too much glare. She looked like a shiny daydream, I wanted to touch her ...

'What's up, gorgeous man?' she said, and snapped me back to the importance of the moment.

'Bill's here, waiting by that palm tree.'

'Bill is here right now? Shit, hand me my sarong.'

She threw her possessions into the beach bag, slipped on her sandals and hurried like a haphazard whirlwind toward the gentleman fanning himself with his hat. I followed behind and calmly picked up the trail of debris she left in her wake. Elena had dropped the towel, a water bottle, and managed to lose her hat while she fiddled with her sunglasses and made sure the sarong was tied tight. I gave her the hat and took the bag off her hands so she could collect herself properly. When she was all set, we accompanied Bill back to the apartment.

Mr Johnstone had cooled down and made himself at home, seated at the dining table with a stack of papers and a tall glass of ice water. Elena disappeared to throw on a shirt more modest than her bikini top and I busied myself removing the bottles of rum from the countertop, which amused Bill as he seemed to understand my motives.

'Don't trust the suits around fine liquor?'

'Koloa isn't cheap and I'm on a budget. Can I offer you boys a beer?'

There was some real struggle in their faces. I knew Bill and the lawyer wanted to say yes, however professionalism won out and they declined. When Elena re-emerged she took a seat at the dining table and Bill launched into his pitch.

'So, after the straight-talking, no bullshit review of Bali by *Mr Eduardo Desah*, my business partners took a step back and did a reappraisal of the situation. Luckily all our eggs weren't in the one basket and there was another option. I'm excited to announce that we are still going ahead with the resort and have purchased land on the Bali oceanfront … and before you say anything, it's on the east side of the island. Not the west. We're on a stretch called Nusa Dua. I understand it's supposed to be more exclusive than Kuta or Seminyak.'

'Incredible, you guys really went full steam ahead,' Elena said.

'Once we had the information we needed, and the right people became involved, it was an easy decision. Things moved very quickly after that. Which brings me to you, Elena. We'd like to bring you on board as senior design consultant.'

I was in the middle of removing the cap from a bottle of beer, and it clattered onto the kitchen tiles with an almost deafening loudness. Elena looked thunderstruck.

I picked my own jaw up from the countertop and managed to convert a thought into words. 'Sorry, Bill, could you please repeat that?'

'We're offering Elena a contract,' he said.

'I'd be honoured. When? Where? How much?' The words spewed from Elena in a torrent. At that particular moment she was existing somewhere between shock, excitement and pure fear.

'We want you to stay on for the duration of the project. I understand you have other clients and aren't a big design firm, but we recognise the talent. *The vision.* We've done our due diligence and are comfortable to move forward. Once all the legalities are taken care of with the Indonesian Government, we aim to start the design process as soon as possible. Barring a disaster, the ground breaking could be in less than a year. Now, onto terms of compensation …' Bill pointed to the contract sitting on the table in front of Mr Johnstone.

Elena spent a minute reading the page in question and began to cry. I stuck my head over her shoulder to see what had set her off.

'Wowsers. That's quite a few zeros.'

'It's not a bad start, but we'd like this to be an ongoing relationship,' Bill said. 'Obviously, once building begins Elena will need to be on site every now and then. We'll take care of that side of things too, with free travel and accommodation when required. After the resort has been completed, you will have VIP status at our entire resort chain — that means your stay is on us. It's all in the contract.' The room was silent except for the constant slow whoosh of the overhead fan. 'What do you say?'

'I don't know what to say … is this real?' Elena asked.

Bill picked up the contract and weighed it in his hands. 'It feels real enough. I'm not expecting an immediate answer. This is a lot to unpack, so it's only fair I give you forty-eight hours to think it over. We'll email the contract to your lawyer. You should talk it through with them to put yourself at ease, but I'm confident you'll sign.'

'Where are you staying, Bill?' I said.

'Five minutes up the road. The Grand Hyatt. Give me a call once you've made your decision and maybe we'll have that beer.'

Everyone shook hands, which was a little anticlimactic when such big news was in the air. More needed to be done. And even though a decision hadn't been finalised, we invited Bill and Mr Johnstone to stay on and celebrate in the only appropriate manner, with champagne and canapes on the terrace. Mr Conroy and Jackie came downstairs to join us and decided that what we had was barely adequate for an occasion of such importance. So, they did what they did best. Jackie got on the phone and called a bunch of friends to come down to Poipu, and Mr Conroy organised food and drink to be brought up to our terrace from the restaurant.

A few hours later the party was in full swing. Folk had arrived dressed to kill, and I had thrown on my finest aloha shirt. I adjusted the bowtie, stroked my goatee to a point and nodded in approval. The top hat sat nicely on my head. My reflection in the glass doors looked sharp. I waded into the frivolity at the exact moment an honour guard of waiters fired a ten-champagne bottle salute to congratulate Elena. Sparkling streams of fizzy burst forth like so many golden fountains. White-coated waiters bussed around with silver trays topped with martinis, champagne and hors d'oeuvres, while jaunty music was played by a three-piece jazz band and several prominent slack key guitarists, including the great Gabby Pahinui.

Everyone was there. At one point I found myself between Bill Billingsley and Duke Kahanamoku while we watched Ernest Hemingway arm wrestle Elvis Presley.

Queen Liliuokalani adjudicated the match, while Hunter S Thompson heckled the contenders and talked foolish bystanders into bets with outrageous odds — people like Mr Johnstone, who made yet another poor life choice when he placed a large bet on Hemingway, which Hunter happily accepted because he knew damn well that Elvis was speeding so hard he would be unbeatable …

Constant cheer filled the air. Elena burst into regular fits of laughter with Zelda and Scott Fitzgerald whenever a fresh bottle of bubbly exploded, and they all tried desperately to fill their glasses before there was any wastage. Onward and around, Jackie was making jokes and drinking martinis with local actor Pierce Brosnan and his beautiful wife, while Gemma and Mr Conroy danced the Charleston on the lawn — flinging their arms and legs between the nene, peacocks and colourful roosters that roamed freely with the other guests who had come to join in the festivities. It turned out to be quite the celebration, and I'm sure there were more people of note present. Sadly, I forget their names right now. My brain is still fuzzy about the details of what happened, something had turned it to happy mush. But, man, that was a most excellent party.

AN EDITORIAL NOTE, COURTESY OF MR CONROY: That boy. I love him, but he is out of his rum-rotten mind. The guest list mentioned is too good to be true. Did he tell you the original line-up of Guns N' Roses was there as well? Just in case you haven't caught on, Eddie is telling the story all wrong. On purpose. That is not what happened. I should know, I was there, and I wasn't even drunk! Just had a slight hangover. Anyway, the time of day and setting are correct — of this I am certain. Everything else? Pure fantasy.

What happened during that hour or so actually went something like this ...

My good friend Jackie Heads and I were sitting on the upstairs balcony when the lawyer and Bill Billingsley arrived. You see, Jackie was feeding me a little hair of the dog to get me into the swing of the day. We had a beer while the meeting took place downstairs. Then Bill and Mr Johnstone went back to the Grand Hyatt. That's it. They did not stick around and sip champagne on the terrace with all our friends. As whimsical a story as that is, and I wish it had been the case, the truth is a little grubbier.

Oh, Eddie and Elena definitely indulged in celebration. Jackie and I heard the whole thing. All thirty-five minutes of it. We even had time to fit in an argument with a passing family, who instead of keeping their head down and continuing on their way, thought it would be appropriate to yell at us about what was happening downstairs ... something about this being America and we don't behave that way here, to which Jackie replied: 'Nonsense! Americans happily involve themselves in such practices every day and society is worse off because of it.' Or did he simply shout: 'Fuck off and mind your business.' The specifics elude me. Anyway, I followed Jackie's lead and decided to get on my high horse and tossed my beer down the lawn, screaming, 'You stole these islands from the Hawaiians!' The high and mighty scuttled away after that.

Regardless, our activities hadn't caused the celebration to miss a beat. They were relentless. The only sure sign we had that they'd reached a climax was a rooster that roamed onto the ground-floor terrace and crowed in appreciation at the very same moment they did. Their celebrating was lewd and vulgar, vocal and noisy, and I can guarantee Eddie had to wash his face afterward ... his fingers too, without a doubt. I can't remember a time when I was more disgusted and proud of my brother-in-law. My sister too; it was exactly the kind of wild gallop a woman of her pedigree deserves.

\*

A few hours after the meeting, we were sunbathing on what had become our favourite spot, the open stretch of perfectly manicured grass between the plantation cottages at the Poipu shoreline. The weather was about as perfect as you could get. It was the good kind of hot. The handful of palms between us and the beach bent to a gentle breeze. Shark patrol aircraft flew by on occasion and gave everyone peace of mind. Waves crashed on the beach below, but only loud enough to serve as ambient background music. Conversation could be had at ease. And the surf shack was only a hop, skip and jump away. The scene struck me as idyllic. A person, no matter how high strung and tightly wound, or those unfortunate souls who suffered from uncontainable energy — all these people would be able to find peace here.

The twins and I were lying on our towels. A cooler bag of refreshments sat nearby. We read books and chatted inanely or stopped to take the odd photo with the Polaroid camera. Jackie was there too, although he was far from experiencing any kind of lasting peace. My brother was on the phone with someone he had trusted to do an important job. Instead, this fool was trying to derail his film. It was a repeat performance of the airport fiasco. Jackie paced back and forth across the grass clearing like an army colonel blasting the troops — except there was no screaming, only agitation to the extreme. We caught enough of the conversation to realise that something deeply unpleasant was going down. I smelled big trouble in little Poipu.

'What do you mean she wants more money? ... Gary, we don't have the budget for that ... She doesn't get to go around me and start making demands, I don't care who she is. Get me another actress ... Why? She missed two scheduled photoshoots for no apparent reason and now she's trying to leverage us for a pay rise. It's dog's bollocks and we can do better ... What do you mean *like who?* Talk to the casting director and go down the list. There are plenty of actresses out there who would be more than happy to do this film for the amount of money we're offering ... *That's your job*, do some work, you shiftless bum! ... We don't need *a name*, if they're good, they're good … What you don't seem to understand is most people are just happy to be offered work — people like to work and get paid … I know there's a difference between getting paid, and *getting paid*, but this isn't a big budget production and we don't live a twenty-four-carat lifestyle. I'm not going to be held to ransom by *any* actor or actress just because their last film was a runaway success, that's flavour of the month bullshit. They either want the job, or they don't … *Oh, right*, now she's a writer as well? Fuck that noise. I don't give a rat's arse if she's not in love with the script anymore … Uh huh … Uh huh … So you would let her re-write half the movie? … Not in this lifetime. You don't get to make those fucking decisions. Do your fucking job and get somebody else … What do you mean we can't? … What the hell have you promised her? … *Say that again* … You let her do what? You dumb sonova bitch … *Look*, I don't care what she did with her mouth … *It wasn't her mouth?* How the hell does that work? … *Jesus Christ* … Yeah, I bet it was, but I don't care … Gary, I want you to listen very carefully — we can't be connected to this kind of bullshit, there is too much at stake. Not just the film but livelihoods … No. You're not employed to live out porno fantasies with the lead actress. If I find out there is photo or video evidence, I will find you and slit your fucking throat … Good. Now fuck off, you're fired.' Jackie hung up the phone. 'Fuck. That.' He strolled over to us shaking his head.

'Trouble in paradise?' I said.

'You would not believe the call I just had with my line producer. What an irresponsible dickhead. This has the potential to be a shit storm of hurricane proportions ... Can I have one of those?'

I reached inside the cooler bag and grabbed a beer and uncapped it for him.

'Thanks dude. I need to get ahead of this, damage control is going to be messy.' We wished him luck and Jackie rushed back to his marching ground, took a long pull on the beer and dove into another unpleasant phone conversation. 'Yeah — Stu, we have a problem. I had to fire Gary ... Yep ... He gave me no choice, he made other arrangements with the lead actress, so we're going to have to dump her too ... I know ... *I know, Stuart*, but the promiscuous slag offered him sex for benefits and the stupid bastard went for it ... I know this is going to rub people the wrong way ... Well, what the hell did you want me to do about it? We would've been crucified if he was kept on ... He was *your friend* not mine ... Look, I'm over here working, location scouting and keeping company with divas, lunatics and sex fiends, while you're sitting back with a thumb up your arse ...'

Mr Conroy and Elena smiled. I could already tell what they were thinking.

'Who do you think is who in that description?' Elena asked.

'Obviously I'm the diva,' Mr Conroy replied, 'and Ed is clearly the lunatic, which makes you the sex fiend.'

'You arsehole!' Elena held a hand to her chest in mock outrage.

'He might have a point, hun.'

Elena smirked. 'Have you heard this one today, babe? Go fuck yourself.'

'You already did that for me this morning. You're the sex fiend remember?'

'Ha! I just finished what you started.'

'As far as I'm concerned, you're both as bad as each other,' Mr Conroy said. 'It's all we hear upstairs, you two grunting it out like a couple of beached harp seals. How do you think the people down the hill feel hearing that all hours of the day?'

'Jealous?' I said.

'Excited?' Elena added.

'Honestly, I'm surprised that couch hasn't collapsed, you ferocious beasts.'

That made me smile. Elena looked mortified, and then appeared to see the funny side, and if I wasn't mistaken, there was a sense of pride in her smile as well.

'We have to shut down the whole film … C'mon, Stu. What choice do we have? … Look, pay her retainer and tell her that we've run into production issues and have to shut down indefinitely. It's a small price to pay instead of being taken to court or having to push through with a movie nobody wants to make except some actress with delusions of grandeur … Uh huh … A totally different film? I guess it's possible. Same location? ... Yeah, I can do that. No problem ... Forty-eight hours tops, I have a writer with me ... Of course professional ... Hey, don't go soft on me now, we can salvage this. You just take care of the rest of this nightmare ... Cool. Talk soon.'

Jackie hung up the phone, took another sip from his beer and came back to join us on the towels. He seemed a lot more relaxed, but it was clear he was still out of sorts.

'What's happening?' I said.

'That was my executive producer. The current film as we know it is dead in the water. Turns out we hired the wrong people. I guess you heard I had to fire the line producer and our lead actress. Not entirely sure who is more to blame between the two of them, just a couple of scoundrels looking for cheap thrills. Sounds like they were cut from the same cloth as you pair of deviants.'

'Come on, we're not that bad,' Elena said.

'The family walking by the apartment this morning would tell it different. Probably the first time since we arrived that I haven't had to worry about what Roy was doing on the balcony because of the scene you two were making downstairs.'

'No way,' I said. 'Were we really that loud?'

'Don't blame yourself,' Mr Conroy replied. 'Elena is just like me, whether she admits to it or not. Underneath her façade of class and modesty is a true hot-blooded Italian. A sexual thoroughbred who is hot to trot. It runs in the family.'

'You're both full of shit, you didn't hear us,' Elena said.

'We're serious,' Jackie said. 'It sounded like you guys were chopping bamboo down there. Is the couch still in one piece or will that appear on the bill when we check out?'

Had the couch been banging against the wall? It was possible. My mind drifted back to the morning, we'd been deep in the moment ... yeah, the sliding door had been left wide open and the rattan couch had definitely suffered a thrashing. How were we to know if we'd disturbed families or attracted a crowd of enthusiastic listeners? And in the end, who really cared? It was a celebration and we had enjoyed the hell out of ourselves.

Jackie continued: 'Anyway, we're going to try a salvage operation and convince the other producers to stay on. We can keep the same setting and style of film; it'll still be in Hawaii. That way nobody is losing money. The catch is we're going to have to re-write the entire script in the next forty-eight hours.'

'That's a lot of work. How are you going to pull that off?' Mr Conroy asked.

'With the writer extraordinaire here. What do ya reckon, Ed? Can you help your brother write a whole new story in two days?'

'Dude, we're supposed to be on holiday, and that sounds exhausting. I have no business sticking my nose in other people's affairs.'

My wife peered over the top of her sunglasses so she could look me directly in the eye, and without a word, let me know I had said something stupid. It was a look that suggested I'd committed a social taboo. And after she had made me feel adequately guilty, she hit me with a hard truth, 'Not your business? Kind of like how it wasn't your business to hijack my conference for your own entertainment, but you did anyway.'

'Good point. I guess that's settled. Am I getting paid?'

'There's twenty grand in it for you if we turn in a script by tomorrow night, otherwise there's no money and no film and we all get to go home and cry about it.'

'*Twenty grand.* Hun, I know we're on holiday and I just got offered the deal of a lifetime,' Elena put a hand on my shoulder and squeezed, 'but if the Billingsley contract doesn't work out we'll need this. You're going back to the apartment right now, and you and your brother are writing that script.'

'Looks like I'm on the job. With the right cash incentive all things are possible. Do you have an idea, dude?'

'I do,' Jackie said, extending the word *do* like he was about to propose something incredibly dodgy and wasn't sure if I would go for it or not.

'Well, let's hear it!' Elena said.

'It's about a bum ... a journalist who was full of potential but has become terrible at his job, just lazy and uninterested. The paper he writes for gives him the sack, so he goes to Hawaii to start over. On the islands he helps three independently successful people overcome personal obstacles to better their lives and learns about himself in the process. Eventually our hero pulls his shit together and makes good … or something like that.'

Everyone was all smiles and sly looks. The twins were leering at me like I'd just dropped my pants and wasn't wearing underwear. Weirdos. Had I missed something? I must have, but who really cared? I was about to be twenty grand richer.

Thankfully Jackie kept the train rolling, super keen to get to work on his new script. 'Alright, that's enough bullshit. Let's get to it. The sooner we finish, the sooner you can get back to breaking furniture with your wife.'

'Right. We'll need supplies. I'm going to need a bottle of rum, a bottle of pineapple juice, a bag of pretzels or whatever salty snacks we can get our hands on, a dashboard hula girl, a scented candle and a pack of dirty playing cards. We better go to Whalers and stock up.'

*

In every homosapien group there is always one maniac. That's a scientific fact. We all know an individual who functions outside of acceptable social norms and whose mental algorithms work in a space beyond the comprehension of your average human. Sometimes these creatures aren't obvious; they're hiding in plain sight and it's not until a specific switch is flicked that they show themselves. Alcohol was always the trigger in our specific case — our maniac was Mr Conroy.

It was mid-afternoon and I was sitting at the table on the upstairs balcony, scribbling crap words on the new script and striking them out again in frustration. It was a struggle getting my head around the broader theme of the story, even with Jackie dictating his ideas and the air thick with so called 'inspiration-inducing incense' — we hadn't been able to get a candle, so the sticks were our replacement — scented vanilla, orange and sandalwood, and named something ridiculous like Rainforest Dream.

Elena lounged on a nearby deckchair with a book and a cocktail. I put the pen down and sipped my own drink, giving the small plastic hula girl a flick. With her perfectly painted smile, she happily began to shake her hips and gyrated to the singing coming from inside the apartment. Mr Conroy was mixing a cocktail in the kitchenette. Spoon clinked against glass as he stirred the drink. And everything went quiet for a moment — the calm before the storm. Metal rattled, a great tearing sound filled the air as the flyscreen was separated from the door, and this was followed by the desperate cry of a half-drunk maniac. 'Help! It's got me! For the love of god, somebody save me!'

Mr Conroy lay on the ground swearing blue murder and struggled like a dying fish on a pier, trying to free himself of the vast mat of black mesh he was somehow tangled in. He'd walked straight through the screen door. Moving from a dark room to a sun-drenched balcony while under the blurring influence of too much rum, washes out even the sharpest vision. First you see spots and then it's like being snow-blind.

We should have helped him, instead we all laughed hysterically at the sight of this insane person trying to liberate themselves from a trap of their own making.

Mr Conroy did eventually free himself, and sat on the ground with his back against the deckchair, breathing rapidly in a sweat-slathered state of shock and overexertion. 'Where the bloody hell did that come from? Which one of you cunty bastards put that screen there?' He became a picture of serious indignity, 'I thought I was going to suffocate. I could have died!'

'It's a flyscreen, you drunk. You were never going to suffocate,' Elena said.

'That may be the case, but the real tragedy is that I've now lost my drink. Has anyone seen my drink? I had a cocktail here, somewhere.'

'It's under your arse,' Jackie said.

A bright red puddle had pooled underneath Mr Conroy's backside.

'Shit. Good thing this was a resort towel. I better get another drink.'

He stripped off the towel, revealing a mostly bare backside decorated with an electric blue G-string. It was the only clothing he wore, and he made sure we all got a good look at it when he bent over to mop up the wasted drink.

'Gah … do you think you're wearing enough coconut oil? I swear every last inch is covered. Although, it was thoughtful of you to wax the rear hallway, Roy. Now it's only half as traumatising.'

Elena wondered what I was talking about and turned her head at the exact moment her twin presented his basket of slimy waxed fruit. She looked horrified.

'*Christ, Roy!* Put on some proper underwear, you goddamned hedonist!'

I gave Mr Conroy a slap across the nearest exposed cheek and immediately realised the blunder. My hand felt tainted. 'Hey, chuck us that towel, my hand is all wet and sticky.'

Jackie leaned on the railing and wiped tears from his eyes, 'Dude, no. You're writing, go and wash up properly. We don't know where that's been.'

\*

That evening Elena and I were out on the terrace, reclined on deckchairs and enjoying the peace and tranquillity of the gardens under a starry sky. It was pleasant and warm. Cicadas filled the air with their shrill song. I enjoyed the simple pleasure of just lying and listening to the insects, until my attention was drawn away by a light thrumming noise. It was an infrequent sound of an unfamiliar nature and origin, but it occurred often enough for me to sit up and take notice.

'Can you hear that?' I said, and realised it was coming from upstairs.

'I've been wondering what that is ... You don't think ...' Elena was cut off mid-sentence by a disaster of mythic proportion unfolding on the upstairs balcony.

'Oh god. Oh my god! Jackie, we're trapped by some sort of invisible barrier ...'

'What the hell are you on about, Roy?'

'I can't get on the balcony.' The strange thrumming sound happened three more times in quick succession, and with greater intensity. 'Yep, definitely a force field.'

'What do you mean *force field?* Get away from there ...'

'The Menehune are back. I saw them in the garden, riding roosters and phasing in and out of reality, shaking spears at me. Papa Benjamin said this would happen ... they've tracked us down and now their advanced technology is blocking the balcony. We're no better than zoo animals!'

The twit was out of his mind with panic. We could hear Jackie saying, 'You need to calm down, man,' but it was pointless. Mr Conroy had his foot jammed on the accelerator and was driving for a top-speed dramatic exit.

'*We need to escape.* I'm gonna test the integrity of the beam ...'

'Don't run at it, you idiot!'

A great crash erupted from the balcony. It was those familiar sounds of rattling metal and folded mesh, and what was probably a beer bottle being dropped on the floor, followed by a frantic cry for help: 'Help! I've fallen into their trap! It's some kind of alien netting — save me, Jackie, before they come for my bones!'

Elena and I looked at each other, her face full of alarm. Mine was about ready to crack. We ran upstairs and I laughed the whole way. They had left the front door open, and we rushed inside the apartment and went straight through to the balcony. The flyscreen had been ripped from the door frame again. We found Jackie sitting on the ground, comforting Mr Conroy in his arms and stroking his hair like a giant man-baby, while Mr Conroy nursed on a fresh beer to calm down from his fright.

I stood there smiling like an idiot.

Somewhere nearby a rooster crowed, and Elena didn't miss the opportunity to lay the boot into her brother. 'You hear *that*, Roy? It's the sound of your people, celebrating the arrival of their new king. You gigantic cock.'

Elena fixed the flyscreen while I got everyone a drink and put on some music that wouldn't incite alien abduction flashbacks in Mr Conroy. Then we chilled on the balcony for a couple of hours. Elena was tired but didn't want to leave her brother, so she went to sleep on the couch. Mr Conroy had already passed out on the living-room floor.

Jackie disappeared into the kitchen, rustled around for a few minutes and returned with two beers, a bag of pretzels, and a notepad and pen. That irritated the hell out of me. I knew exactly what this meant, my relaxed evening was about to come to an end. Brother dear, you're a real bastard.

But sadly, he was also right. If I wanted to make my twenty grand there was no better time to write than now. We had to get back to work, there was two-thirds of a script to finish.

An hour later we had made little progress and I was tempted to start on hard liquor to fire up the creative juices.

'We just need the right spark, dude,' Jackie said. 'Rum will only weaken you at the moment.'

He was right. The good stuff always arrives with a clear head. But this was no good, I was grinding my teeth trying to fill out this script. The passion just wasn't there, and it was like trying to pass a kidney stone. I'd rather have been doing anything else. We were in a creative drought. The well was dry — I'd throw the bucket in and nothing would come back out but useless waste. It was hopeless. Jackie dug in and tried to force a result, but eventually even he looked exhausted. The man was used up and on the brink of defeat. That bothered me. I couldn't let him down like this, not when I'd been trusted to write for him. Plus, all those jobs were on the line.

I made a cup of tea and drank it on the balcony. Leaning against the rail, I watched the crisp moon turn the world shades of black and white, the essence of noir. And something miraculous happened, an enormous wave of inspiration crashed on our balcony and saturated my mind. Kauai had released some of her *mana* and sent it my way. The problem had been obvious, except we were too close to it. We were writing the wrong story. Why struggle on when I had a near-finished story in my notebook?

I pitched the idea to Jackie, who looked at me like I'd suggested we pack our shit and hide out in Waimea until the whole thing blew over. I could see his doubt, this was a natural response — everyone feels the fear just before a high-stakes gamble, but we were desperate men running out of time. However, he was quickly converted when he saw words spilling onto the page at a rate where my hand could barely keep pace with my mind. Roughly two hours was all it took. And there was a decent story at the end. Not a long script, but long enough that it would save Jackie's reputation. It was dark and dreamy, like an early morning, all syrup no waffle breakfast.

*

2 am. Poipu. Was it eight or nine days into this assignment? Did it even matter anymore? I was fit to be committed. Weirder than weird. My brain had been scrambled by rum and sun, tangled by a web of intrigue, and turned inside out by a blonde piece with curves and a shake that would make a hula girl proud and turn a man into a blubbing fool. I wiped a tear from my eye — damn, what a glorious vision. There were too many distractions. Certain women will do that to a man until he's sucked her juice like a ripe piece of pineapple.

Wise up, Eddie. Get your head straight. Why was I walking around tropical Kauai at night wearing a hat and leather jacket? No time to think on that right now. I was in a sticky situation that couldn't even be blamed on the humidity or copious amounts of alcohol … Three bright flashes lit the night. Two of them gunshots.

I ran up the stairs and entered the dark apartment with caution. My hand ran along the wall until it found the switch, and then there was light. Smashed glass glittered on the ground, the carpet was full of it, crunching under my boots as if I were walking along a Moroccan beach covered in gemstones. My nose twitched in air thick with cigar smoke. I recognised the brand; it stank of Hollywood. Furniture had been tossed all over the place, like a yard sale gone mad. And on its back in the middle of the living room lay a bloody body with two bullet holes in the chest. A rooster was pecking at its head, like the bird was trying to revive the poor bastard. Where did this cockerel come from? Never mind that now. The body — it was my loyal photographer. Pierre Conrad was dead. I'd known one of us was going to get it sooner or later. Damn shame. The rooster and I exchanged a gaze, and I understood. It recognised one of its own and would keep a solitary vigil so nobody tampered with the body.

Pierre's camera lay beside him on the floor, the source of that third flash I'd seen from outside. Whoever shot him hadn't stuck around long enough to take the film. They'd spooked. I snatched up the camera — develop this film and you've got indisputable evidence of the murder and a guaranteed conviction. I already had a pretty good idea who killed Pierre. That damn Hollywood director had double-crossed us. It was a dog act; the scumbag may not even make it to trial.

I ran into the night. Fog had settled thick around these plantation grounds. Shadows loomed at every turn. I held my gun with a white-knuckle intensity, waiting for that split second when I would have to pull the trigger or steady my nerve. Somewhere a rooster crowed. I was getting jumpy, even the hibiscus flowers looked threatening. Things had moved beyond hairy. There was no escape. It was like trying to paddle a canoe across a river of lava or navigate shit creek without a compass. Footsteps echoed down the path. The shooter was close, running in the direction of the big old plantation house. I followed.

It all happened quickly. The girl on the reception desk had been dragged out to the looping driveway and was being held at gunpoint by that bastard from Hollywood. He saw the camera and wanted the film.

'Give it,' he said, 'or the girl is dead.'

It was a standoff. If I dropped the gun he would kill me anyway.

A car horn blared. I saw headlights through the fog, racing down the driveway. The girl wriggled free while the director was distracted, and I dove into the garden bed for safety.

The car flattened him. Dead on impact, the coroner would say. A tragic accident due to the fog, is what the cops would say. Never should have been standing in the road on a dark foggy night. I was stunned when I saw who was behind the wheel. The Italian actress. She started all this, and by the look of things she had just finished it. I won't lie, there was something exciting about that.

Everything had fallen into place. It all made sense now. Making 'contacts' at the conference — all a front for dodgy real estate dealings. It was an elaborate scheme where tacky golf course estates were approved for development on sacred land by paying off slimy elected officials with drug money earned smuggling cocaine out of South America, through Hawaii, before hitting mainland USA. All of it hidden inside crates of pineapple and coffee. Nobody would blink an eyelid. Everyone would get rich, and anyone that blabbed would get dead. Just like the journalist at the conference who got too nosey. Just like my photographer, the enigmatic Pierre Conrad. And just like that Port Allen dock worker — the one found choked to death with a sashimi roll in the Hanapepe Adult Theatre. The cops said it was misadventure through autoerotic asphyxiation, but I wasn't so sure, his pants were still buttoned up when they found him. Not even a hard-on.

And there was also this weasel, or what was left of him. The Hollywood director who thought he was going to lose his financial backing, but he lost everything the moment he turned informer. Someone would have gotten to him eventually, I never would've guessed it'd be his starlet, the same firecracker who had stumbled onto the scam and gotten me involved.

She sat on my lap in the garden bed, and up to our necks in banana leaf and exotic flowers, she said: 'You did good, Eddie. You did real good.'

When she kissed me it was like melting caramel on my tongue, and as intoxicating as the finest aged liquor. My head was swimming. A man could get lost on an island like this with a dish like that. But it wasn't to be, not for this private detective. Not yet anyway.

She gave the police her statement, and then she was gone. Case closed.

The sun was up. A rooster crowed — as they tend to do on Kauai. And I was going to miss my flight. The 8.45 am to Oahu. No big loss, I'd get the local boys in blue to reimburse the ticket. I could book a later escape.

My eyes were tired. Right now I needed breakfast, or a stiff drink. Some kind of stimulant to keep me going. Anything but coffee. So I checked my pockets, looking for a packet of cigarettes — and I remembered that I didn't smoke. Never have.

END SCENE.

FADE TO BLACK.

CREDITS.

# Day Nine

Jackie hung up the phone. 'We did it! The producers want to know my writer's name. It's too early to tell them you're my brother, they'll freak and pull the funding no matter how good the script is. Do you have a pen name, a pseudonym?'

'How about Ed Shade? The detective in the script,' I said.

'Shade? What happened to Eduardo Desah?'

'I had to kill him. If those convention types see his name attached to your project they'll come looking for their money, and that's a headache you don't need.'

'You really think they'd try and squeeze *me* for compensation?'

'Yeah — nah. Probably not. I'd be surprised if they ever found out we were freeloading. Wendy said it was covered. Still, let's go with a different name just to be safe.'

'Do you have anything better than Ed Shade?'

'How about Luke E Woodhead?'

'Who the hell is Luke E Woodhead?'

'It's a pseudonym. How should I know who he is?'

'I think we should go with Shade. It just sounds more authentic.'

Elena came running along the garden path and up the grass slope to the terrace. She launched herself at me and I caught her under the backside and lifted her off the ground. After she kissed me, she pulled away. She had tears welling in her eyes but she was showing more teeth than your average crocodile. Something had put her in a fine mood — something that she blurted out at a mile a minute. 'The lawyers went over the entire contract and made some calls. It's bulletproof and one hundred percent legitimate. As good a deal as Bill made it out to be. We're meeting him at the Grand Hyatt in an hour, so dress nice because I'm going to sign!'

\*

'I just need your autograph here … and down here.' The lawyer pointed to a line at the bottom of the page, and I watched Elena scribble her signature on it. Not a second after she had signed, a bottle of champagne was popped by Mr Conroy.

'Cheers!'

Crystal flutes chimed as we toasted to Elena and her fantastic new opportunity. I kissed my wife, and we held it for a period of time that probably made everyone uncomfortable, but I didn't give a shit. I was proud of her. She'd taken the leap, exactly what she needed — and why we had come to Hawaii to begin with. A renewed spark had shown itself early, but I could see now that her fire had returned. There would be no more humdrum and tedium over and over again, and we'd seen the last of those mornings lived in fear underneath a protective blanket. This was a challenge she would attack like a machete to tall grass.

Who would have thought a tall tale about a bogus furniture magazine, started by a writer impersonating a journalist, would lead to an encounter where an instigator of exceptional opportunities would take a chance on the word of that same truth-bender? But that is exactly what happened. And who knew what would happen with the Bali venture? The future was always wild and uncertain. What I did know was Elena working with Bill and his consortium of highflyers would be a rewarding experience.

Being a gentleman, Bill also inquired about the status of Jackie's feature film. And we were forced to relive the whole sordid situation. My brother spilled the details about actresses and producers hooking up to hijack his film. Where one script was discarded, and another, and how it had all been rescued by an out-of-work bum on holiday. Mr Johnstone had downed two glasses of champagne while the story was told. It was the only way he could cope with such a nightmare scenario. The disorganised nature of the process, the threatening phone calls in public, the possible legal ramifications if it had all gone pear-shaped, and the fact that we had gotten away with it. For a lawyer like Mr Johnstone, it was the kind of thing to induce a severe and immediate nervous breakdown, or more likely a week lost in a hotel room — crushed under the dark weight of fear and paranoia brought on by an ever-growing pile of white powder.

Bill reacted as he had when I warned him off Bali during our first meeting in the Hula Grill, by having another drink and taking a deep breath.

'Let me see if I have this straight, Jackie. You had a finished script and the film was moving ahead. The tale of a plantation owner's daughter who falls in love with a local boy. Forbidden love in a time of strict social ideals ... Then all hell broke loose and it was cancelled. However, you had a chance to salvage everything by coming up with a new script — in two days?'

'That's right. So far so good.'

'And you had a solid story ready to go, except halfway through the night you decided against using it and wrote a detective thriller instead.' Mr Johnstone skulled the rest of his champagne as Bill continued, '*But* you somehow turned in a finished draft on time *and* managed to get a decent night's sleep. Jeez, that exhausted me just saying it out loud. No disrespect, Jackie, I realise you know your business, but that sounds like a shit way to work.'

'You're not wrong. But desperate times … Hopefully it's a one off, eh.'

'Stressful, Jackie, awful stressful, like walking up a steep hill drunk and blindfolded. I'd be cautious about repeating the process in future, you're in heart-attack territory there.' Bill had another sip of champagne and gave the lawyer a hard stare, 'Jesus Johnstone, it's not that hot out here. I've never seen a man less relaxed in paradise … brought to the edge of a stroke, and you weren't even involved!'

'I might've looked like Mr Johnstone if Eddie didn't pull this story out of his back pocket,' said Jackie. 'It was an inspired move to make the switch, and a detective noir will be more exciting anyway.'

'So was the end result worth twenty thousand dollars?'

'Can't you tell?' Elena said. 'They've looked pleased with themselves all morning. When Roy and I discovered what they'd done it confirmed what we've always suspected — the Heads brothers are mental.' Elena smiled and winked at me.

'It also confirmed Eddie is a lot more than a bum with a pretty face. So, here's to the new script and a better film!' Mr Conroy said, and he raised his glass.

The toast was a nice touch, however, it's true. I am a bum. But I'm also a hard worker. Out there chasing the goal, playing the game, watching my back as I beg, borrow and steal to try and get an inch ahead in this twisted life. I'll complain about it too, especially if I'm dealing with idiots and selfish arseholes already on the make. And yeah, you might

catch me with a vacant, thousand-yard stare on the regular
— that's the writer and the dreamer. I'm idiosyncratic. A lot
of peculiarities thrown together, *but* into a deceptively calm
package where there is always more happening behind the
scenes than meets the eye. A bit like a shiny present hiding
a spring-loaded boxing glove — lift the lid and you'll get a
nice surprise. I'm no fool, no way, not this little black duck.

\*

We spent our final afternoon at the beach off the plantation.
One last perfect, sun-drenched, hazy-dazed afternoon in
one of my favourite places on Earth. Elena and I had been
floating on the deep water for a while when she got cold and
decided to go back and sunbathe. I said I would join her in
a little while. I wasn't ready to surrender and leave just yet. I
wanted to squeeze every last drop out of this deviation from
reality. My last hurrah, here, at the edge of escapism.

Sunlight glared off pristine sand and azure water.
There were surprisingly few people around. Everyone had
disappeared, most likely for an afternoon siesta. I smiled
about that. For a short while it was just going to be me and
Kauai. I lay back and stared at the sky and listened to the
sound of a world without people. Paradise is what I heard,
along with the smell, taste and enveloping comfort of the
cool ocean. This, accompanied by that pleasant burn of
Hawaiian sun on my chest and face, was a rare vibe that was
perfectly balanced.

And then my perfect little slice of tranquillity was disturbed when I heard a splash of water beside me. Unbelievable. Five minutes of alone time was all I asked, that would have been enough. It must be those fucking snorkelers again, and the thought crossed my mind to drown the bugger if their snorkel came within arm's reach of covering the blowhole. I turned my head, searching for this intruder, this indecent scoundrel who didn't have the good taste to swim around without bothering me. To my great surprise I came face to face with a small white head, speckled with black around its big black eyes. I must have looked as startled as I felt — just an awkward land mammal struggling to right itself in the water — because the turtle was immediately apologetic. 'Sorry about that. I keep sneaking up on you. *Aloha.*'

'No, no, completely my fault.' I coughed out a mouthful of water and took a second to catch my breath. '*Aloha.* I was wondering if we'd ever meet again.'

'It was always my intention. I've been keeping an eye on you and your *ohana*.'

'You have? How?'

'Sometimes I come ashore. I asked the birds to watch you. The birds talk to the trees and trees like to gossip. They talk to the sky and the rocks, and the rocks talk to the water that washes over them and the water runs to the ocean with news from the land. And the ocean talks to me.'

'That's a long chain of conversation. Why not always go ashore and talk with the birds?'

'I don't go ashore often, and birds are *lolo* — crazy pea-brained things that get overexcited and are liable to forget. The ocean is more reliable. I also saw you in the water a few times, one eye watches the interesting ones.'

'I *thought* I'd seen you around. I also thought I was going mad.'

'Not mad, just unusually in touch with the weird. Not many people come to play with the gods and spirits. I'm curious, did you find what you were looking for?'

'We got in some trouble along the way, but yeah, I think we all found something of value. I've been drifting aimlessly for a few years — now I have a purpose again.'

'I'm happy for you. It's good to find your place in life.'

'That's the truth. While you're here, there's something I've been meaning to ask. It's been on my mind since our first encounter, when you told me about the spirit of the islands ... are you *mana*? What I mean is, are we really talking to each other?'

'Does it matter if I am *mana* or just a sea turtle? As long as you and I wish each other well, in the end that is all the truth we need.'

'You make a good point. I keep the experience either way.'

'Now you're on the right path.' The turtle looked at the beach and the sky, soaking in the scenery, and finally returned its attention to me. 'Nice afternoon.'

'You know it really is. And you were right, everything only got better.'

'What will you do now?'

'Go home and write about my adventures.'

'Will you ever come back?'

'I think that goes without saying.'

'Mmm.' The turtle nodded in appreciation. 'It will be nice to talk story again, I wish you much luck with your writing. *A hui hou kakou.*'

'Wait — what does that mean?'

'Until we meet again.'

'*Mahalo.* Take care my friend.'

The turtle winked at me as it slipped below the waves.

*

We agreed as a group that there would be no enormous blowout on the final night, and instead shared an appropriately low-key dinner in the downstairs apartment. When the sun was gone, Jackie put on some tunes. Good music enjoyed with good company. The mood was just right. And bathed in the warm glow of the living room lights, Elena and I danced a half-speed Lindy while Mr Conroy and Jackie played poker with the naughty playing cards, only stopping to snap the odd Polaroid and use up the last of the film. When we couldn't stand to shake it any longer, Elena and I went outside and walked around the gardens. There are few things as comforting as a quiet stroll at night with someone you love, and we stretched that walk for as long as possible, because neither of us wanted to face up to the fact that tomorrow meant we had to leave here and climb on a plane destined for Australia and new beginnings.

*

Sleep was taking a while to find me, so I'd decided to read on the terrace. I closed *Hell is a Hot Bullet!* and stared into the night, coming to grips with the dramatic conclusion. I was surprised and impressed, nothing had been black and white. Who saw that coming? A story ahead of its time, that's for damn sure. And what became of ol' Rick Trickle? Well, he got himself square with his old gang by putting them all in the ground. No real surprise there. Rick got the girl too, but everyone saw that coming. The plot twist was our hero never stopped being the scoundrel and desperado his old gang knew him to be. He saved the ranch, took Belle to bed, had his way with her, and then stole away in the night on her daddy's prize Colt. They never saw each other again. After that Rick tore a streak south, robbed a couple of banks and wound up on a beach in Mexico, drinking tequila and living a drunk, fat, sun-tanned life. Maybe Manny Checkerman should've named his book *Heaven after a Hot Bullet?* Nah, he knew the pulp western game. He was pretty good, and so was this cheap paperback.

It got me thinking again about my own future as a novelist. This was what I had to do. And there was no escape, because I was already in it — like trying to beat that late fee on the Sportster, I was now trying to outrun time on life's superhighway … You can't see it, but you can feel it happening around you. You have become a bullet forever moving forward, trying to finish off this project, and the next one, and the one after that. Got to get it all done while you can. But the harder you work the more the horizon blurs at the edges, and there's no terminal velocity — no slowing down. Not even with drugs or alcohol. Better artists have tried, using every chemical imaginable, all in an effort to take themselves out of the stream or get ahead of it, because everyone on this ride knows, sooner or later, the big crash into that invisible barrier will come and it'll all be over.

It's frightening. It's the great motivator. And there is no better way to live.

The revelation got me so wound up that I considered finishing off the last bottle of rum — even though it was a temporary fix. And I thought, maybe it's time to give up the alcohol? Not completely, but it made sense for now.

# Day Ten

This was the end. It was all over, time to go home.

We packed our bags; the car was loaded, and we drove to reception where Jackie checked us out of the resort. Gemma was on the front desk. Elena hugged her one more time in gratitude for all that she'd done.

Mr Conroy clutched her hand between both of his and expressed deep regret that things hadn't worked out between them, 'Now, I don't want you to lose sleep over that, *bella*. I will be back next year to try again.'

Then we were gone. I was thankful that things moved quickly, when the leaving is slow from a place you love, the harder it always is. There's more time to dwell and wallow in the sadness that you're going away. Nobody wants the long goodbye. It's far better to tip your hat, smile and walk away. Get on with life.

The drive to the airport was pleasant and uneventful. We dropped the Jeep back at the rental office and walked across to the terminal, retrieved our plane tickets, and passed through security. An hour later we were flying away from Kauai. I would miss her charms, although I knew we would be back sometime in the near future. There was a sense of the inevitable about that.

Fifty minutes later we touched down on Oahu again. Everyone was dragging their feet. Nobody wanted to say *ciao, arrivederci* or farewell. Thankfully Jackie made things easy on us when we stepped outside the terminal, 'This is where I leave my people.'

'Wait, you're not coming across to international?' I said.

'Nah, man. My flight isn't until tonight, so I'm getting a taxi and spending the day in Waikiki. One last fling with the beach before I have to go back to Vancouver and winter wonderland.'

'You stay out of trouble, Jackie Heads,' Elena said.

'Ha. No promises.' He gave Elena a hug and European-style kiss — one on each cheek. And then he turned to her twin brother and did the same again. 'Always a pleasure, you dirty rascal.'

'Until next time, my friend.'

I could be mistaken but I think Mr Conroy was holding back tears.

Jackie embraced me in a bear hug. 'Thanks for bailing me out, dude — twice. I couldn't have done it without you.'

'It's what brothers are for.'

'Right. You know this is the story, don't you? Write your novel about this.'

'What do you mean *this?*'

'*This*. Hawaii. Us here and now.'

'This was a working holiday; we weren't really doing anything.'

'I could have sworn we just had an adventure. Some of the best stuff is like that, just real people in real places doing real stuff. You know what I'm saying?'

'Yeah. Stay safe out there, man. Shiny side up.'

'Rock and roll.' He pulled his shades down, smiled and walked over to the taxi rank. Without looking back, he raised his hand in the air and threw up the rock and roll devil horns.

We wandered over to international and checked in. There wasn't a whole lot of time to wait for our flight. Just enough to get a feed, go to the bathroom and change into clothes comfortable for a ten-hour journey. Then we made our final trek to the far end of the old brown terminal. We stood at the windows and inhaled the perfume of classic timber and sixties carpet while we basked in the sun one last time. Even this experience felt uniquely Hawaiian.

Elena appeared to be a million miles away. Lost in some deep thought while she watched a Japan Airlines 737 rise above the distant palm trees to ferry visiting tourists back to their homeland. When she snapped out of her trance, it was like she'd had some kind of life-altering revelation, and she said: 'I can't believe it's over. I don't know if I'm ready. Do you think we'll look back on this experience one day and realise that *this* was the moment where it all changed? And will they be fond memories, or will this all fade away like so many adventures?'

'I don't know about you, sister dear, but for me, this can't be anything but fond memories. In my humble opinion, it has been the complete escape.'

'No one ever realises they're in the special moments while they're experiencing them, but this is a pretty obvious life-marker. Years from now we'll be able to look back and say, there it was — Hawaii. So I don't think a time like this could ever fade. You made a life-changing deal, we saved Jackie's movie, and Roy, well … he got everything he needed.'

'Yes. Yes I did.'

'You're right. It was a bit special,' Elena said.

'And if you're still worried, I've got a way to make sure we never forget,' I said.

I stepped onto the plane and was directed to my seat in business class, which on this Hawaiian Airlines flight was as good as first class. Business class, where they treat you like royalty and ease the pain of having to leave paradise. The sentimental part of me wished that we were at the beginning of the story, about to disembark this plane instead of taking to the sky. I got settled in my seat, and although there was melancholy in my heart that the adventure was over, there was also a fire burning inside. Like Elena, for the first time in years I had a new course to follow, and that was exciting. I was going home to write a novel about our time in Hawaii, and I smiled when the realisation hit me — if I ever got lost again, the whole fantastic experience could be relived any time I wanted, and I could escape to these islands and be reminded where I should be going. And there was comfort knowing that whenever Eddie Heads got on the plane at the end of the story, all I'd have to do was flick back to the start of the book and, like magic, I'd be there again. Sun-soaked on the sand. Fashionable in fresh linen. Drowning in rum and liquid aloha.

The stewardess approached my seat, 'Can I interest you in a mai tai, sir?'

'Please. Actually, better make that two.'

# Acknowledgements

It surprised me when I sat down to write this list, the number of people who helped me get this story out into the world was longer than I expected. So, let's raise a glass to all these lovely folk.

To my wife, Helen, for her tireless love and support.

To my editor, Irma Gold, for helping me make this novel as tight and readable as possible. And for pointing out my unnecessary abuse of the word *then*, which in turn, pushed me to be more creative.

To my cover artist, Sean Longmore, for his spectacular artwork. Let's all take a minute to close this book and bask in its glory — did you have a look? Gorgeous? You're damn right, now go back and have another look.

To Kellie Nissen for proofreading the madness.

To Kerry Cooke for beautifying the interior.

And let's toast another one to Kellie and Kerry for dealing with all those arseholes!

To my parents and their partners (Mum and Pete, Paul and Jeanette, Dad and Julie). To the entire family for always supporting my creativity. To Margaret Hunt, aka Margie, for always being interested. To David Hunt for introducing me to the Flashman series and for leading by example; you can be a gentleman and still enjoy politically incorrect humour. To Liz and Mark Bishop, and Shea Slater for being brave and giving this novel a look through. To my brother, Hayden, for various reasons, some described in the pages you've just read. To Bart Birrell for the enthusiasm and for reading this on the far side of the world. To Kate Taylor, Katrina Carmody, Kate Williams, Michael Nickel, and Suzie Roberts for keeping me afloat and sane during the last two years.

To the people of Hawaii for allowing us to visit your lands.

To the islands for talking to me. To that sea turtle.

To rum. To good times.

To Gianni Ciaccia for the inspiration, the style, the positivity, and for always being interested. And for the introduction to Mark.

To Mark Henshaw for being generous with his time, for putting me on the righteous path with writing, and for the straight-talking, no bullshit, scary-good advice.

To Hunter S Thompson for telling me he thought I fucked up the ending until he read the last sentence. To those muses that sit at my shoulder and whisper their twisted ideas in my ear. And a big thanks to that special individual who told me the word economy of my first draft was good, but the story was sooo boring — that changed everything for me. If you consider where imagination, dreams and thought originate from, all three of the last people thanked may have been the same person. Have you ever been visited like *that* and it altered your path? Yikes ... I've said too much. *Aloha.*

Music always plays a big part for me when I'm in the writing zone, and while I delight in the fierceness and doom of classic heavy metal and hard rock, there was too much sunshine for my regular rotation to play a part this time. Here are the key players that set the vibe for this novel and need a toast. Let's start with Poolsuite FM for their top-shelf easy-breezy synth and bass-heavy tunes — Hangover Club for life, man. To Alice Cooper and his sick sense of humour. To AC/DC, Cold Chisel, James Reyne and Midnight Oil. To Buckcherry, Guns N' Roses, Puddle of Mudd, Saliva (new metal is underrated), Stone Temple Pilots, and the mighty Van Halen. To The Ventures, and any chilled-out surf guitar track I could lay hands on. To Josh Homme. To Billy Stewart. To Elvis Presley.

I'm sure there's more people who need a thank you. Yeah, everyone that took a chance reading this novel and made it all the way through to this sentence. You rock. Especially if you're one of those special individuals that flipped straight back to the start of the book and took the whole wild ride again. Here's to you ... and now here's to me. Cheers!

# About the Author

Luke E Woodhead is an Australian author. He resides with his wife in Canberra where they live in a haunted house at the nexus point of an Aboriginal sacred site and a portal to the other side of who knows where. When he isn't dealing with visitors from beyond the veil of reality, Luke enjoys a good laugh, riding his Harley, bushwalks, exotic travel, and a glass of rum while the sun sets. He sometimes writes too — there's always something to piss and moan about.